"I thought you were nervous,

"but you're not, are you?"

"No." She whispered the denial against his mouth, and it was almost too much for his self-control.

"Maybe you should be," he murmured. "Maybe you should be very nervous."

Thea experienced the same sensation in the pit of her stomach that she felt at the top of the first, terrifying drop on the roller coaster. Half fear, half anticipation, it was a thrill tingling down her spine, a push to be daring. She let her head fall back, lifting her mouth up to his. Luke tried for control.

"Maybe I *should* be nervous." She touched her lips to his, then drew back a fraction, her smile mysterious and wise. "Or maybe you're the one who should worry."

Dear Reader,

This is a special month for Silhouette Intimate Moments, and those of you who have been with us from the beginning may know why. May 1988 marks our fifth anniversary, and what a lot has happened since May 1983, when we launched this new line with no idea how it would be received.

If we'd hoped for the best scenario we could imagine, we still might not have been able to come up with all the good things that have happened to these books and their authors. Silhouette Intimate Moments is selling better and better each month, thanks to you. And in return for your loyalty, we give you award-winning authors, books that consistantly win the highest praise from romance reviewers, and a promise for the future: We will always be proud of everything we have done, but we will never rest on our laurels. In coming months, look for new miniseries from authors like Parris Afton Bonds and Emilie Richards, innovative books from longtime favorites like Kathleen Eagle and newcomers like Marilyn Pappano, and, of course, books that take no new chances at all but always live up to the standards we've set for this exciting line.

One last thing: Silhouette Intimate Moments has always been a line designed by the readers. It came into being because you told us you wanted stories that were not only longer but also bigger, larger than life, stories with mature characters, atypical plots and a strongly sensuous romance. Through the years you've never been shy about writing to me with compliments, complaints and suggestions. Now I want to renew our commitment to bringing you the books you want and to ask you, once again, to please keep writing to me. If we keep those lines of communication open, there's no telling how far we can go together.

Leslie J. Wainger
Senior Editor
Silhouette Intimate Moments

Lucy Hamilton

After Midnight

Silhouette Intimate Moments

Published by Silhouette Books New York

America's Publisher of Contemporary Romance

The Dodd Memorial Hospital series is dedicated to
my grandmother, Thelma June Wheeler Sargeant.
For all the stories you told me, and for teaching me
how to tell stories, thank you. These are for you,
Grandma.

For Dennis, with love.

SILHOUETTE BOOKS
300 East 42nd St., New York, N.Y. 10017

Copyright © 1988 by Julia Rhyne

ISBN: 0-373-07237-6

First Silhouette Books printing May 1988

Printed in the U.S.A.

Books by Lucy Hamilton

Silhouette Special Edition

A Woman's Place #18
All's Fair #92
Shooting Star #172
The Bitter with the Sweet #206

Silhouette Intimate Moments

Agent Provocateur #126
*Under Suspicion #229
*After Midnight #237

*Dodd Memorial Hospital series

LUCY HAMILTON

traces her love of books to her childhood, and her love of writing to her college days. Her training and the years she spent as a medical librarian translated readily into a career as a writer. "I didn't realize it until I began to write, but a writer is what I was meant to be." An articulate public speaker, the mother of an active grade-school-age daughter and the wife of a physician, Lucy brings diversity and an extensive knowledge of the medical community to her writing. A native of Indiana, she now resides in Southern California with her family and three friendly felines.

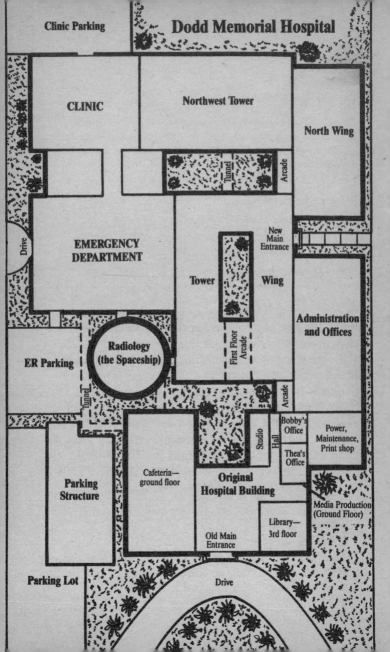

Chapter 1

How about this one?"

"Are you serious?"

"I know he's kind of weak chinned, but—"

"A wimp."

"Hmm." A page turned.

"Here's your boy." A finger stabbed the page. "Now that's a face with character!"

"If the character you want is a psychopathic killer. We don't."

"No imagination at all—"

"Then how about this guy? At least he looks sort of seminormal."

"Fat, sweaty and narrow-minded. Give him a gun and a badge and you've got the perfect small-town sherriff."

"Delightful image."

"I call 'em as I see 'em."

"You'll forgive me if I think your vision is just a teensy bit skewed?" Thea Stevens inquired sweetly, and Bobby Wallace laughed.

He closed the casting book with a slap. "There's nobody in this book, Thea. What's left?"

"This is the last one." Thea Stevens laid the *Directory of Character Actors* aside, and hoisted another fat book from the floor beside her. She dropped it onto the table with a thump. "*The Academy Players Directory, Leading Men*. If we don't find our star in here, we're in trouble."

"But does *Giving the Bed Bath* require a leading man?" Bobby teased.

Thea's cameraman and production technician, Bobby was twenty-five and good-looking in a stylish West Coast way, with short, carefully cut brown hair brushed upward and a single small earring. Today he wore baggy parachute trousers, a blinding Hawaiian print shirt and high-topped leather sneakers.

He looked the part of an empty-headed party animal, but in fact he was a talented cameraman, a meticulous craftsman, and Thea's friend and colleague.

"Why not? As long as he looks like a normal human being." Thea opened the casting book. "Try to remember that these films are about the fundamentals of nursing, not abnormal psychology. We'll save the psychopathic killers for another time."

"But imagine how unique—"

"All-American boys, Bobby. Normal."

"Boring," he muttered, and bent his head next to hers.

They pored over the book together, scanning the rows of small black-and-white photographs. They turned page after page, occasionally muttering comments or rejections.

"This guy?" Bobby asked, and Thea studied the picture for a moment before she shook her head.

"No, he's too—"

"Too what?" Bobby sat back, exasperated. "He looks normal to me. But to you, the perfectionist..."

Thea shot him a glance, unperturbed. "I like to do a good job."

"I know, I know. You're a terrific media coordinator and you've got more talent and ability than anybody I know, but you're too intense. You've got to lighten up!"

Thea laughed and swatted him with a sheet of paper. "You're loose enough for both of us, Bobby. If you were any more laid-back, you'd be comatose. Now let's see if we can find our star." She turned another page and examined the photos, then bent closer. "Hey!" She pointed. "Look at this guy!"

Bobby studied the little picture. "Lucas Adams? Well, he's certainly All-American."

He was blond and light eyed, with a square face that wasn't quite handsome. His easy smile showed even white teeth. He looked relaxed and wholesome and reminded Thea of Kansas cornfields and fresh air.

Thea reached for a notepad and pencil. "This is the kind of look I've been searching for!"

Bobby looked at the picture. "You don't think he's kind of geeky-looking?"

Thea glanced at him and grinned. "I don't even want to know how you define 'geeky-looking.' This guy is just what I want for these films. Normal but not ordinary, good-looking but not too pretty."

Bobby looked at the cover of the casting book. "This book's kind of old, Thea. He may not be this pretty anymore."

"And he may not be available, but I'll call anyway. Hopefully, he'll be around and even be capable of acting." She scribbled the name and phone number of his agency, then stood.

"He doesn't have to act." Bobby grinned. "He just has to lie there and let Vanessa Rice give him a bath." Bobby whistled, long and low. "I wish she'd give me one."

"Why don't you ask her?" Thea suggested with a grin. She picked up the notepad and carried it into her office to make the call.

Media Production, Thea's domain, was located at the end of a dark and depressing hallway in a remote corner of the oldest part of Dodd Memorial Hospital. The offices were on the right side of the hall, the production studio on the left. The outer office held a conversation area, Bobby's cluttered desk and a wall lined with cupboards and shelves which were crammed full of films, tapes, books and equipment. A deep closet in the corner was filled with the overflow.

Thea's office was reached by crossing through Bobby's. It was small, but she'd made it as comfortable as she could in the weeks she'd been media coordinator at Memorial. She had a big, battered desk, two chairs for visitors and one window, which looked out onto a small courtyard. Her walls were lined with shelves full of additional papers, books, films and cassettes.

Thea's daughter, Stephanie, grinned at her from a framed photograph on the desk, and a spindly grape ivy hung in a macramé net in the window. Stefi had given it to her, and Thea was trying, with plant food and lots of water, to nurse it into a state of health.

She touched the ivy as she passed it, then dropped into her desk chair and reached for the phone.

She walked into the outer office again five minutes later, a thoughtful frown on her face.

"Well?" Bobby demanded. "Is he going to do it?"

"I don't know. It was the weirdest thing. His agent didn't seem to want to offer it to him."

"What's wrong? Is he busy?"

"The agent didn't say, but I had to talk him into sending Lucas Adams over here to talk about the part." Thea shook her head. "It doesn't make sense. What agent doesn't want to get work for his clients?"

* * *

"Well? Are you going to do it?" Marilyn Adams Wilcox piled pasta on her younger brother's plate and passed it across the table to him.

Luke regarded his dinner with trepidation. The noodles were red, and there were lumps of white and green beneath the cream sauce and grated cheese. "What is this stuff, Marilyn? You invited me over for spaghetti."

"Not spaghetti, you peasant. This is tomato *fettucelle* with mussels and broccoli."

"Oh, well, of course." Luke prodded the mound with his fork. It did smell good, but it looked odd. "How come you don't make spaghetti and meatballs anymore? Since you and Ed moved up here with all the rest of the successful people, you don't cook anything I recognize."

"When Ed was in law school," Marilyn replied, "all we could afford was spaghetti and meatballs." She served herself and popped a deep red noodle into her mouth. "Mmm, that's good." She waved her fork at Luke's plate. "Eat your dinner, baby brother, or the next time you come I'll make the *tagliatelle* recipe I found today."

Luke rolled his eyes. "What's *that* got in it?"

"Scallops and squid ink."

"Squid ink?"

"That's right," Marilyn smiled. "It colors the noodles black and makes a nice visual presentation with the white scallops and cheese. I might sprinkle red caviar over it for color."

"I'll eat, I'll eat! Compared to squid ink, even red noodles sound good."

"Coward." Smiling, Marilyn turned to her plate.

The family resemblance was strong. They were both tall and blond, with strong-boned faces and blue eyes. Marilyn's hair, with a little help from her stylist, was a lighter blond than her brother's, and Luke's eyes were a clear, bright blue, while his sister's were a smokier gray-blue, but they could never be mistaken for anything but siblings.

They were eating in her big, well-equipped kitchen. Ed was in New York on business, so Marilyn had invited Luke over to test a recipe. Her sons, aged ten and eight, had greeted Uncle Luke and then gone to bed.

Since Marilyn owned and ran a catering business, Luke was used to being an experimental subject. He teased her about her outlandish recipes, and she retaliated by subjecting him to ever-more-exotic dishes. She took another bite and nodded in satisfaction.

"Mm-hmm. That works nicely. Though I may reduce the salt in the sauce, since the cheese is already salty."

"Whatever you say, Mare." Luke sipped his wine and eyed her warily. "You weren't serious about squid ink, were you?"

"For the right client, it would be perfect."

"You mean for people who don't care how the food tastes as long as it looks interesting?"

"People who want something different. I won't serve it unless it tastes good." She studied her brother. "You didn't answer my question."

"Which question was that?" Luke wondered absently. He examined a mussel before eating it, then said, "This is actually pretty good."

"Of course it is. Are you going to do that instructional film?"

"Films. It's a series."

"Film, films, whatever. Are you going to take the job?"

He nodded. "I'm going to interview for it."

"But you just got back from Canada. Don't you need a vacation?"

"I've been back for two weeks, and I'm bored with doing nothing."

"When do you go to Chicago?"

"I was supposed to go next month, but they're having some kind of problem with the Illinois Film Board. It's going to be at least three months before we start shooting, maybe more."

"I guess you've got the time to do the series, then." Marilyn tipped her head to the side and studied her "little" brother. "But educational films? That seems awfully small-time."

"There's nothing small-time about good work," he told her. "And I like the small-film atmosphere. Working with two or three people instead of thirty or forty, you're more involved with the whole project. Besides—" Luke grinned "—I've never done medical films before. It should be interesting."

"As interesting as dancing in an onion suit?"

"I want you to know," he said loftily, "that I was the best damned dancing onion they ever had. I sold a lot of salad dressing!"

Laughing, Marilyn asked, "So when are you going over to—what hospital is it?"

"Dodd Memorial, in Pasadena. My interview's tomorrow."

"Do you think you'll get the part?"

"Yeah." There was no egotism in Luke's voice, only a calm awareness of truth. "This media coordinator person actually talked Morris into contacting me. He didn't want to bother with it, but he said she wasn't going to shut up until he agreed to send me over."

"Does she know you were in Canada for—"

"No. And I'm not going to say anything about it, either."

"Why not, for heaven's sake?"

"Because it could lose me the part. She wouldn't be seeing me as the working actor that I am. And believe it or not, sister dear, I want this job."

* * *

"The media production office," Luke said to the nurse he'd stopped in the hallway to ask for directions.

"Media production..." She thought for a moment, shifting her grip on a tray of medications. "Where they make the films and things?"

"That's right."

"Okay." She pointed down the hall. "This is the north wing of the hospital. I think that office is in the old wing, the original building at the south end."

"How do I get there?"

"Take this hall. It leads you to the main entrance."

Luke knew that; he'd come in that way twenty minutes earlier.

"When you get to the main entrance, take the hallway to the left of the doors. Follow it past the cafeteria and then take the next hallway on the right to Engineering. You'll be in the old building then, and you won't be able to miss it."

Luke thanked her and set off down more of the seemingly endless halls, certain that he *could* not only miss it, he *would*.

Memorial, as he was learning the hard way, was a mad collection of buildings, old and new, loosely tied together by an indecipherable maze of corridors, courtyards and outdoor walkways. The original building was a mission-style fantasy in red tile and stucco, with arches and arcades and enormous palms planted in front. He'd driven past it on his way to the public parking lot and had admired it as a perfect example of 1920s California rococo architecture.

Behind the facade, though, the place was an architect's nightmare. Buildings, wings and additions had been tacked on piecemeal over the years, with utter disregard for aesthetics or design. There were square-edged 1930s structures, squat piles of brick and stone from the 1940s and a round monstrosity that screamed 1950s, with futuristic spikes and curves.

From the outside, Memorial amused him, but the inside was driving him crazy. Hallways jogged to the right and left as they ran from one building to another, sometimes going up or down a couple of steps, as well. When he found himself walking around and around an endless circular hallway in a building like a spaceship, he had to ask directions again. He was forced to stop once more before he reached his goal at the end of a dark, narrow hallway that made him think of moldering dungeons. He resisted the temptation to hunch one shoulder and walk with a limp.

There were two doors, both of them labeled. Both signs read, Media Production. With no hint as to which was the one he needed, Luke flipped a mental coin and tapped on the left-hand door. There was no answer, so he opened it and looked into a well-appointed studio, which was dark and empty. He closed that door and knocked on the other.

"Come in!" a slightly muffled female voice called.

Luke pushed the door open, stepped in and stopped short. In contrast to the dungeon ambience in the hall, this was a large, light, pleasant office. A woman was crouched in the corner with her back to him, doing something to the heavy base of a rolling three-footed stand.

"I'll be with you in just a minute," she said without looking around. "A wheel fell off this thing, and I can't let go until I get it back on."

She was small, with ebony hair twisted into a shining knot at her nape. Her fragile shoulders and tiny waist were outlined by her white lab coat, and when she bent over farther, Luke found himself looking at a small, gently curved derriere.

As he watched, she tipped the stand to the side, struggling to fit the stem of a caster into its socket. All she managed to do was pinch her finger.

"Ow!" She jerked her hand back, and the stand tipped at a perilous angle. She lurched sideways, grabbing for the stand as it overbalanced; then she overbalanced herself and landed on her bottom with a thump. Luke jumped forward and caught the falling stand just before it landed on her head.

"I've got it." He lifted it away from her and tilted it so she could see underneath. "I'll hold it while you put the wheel back."

"Thank you," she said with heartfelt gratitude. As he held the stand, she wiggled the stem into its socket, her small bottom wiggling in unison. Luke smiled, enjoying the view and wondering what the rest of her would look like.

"There." She sat back on her heels, dusting off her hands as he lowered the stand to the floor. She pushed it experimentally, and it moved smoothly. "Good. That should do it, at least until the next time."

"Will there be a next time?" he asked the top of her head.

"Inevitably." She gave the stand another testing nudge. "We only get the rejects to use as props, and age shows." She started to rise, and Luke reached down to help her up. "Here."

"Thank you."

Their hands touched, their eyes met, and they both froze.

That moment of shock and recognition only lasted an instant, but Luke's eyes widened, and he felt his breath catch in his chest as he automatically lifted her to her feet.

She was like a woman from a Byzantine painting, with a wide, pale forehead and classically curved eyebrows, a delicate jawline and a narrow, aristocratic nose. Her skin was flawless, satin-smooth and slightly flushed from her exertions. And her eyes...wide and dark, they should have been brown, but they were blue instead, deep blue. Velvet blue. Midnight blue.

A wave of desire, sudden and stunning, took him by surprise. He worked with attractive women all the time and prided himself on being indifferent to mere physical beauty, but he had to fight this heat that shot through his body, this impulse to pull her into his arms and take her mouth with his. His hand tightened on hers when she tried to draw away, and he held her there for another moment before reluctantly releasing her.

She was small, perhaps five feet two or three, with fine bones and sweetly feminine curves. He wondered if she weighed even a hundred pounds. He wondered what it would be like to touch her, to feel her skin heat under his hands, to hear her whisper his name in that soft, slightly husky voice.

"Thank you for the help." Her prosaic words interrupted the increasingly dangerous train of his thoughts. "I wasn't getting anywhere with that thing."

"My pleasure." He smiled, letting his eyes warm, letting his appreciation show as his gaze drifted from her face to her body. He couldn't believe she hadn't felt what he had. "I'm always glad to help a lovely lady in distress. Do you have any more of these things to fix? Whatever they are."

"IV stands."

Her smile froze as she read the message in his eyes. He could see the the mixture of annoyance and wariness in her look, could sense the mantle of formality she pulled around herself the way she pulled her lab coat closed over her breasts in what was an unconsciously revealing gesture.

"And that's the only one," she said curtly.

"Any other handyman work?" He grinned, an engaging grin that had been known to break down stiff resistance. "I seem to be good at it."

"There's nothing else." Her voice was cool, but a tinge of pink stained her cheekbones. "Is there something I can do for you?"

The obvious answer flicked through Luke's mind, but he pushed it away. "I have an appointment with a Ms. Stevens. Could you tell her I'm here?"

"No need." She extended her hand. "I'm Thea Stevens. You must be Lucas Adams."

She kept the handshake brief, but Luke felt her touch like an electric shock.

"I am, but you must have an old casting book," he said after a moment. "I've used Luke for a couple of years now."

"All right, Luke." Her smile didn't reach her eyes. "If you'll come into my office, I'll tell you about the films."

Unable to stop himself, Luke watched her walk, captivated by the graceful sway of her hips. He jerked his gaze up to the back of her head, staring at the glossy black hair she had twisted into a schoolmarmish knot at her nape. How long was it? What would it look like if he pulled out the pins and let it tumble down her back? If he ran his hands through—

An interview, Luke reminded himself. You're here on an interview. But what would it hurt to see if he could get past her schoolteacher's prissiness to the woman underneath?

Thea had kept her feelings out of her face until she'd turned her back on him to lead the way into her office. Then she'd let her breath out in a silent sigh. She didn't know how she'd kept her jaw from dropping when she'd first looked at Luke Adams.

She'd looked a long way up—six feet, at least—past muscular legs in worn jeans, a narrow waist and a broad chest to a strong-boned face and the bluest eyes she'd ever seen.

In that first stunned moment, she couldn't have said what color his leather jacket was, or even his hair; she only saw those eyes. They weren't just blue, they were the clear, pure, crystalline blue of a summer sky, rimmed by thick, dark gold lashes.

When he'd taken her hand to help her up, her heart had lurched at his touch, her pulse skipping a beat and scrambling along. The movement should have been casual, but she'd felt his hand tighten on hers when she'd tried to pull away. She'd felt a tension in him that had echoed and answered the tension in her.

Such an overwhelming awareness of a man was something she hadn't felt in years. She fought the feeling, because she didn't want to feel that awareness, that weakness. She wanted to feel competent and in control. She had to.

Competent. She marched around behind the solid barrier of her desk. *In control.* "Sit down, please, Mr. Adams."

"Thank you." She folded her hands on the desktop. Clasped together, they couldn't tremble.

He smiled easily as he settled back in his chair, a flash of white teeth and blue eyes against his tan. As far as Thea was concerned, that smile should have been regulated by law. It was warm, flirtatious, laughing, intimate—and downright dangerous. Her own smile stiffened.

He lounged comfortably in the chair, loosening his jacket and resting one arm on the back of the chair, stretching his pale blue sweater across his heavy muscles.

She'd prepared some questions to ask him, and he replied gravely to her conscientious inquiries, but she could feel the laughter lurking underneath. He'd done some local theater and commercial work, including playing an onion in a salad dressing commercial.

"An onion?" she asked.

He wore jeans and leather with an unconscious sexiness that was as disturbing to her poise as his smile. She couldn't quite imagine him in an onion suit.

"Yeah." He grinned ruefully. "A dancing onion. We danced, they played the salad dressing jingle, and I understand that ad sold a lot of dressing."

"I'm sure it did." Thea bit her lip to hide her amusement and scanned the list of credits Luke had brought with him. "Your agent sent a tape of clips from your three-day stint as a murderer on that soap opera and reviews of your theater work in Santa Barbara. That brings you up to about ten months ago. What have you been doing since then?"

Uneasiness flashed across his face. Until this point he'd been utterly relaxed. She wondered why her question should make him uneasy.

"Well," he said after a moment, "it's been kind of a strange ten months."

And then she understood. He'd been without a role and didn't like to admit it. That was nothing unusual; all actors had dry spells.

Thea didn't want to embarrass him. "Have you been busy in another field?" she asked tactfully.

Luke nodded, visibly relieved. "That's right."

Thea knew about the "other fields," which included parking cars, tending bar and waiting tables. Half the waiters in Los Angeles were actors waiting for a part. It was nothing to be ashamed of.

"Okay." She made a note on her pad. "That's everything. You've done quite a bit of work in the last three years. You should be well prepared for this. I've told you that this series is made up of three films on the fundamentals of nursing: *Giving the Bed Bath*, *Ambulation* and *Traction and Care of the Orthopedic Patient*. I have scripts and storyboards if you want to study them before you make a decision, but I'd like to offer you the job."

Luke looked across the desk for a moment, then nodded. "Thank you. I accept."

"Thank *you*," Thea said, stressing the pronoun. "I'm glad you're going to be working with us."

She stood and reached out to shake hands on the deal. When they touched, another faint prickle of electricity ran over her skin. She met his eyes, and her breath caught at the message there. It was frank and intimate and meant for her alone.

"I think—" He shook his head. "No, I *know* that I'm going to enjoy working with a boss as lovely as you." His voice was low and husky. The room suddenly felt small and airless.

"Mr. Adams, I don't think you under—"

"Don't understand?" He smiled teasingly, seductively; it was a smile carefully designed to melt feminine resistance. She tried to pull her hand away, but his grip tightened, not enough to hurt, just enough to hold. "I understand that I'm a man and you're a very lovely woman and we're going to be working together."

"Mr. Adams, I am hiring you to work in my films." She meant the words to come out cold and sharp, but her voice, soft and husky, betrayed her.

"Yeah." His fingertips slid across her palm, brushing over her sensitive inner wrist and the pulse that beat there. It hammered under his touch. "To work with you."

She shouldn't allow this. She should pull her hand away and slap his face with it. Instead she stood there and gazed helplessly up at him, unable to break the spell.

"Thea, have you seen the—"

Bobby flung open the door and burst into the room, then jerked to a halt when he saw them.

Thea snatched her hand away and stumbled back, her face flaming. Luke didn't look the least bit perturbed. He gave her a knowing smile, then turned to Bobby.

Anger ran through Thea, replacing her confusion. He wouldn't get away with this. She wouldn't let him.

Bobby looked from one to the other, his eyes sharp with interest. "Uh, hey, if I'm interrupting something—" he began to back toward the door again "—I can come back later."

"No, don't go, Bobby," Thea said quickly. "I've got news for you." She spoke quickly; a bright, false smile on her face. "Mr. Adams, this is Bobby Wallace, our cameraman and technician. Bobby, this is Luke Adams, and he's just agreed to do the fundamentals series."

"Oh, hey, that's great!" Bobby turned to Luke, grinning wickedly. "You're gonna make a great victim, er, patient." He stuck out his hand. "Welcome to Memorial."

Chapter 2

Thea kept her face, and her temper, under careful control until Bobby had left the office. When she heard the door of the outer office close behind him, she turned to Luke Adams. He was relaxed, one hand in his hip pocket, smiling at Bobby's joke. When he saw her face, his smile widened.

Her anger was showing now, and it rose higher when he gave her that smug male grin, as if her fury only amused him. She contained her temper with an effort.

"Have a seat. I need to talk to you."

He shook his head and brushed back a wayward lock of sun-streaked hair that had fallen onto his brow. "I'll stand."

"If you wish." She leaned against her desk, folding her arms over her chest. "We're going to get something straight right now, Mr. Adams."

"Call me Luke."

"Mr. Adams," she repeated, and his eyes widened in mock awe. Thea's lips tightened in an angry line. "You are going to be working here for a few weeks. You're going to be paid the best salary we can afford, you can eat in the cafeteria at staff prices, and you'll have a discount parking permit to use." She studied his face for a moment, her eyes angry and determined. "There are no other fringe benefits."

Luke rocked back on his heels and folded his arms, mimicking her posture. "By which you mean...?"

"By which I mean me!" she snapped. "You may think that little performance you gave was funny, but I don't." She was glad to see that his grin was beginning to fade. "I'd withdraw my offer of the job, except that I need an actor, I need him now, and I need your physical type."

"So you do like me."

"For this project," she said firmly. "I'm going to make some good films, Mr. Adams. I went through those casting books until I was cross-eyed looking for the right actor. I want the students to empathize with the patient, to understand his feelings when they give a bed bath or care for someone in traction." Her voice dropped, becoming low and emphatic. "I don't just want these to be good films, I want them to be the best fundamentals-of-nursing films available."

There was silence. Luke watched her with an odd look in his eyes, a combination of surprise and something that might have been dawning admiration. She faced him steadily, determined to make him understand.

"It will be impossible for either one of us to do good work if you insist on behaving like an uninhibited adolescent."

He met her steady gaze for several long moments and whistled under his breath. "You don't pull your punches, do you?"

"Could I?" Her sudden smile was full of honest amusement. "And still get through to you?"

Her teasing startled Luke. She'd been so intense that watching her smile was like watching the sun emerge from behind a cloud. It made him want to reach out and touch her skin and hair, to hold her small, soft body against his. He shook his head, stopping the thought before it could go farther. She was right. His smile faded.

"Probably not," he admitted brusquely. "Can I have copies of those scripts? Then I'll get out of your hair."

He waited while she retrieved the copies she'd made for him. They were on her desk in a pile of other papers. As she searched, he picked up the framed photograph on the desk. "Cute little girl."

"I know." Thea looked up with a smile. "That's my daughter."

"Mmm." She didn't look old enough to have a school-age child. Luke replaced the picture as she lifted a stack of papers that had been sitting on her nameplate. He touched the plain plastic strip with cold fingers. It read Mrs. Thea Stevens. *Mrs.* He hadn't even considered that. He looked at her hands and saw the narrow gold band he hadn't noticed before. He felt the heat as his neck reddened. There were few people he despised more than men who pursued married women.

"Here it is!" She extracted the last script from beneath a medical journal. "This is my office number." She scrawled it on the title page. "Call me if you have any questions."

His agreement and his thanks were as scrupulously neutral as she could have wished. In a very few minutes he had agreed to come to work at nine on Monday and politely taken his leave.

Thea stood by the door for several seconds, then moved slowly around her desk to slump into her chair. "Whew!" she exclaimed, unconsciously echoing Luke. She massaged her temples and tried to relax. "I can't believe I did that!"

"Talking to yourself?" Bobby pushed the door open and looked in. "That's a bad sign. And what did you do that you can't believe?" He set a candy bar on her desk, flopped into the chair Luke had occupied and crossed his left ankle over his right knee.

"Thanks." Thea grinned and leaned back. "I told Luke Adams to keep his hands, his eyes and his smart remarks to himself."

Bobby jerked upright in the chair, his left foot hitting the floor with a thud. "You told him—" He seemed to be choking.

"Just what I said, but a little more politely. Not much more, though."

Bobby coughed. "Did he try to . . . ?"

"Not seriously." She hurried to reassure him, touched by his quick, protective anger. She never would have suspected Bobby of having chivalrous instincts. "He was flirting, and I made it very clear that he was going to be working here, not playing."

"I oughta punch his—"

"You don't need to punch him out, not even to defend my honor. He got the message and said a very polite goodbye before he left."

"Yeah, well, if he ever does anything . . ."

"Thank you, Bobby." Her voice was soft and sincere. "I really appreciate the offer."

His face reddened, and he stared at the floor for a moment. "So, do you think he'll work out?"

"Yes." Thea didn't need to think about it. "I think he'll do very well. Especially now that he knows how I feel."

"One thing's for sure." Bobby grinned.

"What's that?"

"Working with him is gonna be interesting."

Interesting? Yes, she was sure it would be interesting. She only hoped she'd be able to keep things under control.

* * *

"Do I have to?"

"Yes, you have to. They're perfectly good peas. And who knows? You might even find out you like them."

Stefi scowled at her plate with the kind of distaste only an eight-year-old is capable of. "Marybeth *hates* peas."

Thea hid a smile as her daughter took three small peas on her fork and examined them with deep suspicion.

"You're not Marybeth," she pointed out blandly. "And you shouldn't let somebody else, even your best friend, tell you what you like or don't like. Personally, I like peas." She took a big bite and chewed with relish.

Stefi put the three peas in her mouth and chewed slowly.

"What do you think?" Thea asked.

"They're okay, I guess."

"I guess," Thea mimicked her. "You know they're good, and they go great with meat loaf."

"You make good meat loaf, Mommy." Stefi grinned, displaying a brand-new pair of front teeth, with gaps on either side.

"Thank you, sweetheart. And you make good mashed potatoes."

"Thank you, Mommy." Stefi smiled graciously and took an enormous bite of her meat loaf. "Did you talk to the actor today?" she asked around her food.

"Yes, I did. His name is Luke Adams, and he's going to work on the films for us."

"Is he a real actor?" Stefi's eyes were wide and bright. She'd just discovered movie and television stars.

"Of course he's a real actor!" Thea laughed. "I told you, we found his picture in the casting book. You have to be a real actor to get in there."

"Yeah, but has he been on TV?" That was Stefi's definition of a "real" actor.

"He's been on TV. He played a bad guy on one of the soaps, and he was in a commercial for salad dressing."

"He's really been on TV?"

"He really has."

"Wow!" Stefi breathed, her eyes like saucers.

They were the same shade of blue as Thea's and fringed with the same dark, thick lashes, but Stefi had her father's brown hair, rather than Thea's gleaming black. Thea could see so much of Marty Stevens in his daughter, in her facial expressions, in the angle at which she held her head, and in her tall, angular body.

Thea was small and curvy, but Marty had been lanky and tall, and his daughter already carried that heritage. Thea glanced at the top shelf of the china cabinet. There was a framed photograph there of a slim, smiling brown-haired man, a man who would never grow old.

He was twenty-four in the picture, and he'd been twenty-five when an auto accident had ended his life. Thea hadn't known about the secrets then; she'd just been the happy young wife of a candy and cigarette distributor, absorbed in her family and her home. Stefi had been almost two, and Thea barely twenty-three, with two years of college and no marketable skills. She didn't remember much of the first weeks after Marty's death. That period had been a black pit for her; without her baby girl, she would have had no reason for living.

By the time she'd climbed slowly out of that pit, spurred by the knowledge that she had a child to provide for, Marty's death, and his secrets, had become old news. She'd lived through the notoriety, and now she hardly remembered it; her mind had mercifully blocked out the memories.

She'd worked to make their lives normal again, taking a job as a secretary in a real estate office while she'd finished school at night, struggling to find time to spend with her growing daughter, struggling to keep her head above water financially.

And she'd made it. Today she had an eight-year-old daughter of whom she was fiercely proud, she was starting the career she wanted, she had friends, she had a good life. When she turned to Stefi again, she was smiling, and her eyes were only a little sad.

"What happened in school today, sweetheart?"

"We had art. We're making pictures of turkeys out of seeds for Thanksgiving."

"That sounds nice. When you finish the picture, we'll hang it over the fireplace, all right?"

"Okay. It'll look pretty up there."

"Mm-hmm. What else did you study?"

"Math." Stefi made a face. "We had a test."

"I thought you liked math. What was the test about?"

"Division." She gave a despairing sigh. "I don't like division, Mom. It's too hard."

"It just seems that way, sweetie. You know what you have to think about when you look at a division problem?"

"What?"

"Division is nothing more than backwards multiplication. If you look at it like that, it's simple."

"Backwards multiplication?" Stefi pondered the idea for a moment. "Really?"

"Really. Like four times four is sixteen, so sixteen divided by four is four!" Thea smiled. "And that makes it almost easy."

"Wow!" Stefi pushed back her chair. "I'm done with supper, Mom. Can I call Marybeth and tell her about backwards multiplication?"

"Yes, for ten minutes. Put your dishes in the sink first."

"Okay, Mom!"

There was a clatter of dishes and a rush of running feet, and then Thea was alone. She smiled and poured herself a cup of coffee. It wasn't easy to be a mother, and it was harder still to be a single mother, but she couldn't have done too badly if she had a daughter like Stefi.

At 8:30 she tucked Stefi, who was wearing her favorite nightshirt and clutching a doll dressed in an astronaut's costume, into bed. "Are you going to do better with division tomorrow?"

"I'm going to do it like backwards multiplication, and it'll be easy!"

"I hope so." Thea smiled. "And I bet you'll do better on your next division test, too."

"I will," Stefi promised stoutly. "Are you gonna start making your movie tomorrow?"

"We're going to start rehearsing on Monday. We'll start shooting on Tuesday or Wednesday." Lying back on the bed with her arm around Stefi's thin shoulders, Thea looked up at the ceiling. "This is the biggest project I've ever done. I hope I do a good job."

Stefi turned in Thea's arms and hugged her tightly. "You will," Stefi assured her. "Because being a mommy is the hardest job there is, and you're the best mommy in the world!"

Blinking away the tears that stung her eyes, Thea hugged her daughter fiercely.

Studying his scripts, Luke had been surprised at the professional quality of the work and then had chided himself for being a snob. It was professional because Thea Stevens was a professional. Now, when he eased open her office door, he saw that she was up to her elbows in a file drawer, filing storyboard sheets. He could have stood there, watching her work, appreciating her prim little sweater and skirt, appreciating the very feminine form they covered but couldn't conceal, but she was married. He moved his gaze from her hips to her hair.

"Good morning."

Thea hadn't heard him enter. Now she gasped and jumped, dropping a fistful of storyboards, which scattered across the floor like giant snowflakes. Flustered at being caught off guard, she looked from the mess of papers to Luke, who was smiling at her. Thea's heart skipped a beat, then scrambled to catch up. She answered his smile with a glare.

"Do you always sneak up on people that way?" she demanded.

"I didn't sneak." Luke stooped and began gathering the papers together.

"You didn't knock."

"The door was open."

"I don't mind you walking in, but I do mind you sneaking up on me and scaring me half to death!"

"I didn't mean to startle you." Luke rose with his hands full of storyboards. "Will you forgive me if I promise to knock, shout your name and come in whistling 'The Stars and Stripes Forever' next time?"

Thea's lips twitched; then a giggle escaped. "Oh, I give up!" She sat back on her heels and let herself laugh. "All right, all right, I shouldn't have snapped at you."

"I should have made my presence known. I'm sorry. Truce?" He offered his hand, and after a fraction of an instant Thea reached out and took it.

She kept the contact light and brief, but the feel of his hard hand engulfing hers lingered long after he'd released her. She'd promised herself that she would be calm and controlled, but she'd forgotten—or perhaps she hadn't wanted to remember—just how attractive he was.

It wasn't just the handsome face or the bluer-than-the-sky eyes, although those certainly didn't hurt. There was something carefree about him, a willingness to be silly, to enjoy without embarrassment, that both attracted and disturbed Thea. The only other person she knew who approached things that way was Stefi, and she was eight years old.

Though Luke Adams was very much a man, his mental outlook and approach to life seemed more like those of a child. Even his flirting had been lighthearted, teasing. Thea knew she'd overreacted. She'd meant the things she said, but she hadn't needed to be so hard on him. And she wouldn't have been if she hadn't been attracted.

She wasn't looking for that right now. She wasn't looking for a man at all, but if she were she wouldn't be interested in an overage teenager, a happy-go-lucky flirt. However attractive he might be, he was the wrong man for a widow with a child.

The thought both sobered and steadied her. When she reached out to take the storyboards from him, he was watching her curiously.

"Is something wrong?"

Thea looked at him in surprise. "No. Why do you ask?"

"You just looked...not sad, but pensive, for a moment."

She gave him a coolly impersonal smile. "Nothing's wrong. If you like, Bobby can show you the studio while I finish up in here. We can start the reading when Vanessa Rice shows up."

He studied her for a moment, but her smile didn't waver. "All right." He turned and left.

Thea looked at the doorway he'd passed through and sighed. She'd looked sad? Yes, perhaps she had; perhaps she'd been mourning the carefree innocence she'd left behind with her childhood. That was inevitable, a part of growing up. Some people grew up at an early age, some grew up later, and some never left childhood behind at all. She shook her head and went back to her filing.

Vanessa Rice sailed into Thea's office fifteen minutes early. Her lab coat was flung on over a sweater and narrow trousers; her dark, shoulder-length hair, dramatically streaked with premature silver at the temples, was flying; and she had a fistful of notes in her hand and a wide smile on her face.

"Hi! Am I late?" She flopped into a chair, her slim frame gracefully draping over it.

"Actually, you're early." Thea grinned. "I'll be another five minutes, so make yourself comfortable."

"I always do." Vanessa grinned, her face alight with laughter. "It's so nice to be out of the nursing school, away from my office and my phone."

"Getting busy?" As head instructor of the fundamentals-of-nursing course, Vanessa was in charge of the curriculum, a team of assistant instructors and 105 anxiety-stricken students.

"Busy? I'm overwhelmed! The term project is due next week, the clinical final is the week after, and there's mass panic among the students. I didn't even tell the switchboard where I'd be. I'll just call for my messages now and then."

"You're a coward, Van."

"You bet!" Vanessa hooked one leg over the arm of the chair and swung her foot. "I'm also anxious to meet our star. Where is he?"

"In the studio with Bobby. Do you want to go over?"

"Tell me about him first. What's he like?"

Thea hesitated. What could she say about Luke Adams? "Well, physically he's the type we decided on, All-American, fairly young, someone the students can identify with. Tall, blond—"

The other woman interrupted her with a laugh. "Good-looking?"

Thea rolled her eyes. "Plenty good-looking, and I've seen his tapes so I know he can act."

"And his personality?"

Thea shook her head and looked away. She didn't want to touch that one. "Why are you asking me all this, Van? I've only met the man twice."

"I know, but I'd like your impressions. What's he like?"

Thea grimaced wryly. "A flirt."

Vanessa leaned forward eagerly. "He flirted with you?"

"Yeah." She grinned. "Bobby offered to punch him out for me."

"And I thought chivalry was dead."

"Apparently not. I told Bobby that wasn't necessary. I'd already made it clear to Mr. Adams that I'm not one of the fringe benefits of this job."

"How did he react?"

"He was very polite." Thea let herself smile and Vanessa laughed. "Actually," she continued, "he seems young, kind of like an overgrown kid."

"He's two months older than you," said Bobby from the doorway.

Thea spun around, her eyes wide in a suddenly burning face.

"No." Bobby grinned and shook his head. "He's not here. He's in the studio looking at the cameras."

"Hi, Bobby," Vanessa said. "How old is he?"

"Twenty-nine, just like Thea, but his birthday's a couple of months before hers."

Vanessa snapped her fingers in mock chagrin. "Too young for me."

"A year younger is too young?" Thea laughed. "You're thirty, Van, not ninety."

"Sometimes it feels like ninety." Vanessa shook her head ruefully. "Much as I love teaching, there are days when I wish I'd gone into something easier—like road construction!"

"I can just see you—" Bobby swung a chair around and straddled it backward "—in a hard hat, waving a red flag at the cars."

"I wouldn't be waving a flag, I'd be driving the bull-dozer. So he's twenty-nine, huh?" She glanced sidelong at Thea. "Just the right age for you."

"He's not going to try anything," Bobby began bellig-erently, but Thea smiled wryly at the idea.

"Don't worry, Bobby. I can handle him." She turned to Vanessa. "Age and maturity don't necessarily go to-gether. He may be my age, but I'm older. I feel as if I'm ninety and he's about sixteen."

Vanessa's reply was forestalled by a series of careful taps on the door. They all looked around to see Luke peering in warily.

Thea laughed aloud at the joke no one else understood, and Vanessa's eyes widened at the sight of her friend's glowing face. She looked back at 'Luke, schooling her expression into a friendly greeting.

"Is it safe?" Luke asked, and Thea nodded.

"Come on in." She turned to the other woman. "He sneaked in here without knocking this morning and nearly gave me heart failure."

She pulled him forward, her hand on his sleeve in an unconsciously familiar gesture. Luke smiled and let her lead him across the office.

Thea made the introductions with her best dancing school manners. "Van, I'd like you to meet Luke Adams, your co-star. Luke, this is Vanessa Rice, R.N., Ph.D., head instructor of the fundamentals-of-nursing class and in-structor of psychiatric nursing. She's the 'NURSE' in all your scripts."

"And I'm delighted to meet my 'PATIENT.'" Vanessa rose and shook his hand. "Thea was just telling me about you."

"Something good, I hope?"

"Nothing to worry about." Vanessa shoved herself out of her chair and briskly changed the subject. "Are we about ready to start rehearsing? Sooner or later I have to go back and face my students, so we'd better get cracking on this."

Thea gathered up her scripts. "Shall we?" she asked, and led them to the studio.

Luke clenched his jaw and tried not to watch her walk. He didn't think she even realized that she'd touched him, but he'd felt that light hand on his arm like a brand. She was another man's wife, another man's lover. Those familiar little gestures of hers were just friendly and casual. Nothing more than that. He was a fool to read anything into them. He was a fool to think the things he was thinking about a married woman.

He strode to the stage, where he waited for his co-star. If he kept his mind on his work, maybe he could keep it off Thea Stevens.

Vanessa joined him, script in hand, and grinned. "Are you ready for a bath, Mr. Adams?"

Chapter 3

Since we're going to be bathing together, you'd better call me Luke." He liked Vanessa Rice, with her dry humor and engaging grin. He was going to enjoy working with her.

In the first script, his role could barely be called a speaking part. Vanessa would talk as she demonstrated the bathing technique and then would add some voice-over narration after the action was shot. Now Luke climbed onto a hospital bed in the center of the stage, ready for her to rehearse the procedure step-by-step with a dry cloth and an empty basin.

"I'm ticklish," he warned with a mock leer.

She leered back at him. "I'll remember that. But you'd better be nice to me or I'll use cold water tomorrow."

Luke appealed to the others. "Make sure she warms the water up, okay, guys?"

Bobby spread his hands, grinning broadly. "*I'm* not tangling with her."

"You're on your own." Thea grinned. "But if I were you, I'd behave myself."

"Cowards, all of you. And if you use cold water—" Luke grinned wickedly at Vanessa "—I just might forget my swimsuit!"

She fanned her face like a Victorian maiden. "Promises, promises, all I ever get are promises."

Bobby snickered, and Luke looked past him to see Thea blushing furiously. Blushing? A woman with a husband and a child blushing because he'd made a dumb joke? There was something sweet about that. Most of the young women he knew wouldn't blush at a male strip show, but Thea Stevens had an innocent, almost untouched air about her, despite her married status.

He would bet she'd been a virgin on her wedding night, too.

Luke had acquaintances—he wouldn't call them friends—who would laugh at the idea of a virgin bride, but he didn't. It would be wonderful to have that kind of love with a woman who was yours alone. If her unseen husband didn't appreciate that, he didn't deserve her.

He grinned at Vanessa. "What do you wash first, nursie?"

"Nursie?" She menaced him with the washcloth, and hilarity replaced pensive thought.

By the time they'd finished the first run-through, they were all clowning around and giggling helplessly. Perched on a stool, script and stopwatch in hand, Thea watched the horseplay. She felt like the only adult at a kids' birthday party, too old and sober to be part of the fun. She couldn't seem to do it, but she envied the others their ability to stop being grown-up, to laugh and make silly jokes.

"Children?" she called, more sharply than she'd meant to. "Can we get back to the business at hand?"

They looked around quickly.

"Sorry, Thea," Vanessa said after a moment. "We'll cut the silliness."

Thea flushed. "No, I'm sorry. I shouldn't have snapped."

"We'll get back to work anyway," Luke said. "What do you want to do next?"

"Time the scene."

"Okay." All business, he returned to the set. "I'm in bed when we open, right?"

"Mm-hmm, and, Van, you enter on cue."

"Okay." She moved into position. "All set."

Thea set her stopwatch. "Ready, and ... action."

This time they moved through the script with no teasing or wasted motion. Thea noted the scene-by-scene time and the total running time in the margin of her script. Her outburst had caused tension, but that eased, and they worked with only an occasional joke when Vanessa muffed a line or Luke moved at the wrong moment.

He had some comments on the script, too. "Why am I lying down when the scene opens?" He propped himself on one elbow and looked at Thea, who was sitting just behind the camera.

"Because the patient's usually lying down when the nurse arrives," she told him. "And Van's demonstrating how to help a weak patient sit up before the bath starts."

"Okay." He lay back. "I didn't get that from the script. Can you add it in?"

Like most writers, Thea didn't like to hear criticism of her writing, but she hid her feelings, because he was right. "Yes," she said after a moment's consideration, "we can put that into the narration easily enough. Van, can you talk about it as you help him up?"

"Sure." The nurse nodded. "What do you want to say, and when?"

Thea was scanning her script. "How about back on page 3, after the voice-over? You can say, 'To help the weak patient sit up, slip one arm behind his shoulders and lift as he attempts to raise his head.'"

Vanessa nodded, but a voice from the doorway replied.

"That's a very good suggestion, Mr. Adams." Jessica Curtis picked her way across the studio to the stage.

"Thank you." Luke sat up and swung his long legs over the side of the high hospital bed. "Have we met?"

"No, but in a way I'm your boss." She was a handsome woman in her fifties who always dressed in carefully proper business suits. "I'm Jessica Curtis, Director of Education." She shook Luke's hand firmly.

Thea bit her lip as she scribbled down the addition to the script and listened to Luke introduce himself. Jessica Curtis intimidated Thea with her polite, businesslike manner. She didn't intimidate Luke, though.

He was charming her with an ease Thea could only envy. Everything came so naturally to him. The charm, the smile, even the flirting—they all made you feel that he was interested in you alone. But how much was genuine, and how much just empty charm?

"I think it's going to work very well, don't you, Thea?"

"Uh, yes. Yes, it will." She cursed the stammer that said Jessica had caught her off guard again. "And he's right." She glanced at Luke Adams, trying unsuccessfully to hide the hostility she felt. "This clarifies the action." She turned away from him. "Did you have any suggestions, Jessica?"

She smiled as graciously as she could and wished fervently that she'd seen the problem in the script and fixed it herself before anyone else could point out her mistake. She wanted to show Jessica that she was competent and effective, not just an unimaginative follower.

"No, no." Jessica waved the idea off. "You folks are the experts here. I'm just an interested observer. Will you start filming tomorrow?"

"I think we can." Thea turned to the others. "If you two are ready?"

"I'm comfortable with that," Luke replied. "I can go over any script changes tonight."

"Van?" Thea asked.

"I just need to rehearse the new lines."

"Then we'll do one run-through in the morning, and if it looks good we'll start shooting about ten. Will you come down, Jessica?"

"I wouldn't miss it. I'll see you then." She smiled. "Is 'break a leg' appropriate in this situation?"

Amid laughter and general agreement that it was, Jessica left. The rest of the group turned to Thea with "what now?" written on their faces.

"We're all done, unless there's anything else you want to go over, Van."

"No, I'm fine. I've got to get back to my students, anyway."

She said goodbye, and Thea turned to her technician. "Bobby?"

"I'll set up for tomorrow, now that I know where the lights should go."

"Okay. Luke?"

"I'd like to go over the script with you. There are a couple of things that aren't clear to me."

Thea bit her tongue. It's *my* script, not yours! she wanted to say, but was immediately ashamed of her childish reaction. She would listen to his comments with an open mind, because she was there to make good films, not to protect her ego. She couldn't quite make herself like it, though.

In her office she seated herself behind the desk, while he stood in front of it, arms folded, regarding her with curiosity and amusement as she rearranged the papers she'd carried in.

"Okay." He leaned forward and slapped his palms on the desktop. "What is it?"

Thea looked up, her face blank. "I don't know what you're talking about."

"Yes, you do, and I'd have more respect for you if you'd just admit it. Something's made you mad, and I want to know what it is."

"I'll tell you what it is. It's you rewriting my script in front of Jessica Curtis!" Thea snapped. She held her breath for a moment, then shoved herself out of her chair and strode to the window to rest her forehead against the cool glass. "I apologize," she sighed. "That was unfair to you."

"Maybe it was and maybe it wasn't. But why are you so upset about it?"

With her back to him, she shrugged. "I'm just being childish."

She jumped when his large hands came to rest on her shoulders. He gently but firmly turned her around. Thea looked up into those impossible blue eyes, then dropped her head and stared at his shirtfront.

"I don't even know what you're apologizing for," he said softly. "I just want to know why you're upset." She said nothing, and he squeezed her shoulders. "Tell me."

"It's the script." Her voice was so low he could barely hear her.

"What about it?" His words were gentle, inviting her to confide in him.

"You keep finding problems with it," she muttered after a moment.

"Just minor ones."

"They're still mistakes I shouldn't have made."

There was a moment of silence. "Are you always this hard on yourself?"

Thea had heard those words before. She looked up and smiled wryly. "I guess so. Marty always said I was at least twice as hard on myself as anyone else was."

"Marty?"

"My husband. My late husband." She didn't notice that his hands stiffened on her shoulders for a moment before she moved away. She was smiling a little at the memories. "He used to tell me I was going to drive myself crazy being a perfectionist. Maybe he was right."

"Your late husband?" Luke repeated. There was a slight emphasis on the adjective.

"I was widowed six years ago." She pushed aside the papers on her desk and picked up the script.

"I'm sorry."

She looked up and smiled. "It's been a long time. What were the other problems you found in the script?"

"Just a few little things." Luke took the chair facing her and forced himself to concentrate on business. She wasn't married. She'd been widowed for six years. She was single.

An hour later, Thea scribbled the last note on her script. "Anything else?" she asked wearily.

"That's it." Luke closed his script and leaned back in his chair. "Everything else was crystal-clear. I wondered if I just didn't have the medical background to understand."

"No, it was my fault."

Thea raised her arms over her head and stretched, arching her back. Luke tried not to watch as her prim cotton blouse stretched over her small, high breasts.

"Whew!" She dropped her arms and shook her head. "I needed that. I'm glad you noticed the weak spots, though I should have caught them myself."

"Nobody's perfect." Luke's voice was husky. He refocused his gaze on her face. "Nobody can be—"

"I'm outta here, Thea." Bobby stuck his head around the door. "I've got a date waiting for a little piece of paradise."

"Go ahead." Laughing, Thea waved him off. "I'll see you in the morning." He disappeared, and Thea grinned at Luke. "He always has a date."

Luke stood. "How about you?"

She straightened sharply in her chair. "I beg your pardon?" Her response was as stiff as her spine.

"Do you have a date?" He perched on the edge of her desk and reached over to close her script.

"No." She pulled the script closer. "I don't."

"Good. You can have dinner with me."

"No, thank you." She pulled open the lower drawer that contained her purse.

"Come on." He took the purse from her hands and set it on the desk, putting his hand over it. "Have dinner with me."

"No, thank you." She tried to pull her purse free, but he wouldn't let go.

"Why not?"

"Because I don't think dinner is a good idea." She tugged again. "Will you please give me my purse back?"

"Do you have a problem getting a sitter? We can bring your daughter along, if you like."

"Stefi's spending the evening with a friend. I'll pick her up at eight, but—"

"Then there's no problem." He handed her the purse, then caught her hand and pulled her out of her chair, overriding her protests. "If we're going to work together on a creative project, we need to iron out our differences."

"We did that already. We're finished with the script."

"But not with the problem. We'll discuss it over dinner."

"We don't have to have dinner for—"

"You want to make good films, right?" He dragged her toward the door.

"Of course I do, but—"

"Then have dinner with me before I drop dead of starvation. You can use the time to tell me what's bothering you."

Thea planted her feet and refused to budge. "You're bulldozing me."

"You bet."

"That's not fair."

He grinned. "But it's working, isn't it?"

"I'm not hungry."

"Your appetite will come back when you see food."

"I shouldn't let you get away with this."

"But you will."

Thea rolled her eyes and sighed. "All right! All right, I'll have dinner with you. Just let me call and tell Stefi I won't be at home."

"Is this so painful?" Luke asked, smiling at her across the small table.

"Excruciating." Her reply was so demure that it took him a moment to feel the sting.

"Oooh!" He winced. "Well, I'm not making excuses. I wanted to have dinner with you."

"And you got your way." She paused. "This time." He flinched again, and she wet her fingertip and chalked up an invisible point for herself. She looked around the restaurant. "This is a nice place."

"I like it. It's quiet, and the food's good." Luke opened his menu. "Especially the steaks."

Thea scanned the menu. Despite the way she'd been manipulated into coming, and despite the fact that being out with Luke Adams made her nervous, she was beginning to enjoy herself. She was immune to heavy-handed flirting, but charm was hard to resist.

From force of habit and lack of appetite, she chose one of the lower-priced items on the menu. Luke requested a big steak.

"Don't you want more than that?" he asked when their order was taken.

"No, the chicken will be fine. Anyway—" she grinned "—it's a treat to eat something that I don't have to cook."

"Don't you ever eat out?" He frowned.

"If you call fast-food hamburgers eating out. Half the time I let Stefi eat and I just have a cup of coffee."

"If you call that stuff coffee." He grimaced. "Since this is a special occasion, let's make it even more special and have a glass of wine."

"That's not necessary." Thea shook her head quickly. Dinner and wine? She didn't think she was quite ready for that. Luke Adams was an attractive man, and when he turned on the charm he was darned near irresistible. She was edgy just sitting across a table from him; if he added wine to the mixture, she'd probably run out of the restaurant in a panic.

"Iced tea will be fine."

"No, it won't. With a glass of rosé and a good meal, maybe you'll be able to relax enough to tell me why you've been so upset." He signaled the waitress and placed their order, requesting a bottle of wine despite Thea's protests.

Half rueful, half annoyed, Thea shook her head. "Why do you assume you know what I'm thinking?" she demanded. "Who made you chief mind reader?"

"I don't read minds."

"Well, *that's* a relief!"

"There's no reason to be sarcastic. I'm an actor, and I know the ways body language and tone of voice can reveal tension. I can tell that you're nervous right now, just like I could tell you were upset this afternoon. It started when Mrs. Curtis came into the studio." He leaned forward, his gaze intent on her eyes. "Was she the problem?"

"Jessica? Of course not." Thea stared at the tablecloth, tracing circles on it with her fingertip.

"I think I know what it is." He trapped her fidgety hand under his. "It's because she heard me make a suggestion, isn't it?"

She glanced up at his face, then looked down at their hands. At that moment she couldn't have said why she didn't pull away but instead left her hand clasped in his.

"You're going to bulldoze me again, aren't you?"

"Yes, I am."

Thea sighed. "It's because she heard you tell me what was wrong with the script. This is my first production job, the first time I've been in charge. I have to prove that I can handle it."

"What do *you* have to prove? It's obvious you're doing a great job."

"Is it?" She didn't look up. "I don't know. All I know is that Jessica walked into the studio just as someone else identified a problem with the script I wrote."

"And that bothers you?"

"Yes, it bothers me!" She jerked her hand free of his and glared at him. "I know it's petty and paranoid, but it bothers me. I'm on probation for six months. I can be fired any time until then. I *need* this job, and I don't want Jessica to think I can't do it."

"She's not going to think that."

"Isn't she? When she walks in just as someone else spots problems in my script? What else is she going to think?"

"She's going to think that you hire good people. And she's going to think that you're open to suggestions, that you're flexible, adaptable."

"I don't know." Thea twisted her hands together. "Jessica is always very formal with me, almost reserved, and that unnerves me. I can't read her, and it drives me nuts, because I want to know if she thinks I'm competent."

"You're kidding, right?" Luke's laughter was incredulous. "You're so competent it's scary!"

"Don't make fun of me, Luke. This isn't a joke!"

"Of course it isn't. It was very clear to all of us that you were in charge of that studio today. When the kidding around got out of hand, you called a halt."

"I snapped. And I shouldn't have."

"Why not? We shouldn't have gotten so silly. You brought us back to the job we were supposed to be doing, and you did it without making a big issue out of it. When we wanted to know what to do next, we all looked to you for direction." He reached across the table to grip her shoulders and shake them gently. "You do a good job, Thea Stevens. Don't let anybody, even yourself, tell you different." He released her and sat back. "You do great work. I'm sure Jessica Curtis knows that."

She searched his face but saw no doubt or uncertainty there. "I hope so," she said heavily. "I hope you're right."

"Hey." He reached out and lifted her chin with a fingertip. "You're gonna do fine. Have a little faith, okay?"

"Do you—"

"Who had the chicken florentine?" The waitress interrupted them, her hands filled with plates.

"The lady has the chicken," Luke told her. "And the steak is mine." They were served their entrées, their wineglasses were filled, and condiments were declined. Then the overhelpful waitress finally left them alone.

"Do—" Thea began, but Luke silenced her with a finger on his lips.

"Yes. I do. Now eat your chicken and don't even think about work." Thea met his eyes for a moment, then nodded and bent over her plate, her usual appetite magically restored.

Chapter 4

I won't allow it," he insisted.

"It's not up to you." Thea reached for the check, but he snatched it away. "Luke, don't be ridiculous. I'm paying for my dinner, and that's the end of it."

"It was my invitation. I'm paying."

The set of his jaw reminded her irresistibly of a stubborn little boy. "Be reasonable, Luke. I know actors don't make a lot of money. I'll pay for my dinner."

Luke's frown deepened, and he shook his head sharply. "No. Not this time." He sat back, and Thea could see him deliberately making himself relax. "I bullied you into coming, so I'm paying. And you don't have to worry. One dinner isn't beyond my limited means. You can pay me back another time, all right?" He was taking bills from his wallet as he spoke.

She gave in reluctantly. "All right. So long as you *do* let me pay you back."

"Cross my heart and hope to die."

Thea smiled at the schoolyard oath and sipped her coffee as he dealt with the bill. She felt amazingly comfortable, even after their wrangle over the check. She'd been tight as a drum at work, tense and worried about her job and Jessica, with the nagging beginnings of a headache at the base of her skull. Now she was calm, at ease, confident, and Luke Adams had effected the transformation. She thanked him for that as he ushered her out of the restaurant into a clear, cool night.

"All part of the service," he informed her with a grin.

"What service?"

"The Lucas Adams Confidence-building Service. Lovely ladies in distress are our specialty."

"Are they now?" Thea hid her laughter behind a long, assessing look. "And have you done a lot of confidence-building for ladies in distress?"

"Once or twice." They had reached their cars, which were parked together in a dim corner of the lot. Luke ignored his battered Jeep and took her arm, turning her to face him. "Got your keys?"

She handed them to him, and he unlocked the door of her elderly sedan, then gave her back the keys, folding her fingers over them. He kept her hand in his. They were standing face-to-face by the car, and Luke was close enough to send a little shiver down Thea's spine.

"Luke?" She looked up at his face, shadowed in the dim light.

He touched her cheek lightly with his free hand, stroking the line of her jaw with a fingertip. "I'm sorry about your husband."

"Don't be. It's been a long time."

"Did you ever get over it?"

Thea looked down at their clasped hands. "Wounds heal," she said softly. "They leave scars, but those fade in time. They lose their tenderness."

"But the scars remain."

When she looked up, he could see the knowledge in her eyes, born of pain and grief. "A scar always remains." Her voice was quiet. "Even if you hide it with plastic surgery."

"I wish I could heal your scars for you." Luke studied her for a moment, then moved closer. "I knew the moment I saw you . . . but I thought you were married."

"You knew what?" Thea whispered. She was having trouble thinking. He was too near, but he wasn't near enough. She wanted to move away, but she couldn't summon the strength.

"I knew what I wanted," Luke murmured, and slid his hands up to her shoulders, then down her back to her waist, pulling her into his arms.

"Luke, no—" Thea pushed at him, but her protest was too weak and came too late to have any impact.

"Thea, yes." His arms slid around her, pulling her close, so that her breasts were pressed against his chest, her hips against his, her hands resting lightly, tentatively, on his shoulders. "I knew the moment I saw you that I wanted this."

Thea gazed up at him wide-eyed as he lowered his face to hers; then her lids fluttered down, and his lips met hers. It was a man's kiss, neither tentative nor exploratory but full of passion and hunger, and it rocked her to her soul.

His mouth teased and coaxed until her lips parted and he tasted the sweetness of her. Thea moaned wordlessly, clutching his sleeves as her body melted bonelessly into his. Without the support of his arms she might have fallen, for her knees had no strength of their own. His kiss was long and deep, hot and demanding, and when at last he released her she wobbled a little, dizzy and disoriented. She leaned against her car to steady herself.

"I knew," Luke said softly to himself. "I knew that was how it would be." There was none of the masculine triumph that she might have expected in his voice; in-

stead, there was a hint of something like awe. "Come on."
With an arm around her waist to support her, he opened
her car door and helped her inside. He reached across her
to fasten her seat belt.

"I'll follow you home and watch until you're inside."

"All right," Thea whispered, then looked up as he
straightened. "Luke?"

"Shhh." He touched his fingertips to her lips. "We'll
talk another time. Good night, Thea."

He swung the door closed and was in his own car before she whispered, "Good night, Luke."

Thea lay awake for a long time, watching reflections
from the streetlights swim across her bedroom ceiling.
Somehow she'd gotten Stefi bathed and into bed, parry-
ing her barrage of questions and listening to an exhaus-
tively detailed account of her evening.

It had been a relief to kiss Stefi good-night and go to her
own room, alone with her confused and chaotic thoughts.
She'd crawled into her wide, empty bed and pulled the
covers up to her chin. Lying there in the darkness, she'd
finally allowed herself to think.

Passion. She'd almost forgotten what it felt like, and the
rediscovery had left her shaken to the core. Passion. After
all these years of burying her own needs in the rush of
working and studying and raising Stefi, how could she find
passion with a man she barely knew?

She punched her pillow viciously and flopped down on
it again. Was it just that she'd been alone, her life empty
of a man's touch? Or was it Thea herself? Had she finished her grieving for Marty and gotten her life in order,
leaving her ready to feel passion again?

Or was it Luke Adams?

Was there something about him that had awakened her
woman's feelings again? Thea turned restlessly beneath the
covers. She refused to believe that. If she were looking for

a man, she would look for a steady, stable, reliable one, not an actor who approached life with the headlong enthusiasm of a teenager. But that was no teenager's kiss, her treacherous brain reminded her. It had been very much a man's kiss. Thea replayed it in her mind, and it was almost dawn before she drifted into an uneasy slumber.

Breakfast with her daughter was difficult. Thea was groggy, her head ached, and she wasn't really up to dealing with all the questions Stefi still had left from the night before. She had postponed the ordeal, but she couldn't avoid it forever. Like the proverbial elephant, eight-year-olds never forgot.

"Where did you go for your date?" Stefi demanded over her scrambled eggs. "Did you go someplace fancy?"

"What do you know about dates and going someplace fancy?"

"On TV, everybody goes to fancy places on dates. There's a band and sparkly lights, and people dance with each other. Did you dance with Mr. Adams?"

"No, honey, I didn't. We didn't go to a place with dancing."

"You didn't?" Stefi was crestfallen. "Where did you go?"

"To a restaurant. A quiet restaurant where they just have food. No band, no dancing, no sparkly lights."

"Oh." Stefi took a bite of her eggs. "What did you have to eat? Pizza?"

"No. I had chicken, and Mr. Adams had steak."

"Steak? I didn't know actors liked boring stuff like steak."

"Lots of people like steak," Thea pointed out. "You like steak."

"I know, but I thought actors ate special stuff."

"Like caviar? You tasted that at Mrs. Cudahy's Christmas party last year, remember?"

"Yuck!" Stefi grimaced, tongue out and eyes crossed. "Is *that* what special food tastes like?"

"'Fraid so." Thea hid her grin. "And anyway, Stefi, Mr. Adams and I weren't on a date. We had a business dinner so we could talk about work." Her voice was calm, but she could feel her color rising. Apparently her tone wasn't as convincing as she wanted it to be, because Stefi wasn't buying it.

"It was so a date, Mommy! Jamie's mother goes on dates a lot, and he says she always goes out for dinner."

"I think that's a different kind of date, honey." Stefi looked so downcast that Thea relented a little. "It was a nice dinner, though," she added.

"It was?" Stefi brightened. "Is Mr. Adams cute?"

"Is he what?" Thea's head jerked up.

"Is he cute? Actors are cute, aren't they?"

"Some of them are." Stefi waited hopefully until Thea gave up and said, "Yes, Mr. Adams is cute."

She was rewarded when Stefi's face broke into a wide grin. "That's great, Mom!" Her chair screeched as she shoved it back. "I'm done with my eggs. Can we go to school now?"

"Sure, if you don't mind getting there a little early."

"That's okay." She ran for the hall closet with a thunder of saddle shoes. "I want to tell Marybeth that my mommy had a date with a cute actor!"

Thea was smiling as she shook her head and poured herself another cup of coffee.

She wasn't smiling when she walked into the hospital, though. She was a jittering bundle of nerves at the prospect of facing Luke Adams.

"Stop it!" she whispered to herself. Two lab technicians walking along the hall looked at her curiously. She flushed and walked on quickly.

Thea pushed the office door open and froze. Bobby wasn't due for another half hour, but there was a dark shadow on the small couch. Thea held her breath and groped for the light switch, poised to flee. The lights flashed on, momentarily blinding her. When she blinked, the shadow from the couch was advancing on her. She turned to run, but he caught her arm, pulling her back.

"You!" Thea stared at his face and sagged against the doorframe, her heart thundering in her ears. "My God, you've got to quit doing this to me!"

"I didn't sneak up on you this time," Luke protested.

Thea crossed to her office, turning on lights as she went. "But I didn't expect to find somebody sitting here in the dark this early in the morning."

"What time is it?"

"Don't you have a watch?"

"I have a couple. I don't wear them much."

"Why not?" She unlocked the door and led the way into her office.

"I don't like being tyrannized by a timepiece."

Thea looked at him curiously. She hadn't heard that kind of comment since her schooldays, and associated it with remnants of the sixties counterculture. "Don't you have trouble getting to your appointments on time?"

Luke shrugged. "I got here on time, didn't I?"

"You got here early." She put her briefcase down, locked her purse in a drawer and began arranging her papers and possessions. "Do you get everywhere early?"

"No. But I'm rarely late, and I even drag the old watch out when the occasion seems to warrant it."

Unconsciously Thea adjusted the pretty gold watch Marty had given her for their first anniversary. She took it off only to sleep or bathe, and even the scratches on the crystal were old friends. She couldn't imagine being without it, but perhaps that was because she was a working mother, constantly juggling her schedule and Stefi's. She'd outgrown the stage in her life when she could afford to regard a timepiece as a tyrant.

But Luke hadn't. Thea looked at him, slouched in his chair, scanning his script as he waited for her. A vast gulf separated them. At twenty-nine, Thea was weighed down and hedged in by responsibilities. Luke at twenty-nine re-minded her of herself at eighteen, casual, carefree, re-sponsible to no one.

She closed the drawer and laid a clipboard and pencil on her desk. Luke looked up from his script.

"I had a reason for coming early," he said, and Thea's heart lurched. "I want to talk to you."

"We need to get to work," she said quickly. "We can talk later."

"We can talk now." Luke leaned forward, resting his elbows on his knees. "We need to . . . clear the air." He looked around the room. "I can feel the tension in here, even if you can't."

Thea began doodling on her blotter, watching the end of her pencil with intense absorption. "I don't know what you want to say, but there's something I need to say." She dropped the pencil and looked up, her face tight with em-barrassment. After a moment, Luke nodded. "I . . . I've thought about . . . last night."

"And?"

She took a deep breath. "And I realized that I'm not ready for that."

"Not ready for what?" he smiled.

"You know perfectly well!" she snapped as her tension broke through. "I'm not looking for involvement right now, or for dates, or even flirting. To be blunt, I'm not looking for a man. My life isn't just full, it's crammed, and I don't need anything else to complicate it."

Luke stood and smiled, not the least bit put out. He reached over the desk to touch her cheek. "The oddest things turn up when you're not looking for them." He turned toward the door, then glanced over his shoulder. "I'd better go get ready for my bathing debut."

Thea gave herself five minutes of calm thoughts and slow breathing before she left her office. By the time she walked into the studio, she was confident that she was right and that Luke was indulging in wishful thinking. She didn't have room in her life for a man. And Luke Adams was the wrong man for her, anyway.

Besides, they had a film to shoot. In the studio, Vanessa was dressed for her role in a crisp white nurse's uniform with a starched cap. She had made herself up for the camera, with more color on her face than she wore for everyday. A headset dangled around Bobby's neck as he tested the microphones.

"Hi, guys." Thea set her things down. "Is Luke dressing?"

"For what it's worth." Bobby grinned. "Where do you think his makeup will stop?"

"At his navel?" Vanessa suggested. Thea shook her head, still playing the adult in the schoolroom.

"You two are worse than a couple of kids! You look good, Van. Everybody's idea of the efficient nurse."

Vanessa looked down at herself. "Am I too starchy? I don't want to turn people off."

"You're fine. You want to be an authority figure."

"Yes, but an approachable authority figure, not like the warden at the state pen."

Thea grinned at that. "Don't worry, Van, you're not the state-pen type."

"State pen?" Luke asked from the dressing room door. "I'm not sure I like the sound of that."

He was wearing a navy-blue terry-cloth robe that reached his knees. Below it, his legs were muscular and tanned, dusted with dark-blond hair. Above the robe, Thea's gaze skipped skittishly over a deep V of tanned chest and more dark gold hair, then focused on his face. He'd done his makeup skillfully, darkening his face to a shade that would photograph perfectly, though it looked unnatural to the naked eye.

"I forgot to ask if I'm supposed to have any particular illness. I can turn myself pale and sickly if you want."

"Healthy is fine." Somehow she managed to smile, ignoring mental images of the body she couldn't see beneath the robe. She would see the reality too soon for her peace of mind, anyway. "We don't want you to look as if the evil nurse over there has been abusing you."

"I'll have you know I am the essence of gentleness and consideration," Vanessa informed them loftily. "And I resent all this evil nurse business."

"Actually, we need to get started." Thea broke in before things got out of hand. "Luke, would you get in the bed so we can light you?"

"Sure." He dropped his robe over a chair that stood just off-camera and picked up the hospital gown Bobby had left for him. He stuck his arms into it, then craned his neck to see the rear view.

"I thought this was supposed to fasten in the back."

"It does." Vanessa's voice was filled with laughter.

"Yeah, sure." He pulled at the edges, but a gap of several inches remained. "If you want a draft. Who thought these things up, anyway?"

"Somebody with a sense of humor." Vanessa joined him on the stage. "Don't bother tying it. I'll just have to undo it later."

"Yes, sir, ma'am."

"If you don't behave, I'm putting ice cubes in the water," Vanessa threatened absently as she arranged her supplies.

Chuckling, Luke climbed into the high hospital bed and tucked what there was of the gown around him. Fortunately, his back was to Thea. By the time he looked at her, she had her face under control.

Her mind was another matter. It spun wildly, filled with images of a lean, muscular body, tanned and smooth skinned, of golden hair sprinkled over strong limbs and across a broad chest. It was a man's body, with the powerful muscles and heavy strength of maturity. His back was broad, his hips narrow, and his strength was evident in the muscles of his legs and arms. His swimsuit, a brief sliver of black nylon, was practically nonexistent. Thea had never seen anyone so beautiful.

She couldn't banish the image of those arms around her, of that mouth kissing hers. She licked her dry lips and tried to steady her shallow breathing. If she didn't get hold of herself, she'd be blushing and staring like a schoolgirl.

She concentrated fiercely. Today they would do the full-frame shots of Van moving around the bed, demonstrating the bath. Tomorrow they would shoot close-ups; after that they'd reshoot things that hadn't turned out, then add the voice-over and any dialogue that needed improvement.

Bobby stepped aside when she walked over to the camera. She looked through the viewfinder, then stood back, nodding.

"Looks good, Bobby. You all set?"

"All set."

"Okay. Van, Luke, are you ready?"

They nodded, and Bobby put his headset on, positioning the microphone in front of his lips. Thea donned a similar headset so she could hear what the microphones heard, then said, "Van, the blanket's caught on the bed frame over there."

"Okay." She straightened it.

"Are you comfortable, Luke?"

He patted the blankets arranged over his chest. "I'm fine."

"Bobby, how's the sound?"

"Say something, Luke," Bobby called.

Luke placed a hand on his chest and flung the other one out dramatically declaring, "There was an old man from Chicago—"

Bobby interrupted him quickly. "Thank you! We may have to adjust when Van starts moving around, but it's fine now."

"All right." Thea picked up the clapper slate with Scene 1, Take 1 printed on it and walked into camera range. "Scene one, take one," she announced to the lens. "Marker." She snapped the clapper shut and stepped out of range. "Action."

Vanessa walked into frame, greeted "Mr. Smith" and began listing the supplies necessary for a bed bath as she took them from the stand. Thea watched both the stage and her black-and-white monitor, prompting from the script when necessary, signaling Bobby for a different camera angle or a sound adjustment.

As she worked, Thea found herself almost able to ignore the large expanses of Luke's body that were systematically washed, dried, lotioned and powdered for the camera.

Almost. They would use a plastic model to film the "personal" segment of the bath, but there was entirely too much man on view for Thea's peace of mind. She tried not to look at him at all, and when she had to, she tried to look at him as a piece of equipment, a prop for the film. Unfortunately, it was impossible.

"Cut!" she called as Vanessa washed Luke's left leg.

Vanessa straightened and turned toward her, squinting to see beyond the bright stage lights. "What did I do, Thea?"

"It's not you," Thea replied. "It's Luke's leg."

He regarded the limb in question. "What's wrong with it?"

Not one little thing. Thea tore her eyes away from all those finely sculpted muscles and that tanned skin. "Your leg's fine," she replied with a laugh that she managed to make sound natural. "But we're getting some flare off it now that it's wet. We need to reset the lights."

While Bobby took care of the lighting, Vanessa and Luke began clowning around, just as they had done at rehearsal. Thea found herself irritated—and inexplicably jealous.

"Children, children!" She tried to hide her feelings with a schoolmarmish voice and clapped her hands for attention. "Time to get to work."

Luke arranged himself on the bed, and Vanessa lifted the blanket off his left leg.

"Could you wet his leg again, Van?"

Vanessa dipped her cloth in the basin and stroked it down the length of Luke's thigh. Thea followed the movement with her eyes, unable to help herself.

Bobby's voice brought her out of her daze. "It's okay now, Thea. See for yourself."

He stepped back, and she looked through the camera, nodded and picked up the slate. "Marker." She clapped it shut. "And . . . action."

Vanessa resumed her washing and narration, and Thea tried not to look at Luke. Every time she did, she lost her train of thought.

As the day wore on, paying attention to business required more and more effort.

"Thea? What do you think?" Bobby's question jerked her away from an intent study of Luke's chest.

"Think? I'm sorry, Bobby, what did you ask?" She was blushing, and she knew Bobby could see it. She hoped Luke and Vanessa couldn't.

"Take a look in the monitor," Bobby said, watching her curiously, "and tell me if you like the way the shot's framed."

Cheeks hot, she looked. "That's good, Bobby. Thank you."

"Glad you could make it back," he murmured.

"Back?"

"From Mars," he answered dryly, and Thea flushed again.

She simply had to concentrate on her work, she realized. Vanessa was washing Luke's chest, and it couldn't be comfortable for him, since this was the third washing his chest had received. Luke was a professional, though, responding to Vanessa's comments and instructions as a real patient would when receiving a bath that made him more comfortable, not less. He stayed in character until the take was finished and Thea called, "Cut!"

"Aghh!" Luke grabbed for a towel. "That water's freezing!"

"Well, why didn't you say something?" Vanessa passed him a second towel. "You don't have to sit there and get pneumonia."

"I didn't want to blow the take." He rubbed the towel vigorously over his chest and arms. "You were on a roll, and I didn't want to throw you off."

"Next time throw her off," Thea told him. "You're here to act, not catch your death. Give me the basin, Van. I'll put warm water in it." When she returned, Luke was dried off and repositioned for the final scene. It was getting late, and they were all ready to finish up for the day.

"Think we can get it in one take?" Luke asked.

"I'll do my best," Vanessa said, and turned toward the camera. "Ready, Thea?"

"All set." She clapped the slate shut, and the action began.

As Vanessa described the way to wash a patient's face, Thea heard the studio door open quietly behind her, and she glanced around to see Jessica slip inside. She nodded a silent hello and turned back to the action while Jessica walked up beside her. She willed herself to be calm, but she could feel her stomach tighten and her palms dampen with tension.

Everything was going well when Bobby suddenly swore. "Oh, hell!" He stepped back from the camera. "Cut, guys! Cut it!"

"What's the matter?" Thea walked over to him as Van straightened, washcloth in hand. Nothing had gone wrong all day, but as soon as Jessica walked in . . .

"What happened?" Thea asked quietly.

"I goofed," Bobby said in disgust. "I was trying to get closer on his face and I blew the frame. Van? Luke?" he called to them. "I'm sorry. My fault!"

"That's okay," Vanessa called back. "Thea, where should we start?"

Thea was scanning her script. "Can you start with the washing again, Van? We can edit that in after the narration."

"Okay." She took her position, but before Thea could mark the take, Luke pushed himself up on one elbow.

"Just a minute, please."

Thea walked up to the stage. "Yes?"

"I wondered about something."

"What's that?"

"When you wash my face," he said to Vanessa, "I'm kind of uncomfortable when you cover my eyes."

"You are?"

"Yeah. I think I'd be happier if you didn't cover both eyes at the same time. If I were helpless in this bed, I'd like to know that I wouldn't be blind, too."

"That makes sense." Vanessa turned to Thea. "Can we work that into the script?"

"Sure." Thea scanned the page, looking for a good spot to insert the narration. "How about the bit about keeping soap out of the eyes? You can add a line there. Something like, 'For the patient's comfort, don't cover both eyes at once.' You can demonstrate as you say it."

"Okay." Vanessa mumbled the lines to herself. "I think I've got it."

Luke lay down again. Bobby framed his shot and focused, Thea marked the take, and they did it again. The new line blended smoothly into the narration, and as Vanessa went on, Jessica turned to whisper to Thea.

"I want to congratulate you, Thea."

"What for?" Thea whispered back.

"For hiring Luke. I can see he's going to be an asset to this project."

"Thank you. He is good, isn't he?"

"He certainly is." Jessica smiled. "You'll be able to learn something about the actor's perspective on things from him."

"Yes," Thea agreed with as much enthusiasm as she could muster. "I'm sure I will."

She turned to the stage again, biting her lip. Did Jessica see Luke as a valuable source of information, or did she think that Thea didn't know enough to do her job?

She frowned as she watched Luke. It wasn't his fault; he hadn't done anything wrong. The problem seemed to be that he did everything right. He was so good that his mere presence highlighted her own weaknesses. She glanced out of the corner of her eye at Jessica, who was raptly watching the action on the stage. What was she thinking about Luke? And, more to the point, what was she thinking about Thea?

Chapter 5

Thea's head was splitting. She gingerly touched the muscles at the back of her neck and winced. She wasn't surprised to find them as taut as piano wire. The cumulative tension of the rest of the day had been nothing compared to the tension of the last half hour.

When they'd finished the final scene, Jessica had congratulated Luke effusively on his work. Thea had told herself to be mature and reasonable, but it hadn't worked. She wanted so badly to do a great job, to be perfect. Maybe she wanted it too badly.

It has to be perfect. She shook her head ruefully at her own conceit. *I have to be perfect.* There was irrational, there was perfectionist, and then there was just plain stupid.

"And I'm just plain stupid," she muttered, and rested her head on the desktop. The tension was a hard knot at the base of her skull, and she reached back to massage the tight muscles with her fingertips.

"I still say you're too hard on yourself."

Luke's deep voice brought her head up with a jerk. The sudden movement made her wince, and she scowled at him as he entered the office. He moved behind her and brushed her hands away from her neck.

"What hurts?"

"Everything."

"Well, you won't do yourself any good that way. Let me."

At first the firm massage was almost painful, and Thea tensed when his hands touched her shoulders. Then her neck muscles began to relax and she let her head drop forward, her breathing falling into the same rhythm as the hands moving in circles on her skin.

"Hmmm." She sighed and let her head sag lower as the kinks eased out. Her forehead rested against her arms, which were folded on the desk.

Luke couldn't massage the base of her neck, so he reached around to open the top two buttons of her high-collared blouse. She didn't even move. He eased the fabric back and slid his fingers inside to massage her shoulders. His fingertips were slightly rough on her skin, and his palms were warm and hard as he pressed and kneaded. Thea wasn't even aware when he pushed the narrow straps of her camisole off her shoulders.

Luke breathed deeply as he massaged her. Her fragrance, light and warm, drifted up as he stroked her skin, which felt like satin under his hands. His fingers moved around and around in a steady, soothing rhythm. He could feel that she was half-hypnotized, and he was close to being dazed himself. Talking was a way to divert his thoughts.

"What was it?" His soft-voiced question didn't startle her out of her trance. "What made you so tense?"

It would have required an effort to think of an evasion, so she just answered honestly. "Directing. Jessica. You."

"Because Jessica came in, you mean?" He knew she was anxious about Jessica and her job. It was easy enough to put two and two together.

"When you made another brilliant suggestion," she mumbled against her folded arms. Luke could barely understand her. "She came in just then."

"It was nothing much."

"It was another of your good ideas. You were right about having your eyes covered, of course. Anybody would hate that, and she knew it."

"I just told you how I felt. You wrote the new line."

"Anybody can write a line to order. You had the idea. What did I do? Nothing!" She snorted inelegantly against her sleeve.

Above her head, Luke grinned. She looked like a Dresden doll, but there was a tough streak in his Thea. His hands faltered. When he set them back into their cadence, his mind was far away. *His* Thea? Why had he called her that, even in his thoughts?

His fingers moved automatically over her skin, warming and soothing, the way he'd learned as a boy. His grandmother, who'd been subject to severe headaches, had taught him how to relieve them years ago. Even now he could close his eyes and smell the glycerine and rosewater lotion she'd used. Her skin had been papery, her flesh spare over fragile bones. The skin beneath his hands now was smooth and fragrant, the flesh firm and supple....

Luke caught his breath at the quick rush of heat through his body and snatched his hands away. He backed away from the chair almost fearfully, his hands clenched in tight fists. He had to put distance between them, had to think. She'd told him that she wasn't looking. Well, he wasn't looking, either, not for something like this.

The massage over, she roused herself from her trance. "Thank you." She blinked sleepily and experimented, rolling her head from side to side, reveling in the absence of pain. "That was marvelous. Another two minutes, and I'd have been asleep."

"A little something I learned from my grandmother."

Thea straightened in her chair, pulling her blouse back up on her shoulders, a little embarrassed at the way she'd let her guard down.

Luke walked across to the door and picked up his jacket. "You're worrying about nothing." The grin he gave her as he pulled the jacket on was deliberately engaging. "I made an observation, but Jessica saw you work it into the script. She's no fool. She can figure out that you know what you're doing."

Thea shook her head, not falling for his easy consolation. "Thanks for the thought, but when you're around, all my failings seem to be highlighted."

"What?" He stopped moving, astonished.

"It's not your fault. You don't do anything deliberately. It's just that you have an instinct for what will make a script or a scene better."

"Failings?" Luke repeated incredulously. "What failings?"

"I should have realized that point needed to be added to the script."

"Why should you? You're not a nurse, you're a producer. If anybody should have thought of it, Vanessa should have, but you'll notice she's not hitting herself in the head over it." He wasn't going to allow Thea to be depressed. "Nobody knows everything, Thea. Perfection is only a concept."

"That's a cute little philosophy, Luke. Glib, but—"

"But *nothing*!"

He pushed himself away from the doorway in a quick movement that was too revealing of his inner feelings. Thea looked sharply at him, and he made himself relax, hiding his anger behind an easy smile.

"This is turning into an endless argument," he said. "And I'm too hungry to stand for it. You should be, too, after working as hard as you did all day. Come and have supper with me, and after I'm fortified with something, maybe I'll have the strength to argue some more."

"I didn't do that much." Thea began to smile, a teasing grin that lit her from within and warmed Luke with its glow. "You're the one who spent the day all wet."

"Don't forget powdered and lotioned." He sniffed at his arm. "I'm so clean I should squeak, and I smell like a drugstore. How does pizza sound? Or would you rather have Chinese or Mexican?"

"Thanks anyway, but I can't. I'm spending the evening with Stefi."

"That's fine." Her refusal didn't slow him down. "I'll pick something up and bring it to your house."

"No, thank you, Luke. I'll see you in the morning, okay?"

His smile faded. "Not really."

"Not really what?"

"It's not really okay." He shifted his feet and looked down at the floor, then gave her a wistful grin, appealing to her soft heart. "I really hate eating alone. I'd love to have supper with you and your daughter, if you'll let me."

He'd known she wouldn't be able to resist. With a slow smile, she relented. "All right, you can come. Stefi's dying to meet you. You fill her criterion for a real actor."

"Which is?"

"Acting on TV." She pulled out her briefcase and zipped it closed, then took her purse from a drawer. "The commercial was a point in your favor, but the soap role clinched it."

Luke stared at her for a moment, then gave a shout of laughter. "That's great! What if I'd been onstage? Broadway or something?"

Thea shook her head, fighting back laughter. "I think it had to be TV." She led the way out of the office, turning off lights and locking doors as she went. "There's one condition to this dinner, by the way."

"What's that?" Now that he'd gotten his way, Luke was prepared to be indulgent.

"I'm paying for the pizza."

Luke stopped in front of the elevator. "No."

"Then the deal's off." Thea walked in as the doors slid open and turned to face him. "I'll see you tomorrow, Luke."

"Wait a minute!"

With control of the situation slipping through his fingers, he jumped into the elevator just before the door closed. How did she manage to keep him just a little off balance without even being aware of it?

"I asked you first. I'm paying."

"Either I pay," Thea replied with maddening calm, "or you go wherever it is you go for dinner and Stefi and I have leftover meat loaf."

There was a finality to her ultimatum that made argument pointless.

"Why?" he demanded in frustration.

"Because I said I'd pay for the next meal, and I meant it." She walked out of the elevator, her back straight, her head as high as it would go.

Luke followed, admiring the smooth rhythm of her walk. "Even though it's my invitation?"

"Even though."

"All right." His concession was less than gracious. "I don't like it, but all right." Luke paused outside the old main doors. He didn't know where her car was, but his was around the corner, probably sporting a ticket. He'd have to ask about that parking pass she'd promised tomorrow, or the local parking authority would eat him alive. "What do you and Stefi like on your pizza?"

"Anything but anchovies and pineapple. Can you find the house? You hardly saw it when you followed me home."

"I'll find it. I'll be there, pizza in hand, in half an hour." He started one way, and she went the other; then he paused and turned back. "Thea?"

"Yes?" She looked over her shoulder.

"What's Stefi's idea of the ultimate, all-time, perfect pizza?"

Thea grinned. "Pepperoni, Canadian bacon, green peppers, mushrooms, olives and extra cheese."

"No onions?"

"No onions."

"Got it!" He waved and trotted around the corner to where his Jeep sat, a pink slip tucked under the wiper blade.

Half an hour later, a pizza box was sitting on the seat beside him. He scowled at the check stapled to the lid. He would have torn it off and thrown it away, but he knew Thea would suspect him of telling her the pizza had cost less than it actually had. She would be right, but that didn't lessen his irritation.

He hated taking money from her, *hated* it. It wasn't just chivalry or chauvinism, either. It was a bone-deep distaste for accepting money under false pretenses.

Thea thought he was a struggling actor, waiting for work, eking out a meager income from part-time jobs that left his days free for auditions and cattle calls. Bartending, parking cars, and waiting tables all offered flexible schedules and low pay and were sought after by aspiring actors chronically short of cash. Thea didn't know that he wasn't one of them.

Even if he told her that he had plenty of money she wouldn't believe him. She'd think he was salving his pride, and she'd probably try to slip him an extra five dollars, money she couldn't spare.

His first good look at her house didn't make him feel any better. Small and neat, it sat in the middle of a block of similarly small, neat houses, which were all ranch-style and looked about twenty-five years old. The yard was well kept, and he could see an ancient lawn mower in the garage. So she didn't pay a gardener to cut her grass; she did it herself with that dinosaur of a mower. It must have weighed more than she did. Luke's jaw tightened. She was too small to shove that thing around.

The front door opened before he rang the bell, and a slender little girl, tall for her eight years, grinned up at him.

"Hi! I'm Stefi," she announced. She pushed the door open as far as it would go and waited for him to carry the pizza inside.

"And I'm Luke." He stopped as she closed the door and carefully replaced the safety chain. "Glad to meet you. Can you show me where to put this?"

"In the dining room." She led the way, obviously feeling very important. "And I know who you are. You're Mr. Adams and you're working on Mom's movies and you're bringing us a pizza."

As Luke followed her across the living room, he saw a well-kept home, cozy and comfortable. Everything was pleasant, but the only expensive items were a crystal candy dish and a pair of silver candlesticks on the mantel, which had probably been wedding presents. It was a warm and welcoming room, but he could see the signs of a tight budget.

"Mr. Adams?" Stefi was eyeing the pizza box.

"Yes?"

"What's on the pizza?"

"Well," Luke said, keeping his face absolutely straight, "I got all my favorite stuff: pepperoni, Canadian bacon, green peppers, mushrooms, olives and extra cheese."

"You did?" Stefi's mouth opened in surprise, and so did her dark blue eyes, Thea's eyes. Her hair was a rich mahogany brown, not Thea's jet black, but her child's features, even with a snub nose and a dusting of freckles, bore a clear resemblance to her mother's. The gamine child would grow up to be a lovely woman. "That's my favorite kind of pizza in the whole world!"

"Is it really?" Luke stooped to look her in the eye. "We must be meant for each other."

"You're silly!" Stefi laughed and skipped to the table. "Mom said to put the pizza on the mat."

She pointed to a quilted pad in the center of the smallish table, which was already laid with plates and silverware. Luke set the box down, and Stefi sniffed the spicy-cheesy aroma longingly.

"Do you want a taste?"

Stefi glanced from the box to Luke and back again. Then she shook her head and squared her thin shoulders. "No, thank you, Mr. Adams. Mom says I have to wait for dinner."

"Then we'll do what your mom says. But you can call me Luke, okay?"

"Okay."

Luke looked around. "Where is your mom, Stefi?"

"In the kitchen. She's makin' a salad." Stefi wrinkled her nose.

"Mmm, good. I like salad, don't you?"

Manners warred with honesty, and honesty won. "No. It has carrots in it."

"You don't think much of carrots?"

"No! Marybeth says they're gross." Stefi screwed her face into a grimace.

"Who's Marybeth?"

"She's the third grade's final authority on dietary matters, and there aren't many things she likes," Thea answered from the kitchen doorway, where she stood with a salad bowl in her hands. For an instant Luke just stared at her.

Where was the conservative, faintly starchy woman who made videotapes and kept him off balance and intrigued him so? She had traded her prim skirt and blouse for snug, well-worn jeans and a cotton polo sweater. Her hair, released from its neat knot, hung in a thick braid to the center of her back. He watched her move across the room, fascinated by the fit of her jeans.

For some reason, he'd never imagined Thea in jeans. He'd imagined her in a sheer negligee, in a bubble bath, in an evening gown, even in nothing at all, but he'd never imagined her in jeans. If he had, he wouldn't have guessed how great she'd look in them.

"Have a seat, please, Luke." Thea set the salad on the table and grinned at him. "I'll get the drinks, and then we'll be ready."

"Let me help," he began, but she shook her head.

"No need. It's just a couple of glasses. Stefi, spare us Marybeth's opinions on food, okay?"

"Okay, Mom." She slid onto a chair and gave Luke a conspirator's grin. "Marybeth *really* hates pizza."

"So you don't believe everything she says?"

Though he was looking at Stefi, Luke felt Thea reenter the room. Perhaps it was a change in the magnetic field, but he could tell that she was there. When he looked up at her, his smile was easy and natural.

"Is iced tea all right for you, Luke?"

"Of course." He stiffened when she pulled the receipt off the pizza box. An actor made his living through pretense and deception, but this pretense left a sour taste in his mouth.

Stefi offered the box with her best company manners. "Will you have a piece of pizza, Mr. Adams?"

"Thank you very much," he replied, serving himself. "And call me Luke, like I said."

Stefi glanced at Thea, who nodded her permission. "You're welcome, Luke."

She pronounced his name with relish, obviously feeling very adult. Luke gravely passed the pizza to Thea. When he'd served himself some of the salad, he began to eat.

Stefi's chatter ceased abruptly, and she fell on her pizza like a hungry puppy. Luke watched in awe as she devoured two pieces to his one and then went on to eat a small salad, after carefully extracting all the shreds of carrot and cabbage and piling them on the edge of her plate. Thea watched but didn't comment, meeting Luke's glance with a wry smile that said she'd decided to save her battles for more important issues.

Stefi picked another carrot out of her salad with great care, and Luke had to cough to disguise a laugh. He cleared his throat and took a sip of water. "What things do you study in third grade, Stefi?"

"You mean like what subjects?"

"Uh-huh. Do you have math and reading and things like that?"

"Yeah. We do math homework on Tuesdays, and this week it's going to be long division. I hate long division."

"I think most people do." Luke grinned. "Have you figured it out yet?"

"Mom told me a secret."

Luke listened with interest as Stefi launched into a complicated explanation of Thea's backwards-multiplication theory.

Thea smiled, but her eyes were pensive. Luke seemed so like Stefi, willing to share the simple silliness that had gone out of her own life when Marty had been killed.

Tragedy had forced maturity on her, and her life had been packed solid with responsibility ever since. Though still a young woman, she had almost forgotten what it was like to feel young. Luke and Stefi giggled their way through dinner, but she ate quietly, feeling like an outsider. Feeling old.

"Who wants the last piece?" Luke hawked it like a carnival barker. "Thea?"

She shook her head, smiling at his performance. "I couldn't eat another bite?"

"Stefi? Can I interest you in this one, last, lonely slice of delicious, almost-cold pizza?"

Stefi shook her head, giggling. "My tummy's too full. Why don't you eat it?"

"Because if I eat another bite, I'll explode."

"Then we'll save it, and Stefi can have it for a snack after school tomorrow," Thea said, solving the problem.

"Okay!" Stefi pushed her chair back. "I'm all finished, Mom. May I be excused?"

"Yes, you may. Do you have homework to do?"

"Just reading."

"Do your reading, then, and when you're done you can play for a while before bed, okay?"

"Okay!" Stefi thundered out of the room, leaving an unnatural silence behind her.

Luke watched with a slightly bemused smile. "Where does she get the energy?"

"Kids come with good batteries. Would you like a nice quiet cup of coffee while she does her homework? I have some ice cream in the freezer, or—"

"Coffee will be fine." He rose with her, picking up his plate.

"You don't have to do that. I can take care of the dishes."

"Oh, no." She was reaching for the salad bowl when he plucked it off the table. "My mother trained me better than that. Come on." He led the way to the kitchen. "If we work together, we can clean this up in three minutes."

By the time Thea caught up with him, the dishwasher was open and he was loading the plates onto the rack. She didn't need a second glance to see that he knew what he was doing, so she left him to it, clearing the table and putting the leftovers away.

She was standing by the refrigerator with a plastic bowl of salad in her hand when he turned and caught her watching him.

"Did I do something wrong?" He glanced at the dishwasher, then at Thea again.

"No, you didn't."

"Then what . . . ?"

"I'm sorry. I was staring." She could feel herself blushing in embarrassment. "I guess I'm just surprised."

"That I can do dishes?" He grinned. "I have an older sister, too. She and my mother trained me well."

"I can see that." Thea put the salad away and closed the refrigerator door. She stood with her hand on the white enamel, smiling gently at the memories. "Marty didn't have the faintest idea how to load a dishwasher."

"Your husband."

"Yes." Her eyes were vague, looking inward. "He came from a very traditional family, Greek, like mine. Their last name was originally Stefanides, I think. Anyway, his mother wouldn't let him near the kitchen. When I was in the hospital after Stefi was born, it was the first time he'd done any kind of housework or cooking. He cleaned the house to get it ready for the day we came home. I never told him that when he went back to work I had to clean it all again. It was sweet of him to try, but he didn't have any idea what to do."

"An old-fashioned guy," Luke said softly.

"Yes," she said softly. "Old-fashioned."

"And helpless," he said grimly. "Mothers don't do their sons any favors that way. They just leave them ignorant and unable to cope."

"It was all she knew, her way of loving him."

"I'm glad my mother chose another way. I'd hate to think that being loved meant being smothered."

"It's obvious you don't have to worry about that." Thea grinned. "Apparently your mother loved you by making you do dishes."

"And laundry and vacuuming and washing the car and cutting the grass—"

"Oh, stop it!" Laughing, she cut him off in midlist. "You sound like the mistreated urchin in a Dickens novel."

"Oliver Twist?"

"More like David Copperfield." She tipped her head to the side, studying him with teasing curiosity. "Or the little prince in *A Tale of Two Cities*. There's a lot of arrogance lurking under that boyish facade."

"Arrogance?" Luke's haughty outrage would have satisfied the most demanding director. He looked down his elegant nose at her, watching her giggle, until her laughter infected him as well. "You need to learn the proper respect for an actor's talent, you know that?"

"For an actor's ego, you mean!" She let him tuck her hand in his elbow and lead her to the front door. "And if I give yours too much respect, it'll get too big for you to carry it around."

At the door, the laughter faded from his face. "Will you say good-night to Stefi for me?"

"Or good morning." Her smile was gently maternal, and something Luke barely recognized stirred inside him. "Since she hasn't been out here ninety-nine times to see what we're laughing about, I imagine she's already asleep."

"Will you wake her up?"

"No. Once she's asleep, that's it. I can get her into her pajamas and put her in bed without her knowing anything about it."

"Will you kiss her good-night?"

"Of course. She's very precious to me."

Luke studied her face for a moment. "How about me?" he asked, very softly. "Will you kiss me good-night?"

Though she'd thought of him as a kid, there was nothing boyish about the man who looked down at her now. His eyes were shadowed and mysterious in the dim light, his smooth, handsome face reduced to hard angles and male strength. Her heart began to pound in a slow, heavy rhythm.

Without realizing she'd moved, she swayed closer to Luke, the initial instant of trepidation replaced by something new and unfamiliar. Excitement sang through her veins, hummed over her skin and melted her cautious reserve like ice cream on a summer day.

"I don't know," she whispered with a flirtatious daring that astonished her. "Why don't you try it and see?"

There was a flash of startled surprise in his eyes; then one corner of the beautifully curved mouth lifted, and he bent his head toward hers. One large hand caressed her throat, then slid beneath her hair, cradling her skull, tipping her face up to his. He brushed his lips across hers in a butterfly caress. "I thought you were nervous, but you're not, are you?"

"No." She whispered the denial against his mouth, and it was almost too much for his self-control.

"Maybe you should be," he murmured. "Maybe you should be very nervous."

Thea experienced the same sensation in the pit of her stomach that she felt at the top of the first terrifying drop on a roller coaster. Half fear, half anticipation, it was a thrill tingling down her spine, a push to be daring.

She let her head fall back, lifting her mouth up to his. Luke tried for control, but in a way he didn't quite understand he had to kiss her. He had to taste her sweetness.

"Maybe I *should* be nervous." She touched her lips to his, then drew back a fraction, her smile mysterious and wise. "Or maybe you're the one who should worry."

Chapter 6

They were supposed to do close-ups the next morning. Taping was scheduled to begin at eight, but Thea's phone rang at 7:15.

"I have a breakfast meeting," Luke told her. "I'm sorry to let you down, but I'll be there by nine, I swear."

"A meeting for breakfast?" Thea held the phone on her shoulder as she braided Stefi's hair and looked longingly at the coffee steaming gently on the kitchen counter. "What on earth do you talk about over bacon and eggs?"

"Business. And breakfast is the new power meeting time. Lunch is passé."

"Well, of course it is," she drawled, exaggeratedly blasé. "Who am I to argue with power meetings?"

"Thanks for understanding. I set this thing up for 7:30 because lunch would break up the day. So once I get to the hospital, I'm all yours."

Thea could hear a smile in his voice as he said goodbye. She replaced the receiver and snatched a sip of coffee before returning to Stefi's hair.

"Was that Luke?" Stefi looked over her shoulder.

"Mm-hmm." Thea took her daughter's head in gentle hands and straightened it. "Turn around, honey, so I can get this finished. We're going to be late as it is."

"Okay." Stefi faced straight ahead, sitting very stiff and tall. "Did you tell Luke I had a good time last night?"

"I think he knows you did." Thea smiled as she braided Stefi's silky hair with quick, deft hands. "You were certainly laughing enough."

"He was laughing, too." Stefi turned as Thea finished the braid and fastened its end with two red beads on an elastic band. "And so were you."

"I know. We had a nice dinner, didn't we?"

"We sure did!" Stefi hopped down from the stool she'd been sitting on. "Is Luke coming to dinner tonight?"

"I don't think so." Thea saw Stefi's face fall. "Last night was nice, though, wasn't it? I'll tell him you had fun. Go get your jacket and book bag, okay?"

"Okay!" Stefi took off. "Race you to the car, Mom!"

Thea got Stefi to school on time, though just barely, and was at her desk by ten to eight.

"Where's Luke?" Bobby followed her to her office, a grin on his face, his earring glinting next to his cheek.

"Am I supposed to have him in my pocket?"

"Whatever turns you on. I thought he was going to be here at eight."

"He was, but he called me and said he had a breakfast meeting. He'll be here by nine."

"A breakfast meeting, huh?" Bobby raised an appreciative eyebrow. "Our boy must be moving into the big time."

"Do you think so?" Thea sat down and unlocked her desk. "He just said he scheduled it for breakfast so he wouldn't have to break the day up with a lunch meeting."

Bobby draped himself over an armchair, one leather-sneakered foot swinging. "Doesn't that strike you as strange?"

"Not really." Thea put her purse in her desk drawer and glanced up at him. "Should it?"

"Maybe not." Bobby gazed out the window at a moth-eaten azalea growing in the courtyard. "But it's usually the one with the clout who sets the meeting. It's a Hollywood power thing, you know?"

"Not really, but I'll take your word for it." Thea's voice was dry. "Don't you think you're making too much out of this power business?"

"Maybe." Bobby unwound his length from the chair and stood. "Nice for him, though, that he can schedule meetings at his own convenience."

"Mm-hmm," Thea agreed absently, reaching for the phone. "I'll call Van and tell her she doesn't need to come down until nine."

"Okay. You want to look at yesterday's tape? We can find most of the problems in an hour."

"Sure. I'll be with you in a minute."

Thea dialed quickly, but her mind was on Bobby's half-serious remarks. Was there any significance to the fact that Luke had been the one to arrange the meeting, or was Bobby just imagining things?

They were absorbed in the tape when Luke walked into the office.

"How does it look?" The deep-voiced question came from scant inches behind Thea's head.

She whirled around with a gasp, then sagged back into her chair when she saw it was only Luke. She pressed a hand to the pulse thundering in her throat. "Don't *do* that!"

"I didn't know you were going to jump that way." Luke took her hand from her throat and rested his fingertips on the hammering pulse. "Whew! I'm sorry, Thea. I didn't mean to give you heart failure."

"Well, you almost did." She scowled at him. "Quit sneaking up on me, will you?"

He studied her face, concerned. "After this, I'll announce my presence with drums and cymbals."

"A simple knock on the door will do fine."

Thea sat up in her chair, but Luke didn't move back, which placed his face very close to hers. His skin was smooth and freshly shaven, and his breath feathered her cheek, warm and coffee-scented. Her breathing quickened, and she stiffened automatically against the seductive pull of his nearness. Luke's gaze flicked to her sweater, soft gray wool over softer curves. The rhythm of her breathing could be read there, and he smiled into her eyes before he straightened and moved away.

Thea could feel the heat scorching her cheeks. If Bobby noticed, she'd blame it on her fright, but to her relief he had other things to concern himself with. He'd nodded to Luke, then returned to the videotape. Now he gestured to her.

"Thea?"

"Yes?"

"Van will have to redo these lines. The blanket rustled and covered her up."

"What page is that?"

"Twenty-three. I've marked it."

"Thanks, Bobby. Luke, if you'll get ready, I'll call Van. You know which close-ups we're shooting, right?"

"I've got 'em." He tapped his copy of the script. "I'll get changed."

Bobby switched off the VCR. "I'll set up." Thea dialed Vanessa as he followed Luke out the office door.

That day's filming was easier for all of them than the previous day's had been. The close-ups were shot in brief segments, so Vanessa had to remember only short bits of action and narration and Luke had to uncover only the small part of his body that was involved. He was vocal about his relief that he didn't have to spend long periods of time wet and cold.

Thea found it much easier to concentrate on her work when she didn't have to expend so much effort on ignoring his body. She kept her professional cool, spared the schoolgirlish confusion that had tormented her on Monday. Even Bobby had an easier time, framing small, close shots and focusing on a shallow depth of field.

The rest of the week slid quickly past, and by Friday afternoon the taping was complete. They had finished a preliminary editing job that morning, and at 4:30 Thea was watching a rough cut of the tape on the VCR in her office.

She looked up at the sound of a hesitant tap on her door. With exaggerated caution, Luke peered around the doorframe. "Is it safe to come in?"

"Come on in!" Laughing, she stopped the machine and watched him enter.

He'd kept the running joke going all week, knocking on every available door and making his presence known with whistles, tap dancing and bus-station-style announcements.

"Is that the tape?"

"The first rough cut."

"How is it?" He walked around to perch on the end of her desk, where he could see the screen.

"You can see for yourself." Thea rewound the tape, then started it up again. She appeared on the screen and clapped the slate. "Action." Vanessa walked onto the set and greeted her "patient," and the tape proceeded. Close-ups were intercut with long shots, with some bobbles and breaks that would be smoothed out in the final editing.

Thea watched for flaws in the logical order of presentation, but Luke watched his own performance critically.

"There!" His sharp interruption startled her. "Damn!"

"What is it?"

He reached over her shoulder to pluck the remote control from her hand, then ran the tape backward until he reached the point he wanted. He pushed the start button and Vanessa rewashed his arm.

"Right there." He pointed at the screen. "I'm helping too much. She's supposed to be holding my arm up, but I'm doing it for her, making it look easier than it really is. It looks staged."

Thea ran the tape back and watched the segment again. "I don't see anything like that."

Disgusted with himself, Luke sat back. "Let's see the rest. I might as well get all the bad news at once."

Thea pushed the pause button and looked at him curiously. "Are you always this hard on yourself?"

He didn't seem to notice that she'd turned his question back on him. "I want to give a good performance."

"You did. I've been editing it, and I know a good performance when I see one."

"Why don't you let me be the judge of that?" He pulled her arm up and took the remote, setting the tape in motion again. He grumbled steadily under his breath, then erupted again. "Hell!"

Thea sighed. "What is it this time?"

"Look at the beginning of the take, where you cut back from the close-up." He scanned back. "Right there. I'm laughing, see?"

Thea watched, then shook her head. "You look fine to me."

He scowled at the screen again. "Look, right there. Van said something funny just before the take and broke me up. I'm not hiding it well enough."

"Luke, I don't see a thing. And if I don't, nobody else will. You're being too hard on yourself."

"I'm being realistic. You're biased."

"I'm supposed to be the perfectionist here, remember?" she protested with a smile. "I didn't see anything wrong with any of the takes I edited into this cut. Let's just watch the rest of it quietly, okay?"

He watched, grumbling and muttering under his breath. At the end, Thea stopped the tape and sat back, smiling and satisfied.

"I like it."

"Van did a great job. You'd never know she wasn't a professional."

"She is." Thea grinned. "A professional nurse."

"Are you sure she doesn't have a Screen Actors Guild card hidden somewhere?"

"No SAG card, only a Ph.D. in nursing."

"A Ph.D.," he mused. "Makes my undistinguished B.A. in history seem pretty thin."

"To say nothing of my night school B.A. in film and media." Thea ejected the tape from the machine and placed it in a locked cabinet, then stood and faced him, her hands on her hips. "There is *nothing* wrong with this tape," she told him severely. "Do you understand me, Luke Adams?"

He hid his grin. "Yes, ma'am."

"And you gave a fine performance. Understand?"

"Yes, ma'am."

She stepped closer, leaning threateningly over him as he sat. "And I defy anybody to find anything wrong with it. *Including you!*" She glared.

"Yes, ma'am."

His meekness was her undoing. She bit her lip, but giggles seeped out anyway. She collapsed into her chair and let the laughter run its course. "You," she gasped, "are certifiable."

Luke lounged against the wall, arms folded across his chest. He lifted one hand, dusted his fingernails across his lapel and examined them with interest. "It's part of my charm," he informed her, sending her into another spasm of laughter.

"I must be so tired I'm slaphappy." She brushed tears off her lashes. "It's been a long week."

"Especially for you." Luke touched the stacks of papers and tapes and slides on her desk. "Do you always work this hard?"

She shrugged. "I do what has to be done. This week was unusual, doing the first tape of the series." She looked up at him. "Making a tape is a lot harder than doing slides and things."

He smiled. "I'll second that. Are we starting epic number two on Monday?"

She nodded. "We are. If we can tape each one in a week to ten days, we'll be ready to begin duplication and distribution in a month or so."

"And you'll be exhausted." He lifted her chin with gentle fingers. "You push yourself too hard, woman." He looked her up and down, as if to emphasize the accuracy of his statement.

Thea held his gaze for a taut moment; then she flushed and looked down at her desk. The next script was in front of her, and she picked it up in hands that only shook a little.

"I think you'll like this tape better than the bed bath."

"The ambulation tape?"

She nodded. "*Bed bath* didn't require much acting, but this one will give you more of a challenge."

"Sometimes it's more of a challenge *not* to act too much." He slid off the desk. "I'd like to come in sometime over the weekend and observe the things I'll be doing. I don't understand all the techniques you describe in the script."

"I can arrange for you to observe. That's no problem. But if you'd like to stay for a while tonight, I can show you the equipment and how it's used."

Luke looked out the window at the early darkness. "I wish I could, Thea, but I've got an appointment in an hour."

"Seven-thirty in the morning and Friday night, too?" Thea asked, teasingly. "You have appointments at very weird hours."

Luke shifted his feet. "Most actors have meetings at odd times."

"Since I've never been an actor, I wouldn't know." She watched him. There was something about nis averted face, the stiff set of his shoulders as he looked out the window, that spoke of tension. But why should he be uneasy? "If you don't mind spending your Saturday working, I can go over that stuff with you tomorrow."

He turned around. "I'd appreciate it. But won't you be spending Saturday with Stefi?"

"Not tomorrow. She'll be on a Girl Scout campout until Sunday. Since I'll be on n y own anyway, I might as well be doing something constructive."

"Okay. What time shall I pick you up?"

"I have to drop Stefi off at 9:30, so I'll meet you here at ten, all right?"

"It's a date, sweetheart."

He slung his jacket over his shoulder with Bogart panache, leaned across the desk to press a quick kiss to her lips and then was gone. Thea sat there as seconds ticked past, unaware that her fingertips were pressed to her tingling mouth.

Saturday morning was gray and cool, the sky heavy with the threat of winter rain. Thea dressed Stefi in jeans, a sweater and a warm jacket and wore almost the same thing herself. When she arrived at the hospital, she found Luke already waiting for her.

She stopped at the bottom of the stairwell, looking at him. He wore a battered leather jacket, and his jeans were as worn as hers. He was sitting on the hall floor with his arms folded and his chin resting on his chest, apparently asleep.

The overhead light gleamed on his hair, picking up shades that ranged from wheat to gold to sun-bleached platinum. His legs stretched halfway across the hall, long and lean, his strong muscles outlined by the much-washed denim of his jeans. He filled the hallway with a vibrant male presence, bringing life to the sterile tile and linoleum.

Thea watched for several seconds, but Luke didn't move except for the regular rhythm of his breathing. A slow smile spread over her face, and she tiptoed carefully toward him, flinching when her rubber soles squeaked on the linoleum. She stopped beside his legs and nudged his foot with her toe.

"Most people say hello." The deep-voiced comment was completely unexpected. Thea jumped back and stood glaring at him as he slowly got to his feet.

"I thought you were asleep!"

"And you thought you'd sneak down the hall and wake me up." He unfolded himself to his full height and grinned down at her. "Sorry to disappoint you, Thea."

"No you're not." She marched around him and shoved her key into the lock. "You're congratulating yourself on your little joke." She led the way into her office, snapping on the lights as she went. "Actually—" she turned to him, her face alight with laughter "—I must have looked pretty silly tiptoeing down the hall."

"I don't know if I'd say *silly*...." His eyes sparkled with suppressed laughter.

"Then what would you say?"

A dimple appeared at the corner of his mouth, and his handsome smile became devastating. Thea was very conscious of how close he was standing, with only a few scant inches separating them. "I think I'd say—" he bent closer "—cute."

"Cute?" Thea demanded, outraged. She stepped back, out of range of that dangerous closeness, and moved behind her desk. "A professional woman—and, I might add, your current boss—cute? Next time I decide to sneak up on you, I'll make sure you don't see me coming."

"Promises, promises." She was grateful when he turned away to examine the pile of equipment stacked against the far wall of her little office. "You've got a lot of stuff here."

"You saw the prop list for that script."

"I just didn't know how much stuff it would translate into."

"It makes quite a pile, doesn't it?" She found the script on her desk. "How was your meeting?"

Luke went very still. "My—"

"Your meeting. The one you had last night. How did it go?"

She looked up to see Luke watching her, but when their eyes met, his gaze slid away. He looked at the floor for a moment, then grinned at her. She didn't notice that the grin didn't reach his eyes.

"It was fine."

"That's good. Did you see your agent? I liked talking to him, even though he didn't want to offer you this job."

"Yeah, Morrie's a funny guy."

"Was your meeting with him?"

"Morrie? No, not last night. It was just . . . one of those general things. You know."

Thea didn't know, but she didn't ask him to elaborate, because he had lifted a tangle of leather straps off the pile of equipment and asked, "What's this?"

"An ambulation belt. It fastens around the patient's waist, and the nurse holds those handles while walking with the patient in case he becomes weak or dizzy."

"Hmm." Luke turned the belt over in his hands, sorting out the apparent confusion of straps until he saw how the device was used. "That's a good idea."

"I imagine the nurses think so." He looked up and saw her grinning.

"That's right, laugh at me," he said huffily. "All I'm trying to do is learn."

"Far be it from me to stand in the way of education." Thea walked across to him. "That's why we're here. What else would you like to know about?"

"How about this?" He lifted an aluminum crutch from the pile. "I know it's a crutch, but are there trade secrets to using these things?"

"A few." She took it and moved to his side. "Crutches have to fit you. You have to use the right technique to walk or you can end up with damage to the nerves in your armpits. And you have to go upstairs feet first and downstairs crutches first and—"

"Whoa! Let's start at the beginning. How do you make the crutches fit you?"

"Lift your arm and I'll show you." She loosened the wing nuts that adjusted the crutch's height and moved to his side to demonstrate.

Even absorbed in her work, it was impossible to forget who she was working with. She had to assist him with the crutches, stand behind him as he used the walker and buckle him into the belt to demonstrate how Vanessa would move with him, one hand on his waist, the other arm around his back.

They were pacing slowly across the outer office when Luke stopped short. She swung around his suddenly immobile body and thumped into his chest. Before she could recover her balance, Luke wrapped his arms around her, holding her firmly in place.

"Is—" A thin squeak emerged instead of her voice. She cleared her throat and tried again. "Is something wrong?"

"Not anymore."

The smile on Luke's lips echoed the smile in his voice. Thea's chin was resting on his chest, and when she looked up, all she could see were his blue, blue eyes.

"I think..." He bent his head and brushed his lips across her forehead, very lightly. "...that everything is very..." His lips touched her cheekbone and the tip of her nose. "...very..." He bent lower, and his breath warmed her lips. "...very right." And then his mouth closed over hers.

Chapter 7

Thea's eyes drifted closed, all her senses concentrated on the magic he was working on her mouth. She didn't know when her hands slid up Luke's back to clasp his shoulders. She didn't know when her body softened and molded to his, when her knees weakened, but without his arms to support her she might have fallen in a heap at his feet.

It was heat and light and dizziness, and yet it was no more than a kiss. His lips brushed over hers, moving slowly, teasing and tempting until she reached for him, opening her mouth with a little mutter of protest as she sought to return the kiss.

Luke tightened his arms and shifted to take more of her weight against him. The flex of his muscles against her body excited her with its intimation of strength and protection, and the taste of his mouth was a sweet temptation to step into madness with him.

It was only when Luke lifted his head that sanity's cool breeze touched her again. She gazed up into his face, the haze of passion clearing slowly from her mind. Her eyes widened in alarm, and she stiffened in his embrace, pushing against arms that automatically tightened to hold her.

"I'm not going to apologize," he murmured, and traced a fingertip across her swollen lips. "I just couldn't wait any longer."

"Wait?"

He smiled. "To kiss you."

Thea stiffened again. Luke stroked her back, his hands warm, comforting and just a little seductive. When she didn't relax, he tipped his head to one side, looking into her face.

"Hey," he whispered, "don't be afraid, not of me."

"I'm not!" Her hotly whispered denial was a bit too quick.

Luke smiled gently. "I'd never hurt you, Thea. You know that."

Thea flushed. His clear blue eyes saw too much, and she didn't want him to discover that she wasn't afraid of him, but of herself. She was lost on shifting ground, uncertain where security lay. Luke stroked her cheek, and she instinctively turned her face into his palm, accepting the comfort he offered without even knowing that she needed it.

"Hey." He slid his fingers under her chin and tipped her face up. "Thea?"

"What?"

"It's not so bad. You need to have a little fun along the way."

She could have said he was wrong, that the only way for her to take life was seriously, but his words struck a nerve. Maybe he was right.

"You think so?" Her face lightened.

"I think so." Smiling, he loosened his arms and let her lean back. "And I know just what you need."

"Oh, do you?"

"Dr. Feelgood's got the answer. You need a picnic."

"A picnic?" She looked out the window at the sullen sky. "On a day like this?"

"Why not? It's a perfect day for it."

"Sure it is. If you like to picnic in the rain."

"Don't be a wet blanket." He ignored her groan at the pun. "Are we finished here?"

"We've gone over all the equipment you'll use. Do you need to see anything else?"

He shook his head. "I've done what I came to do. It's one in the afternoon and I'm starving, so will you come on a picnic?"

"Even though it looks like rain?"

"Don't be closed-minded. With a little positive thinking, it'll hold off just for us."

Thea burst out laughing and threw up her hands. "Who am I to argue with logic like that?"

When Luke Adams set out to have fun, he didn't waste time.

In less than an hour they were on a steep hillside in Griffith Park, unloading a blanket, a radio and a sack filled with food. Luke had parked his Jeep beside the winding road that led up to the observatory, where a patch of level ground boasted an ancient olive tree, soft grass and a view of Los Angeles. The view should have been panoramic, but the air, hazy with moisture and low clouds, reduced visibility to the nearby Hollywood and Silverlake Hills.

"Your sister fixed all this food?" Thea was still puzzling over the fact that Luke had driven into an alley behind a Bel Air mansion, left her in the Jeep with instructions to drive around the block if a policeman tried to ticket them, disappeared into the enormous house and reappeared with the food.

"Yeah." He was absorbed in tuning the radio to an oldies station. "She's catering a party there tonight. What looks good?'' He reached into the sack, took out a plastic bowl and shook it experimentally.

"I can't tell," Thea took out another bowl and studied it. "Everything's wrapped up so that it all looks the same."

Luke began easing the lid off. "Let's hope it's not pasta with squid ink."

"Pasta with *what*?"

Before Thea could repeat her question, Luke motioned to her to be quiet and reached for the radio. He turned up the volume in time to hear, "…seventy percent chance of rain today, tonight and tomorrow. Heavy swells on the west-facing beaches, so all you surfers beware. High temperature this afternoon—"

He switched the power off.

"Turning it off won't help," Thea said with a wary look at the clouds overhead. "You knew the forecast was for rain."

"It's not the forecast I'm worried about," he retorted, putting their lunch back in the bag with more haste than care. "It's that."

He pointed toward the ocean. From their vantage point on the hill, they could see a dark, heavy mass of clouds sweeping in from the west, the rain it carried with it clearly visible. It was equally clear that the clouds were heading straight for their hillside.

"Oh, boy!" Thea scrambled to her feet, yanking the blanket into her arms. "We'd better hurry!" Fat drops had begun to rustle the leaves overhead and spatter on the ground before they had a chance to collect everything.

"Ready?" His arms full, Luke grinned at her. The rain was gathering strength, wetting the blacktop and penetrating the thick umbrella of the olive tree, and beating it was a game to him, a challenge. "One, two, three, *run*!"

Laughing, they sprinted toward his Jeep, through rain that suddenly became a downpour. They were soaked in the first few yards, and Thea could scarcely see by the time they reached the Jeep. Breathless and drenched, she huddled against the passenger door while Luke unlocked it. He boosted her into the seat with a hand under her bottom, dumped the food in her lap and slammed the door to sprint around to the driver's side.

The drumming of rain on the canvas top was deafeningly loud, but at least it was dry inside. In fact, the Jeep was drier than they were. Thea wiped the rain from her eyes, looked at the dripping man beside her and burst out laughing.

"I don't know what you're snickering at," he said haughtily. "You look like somebody stuck you under a shower."

"You did." She giggled. "When you insisted on picnicking on a rainy day. And you look like a drowned rat!"

"How about a wet dog?" There was a wicked gleam in his eyes as he leaned toward her and shook his head hard, spraying her with water from his hair.

"Stop that! Luke, stop it!"

Laughing and dripping, she tried to fend him off, but he caught her hands and held her close, sprinkling her thoroughly. When he stopped, they were nose-to-nose, his tangle of wet, dark-gold hair falling into eyes alight with laughter.

He pulled her closer. "Take back the drowned rat?"

"Never!" She raised her chin, defiant.

"Not even if I torture you again with my wet hair?"

"Not even then. I can't get any more soaked than I am now."

"I see." He scowled, an acting class study in deep thought. After a few moments, one eyebrow lifted and a sinister twist altered his features. "Ve haff ways of making you talk," he warned her.

"*Nevair* shall I talk!" Her French accent was as bad as his German one.

"You'll talk," he murmured in his own voice, and kissed her.

The rain was cold on his lips, but the blood beat hot under his skin. It was warm where they touched, banishing the rain's chill, heating her mouth, and her blood. He stroked over her hair and down her arms, and her body began to burn.

Thea smoothed her hands over his cheeks, stroking away the rain, pushing his wet hair back, learning the shape of his face and the texture of his skin. He lifted his head and touched his lips to her cheekbone and her jaw, then brushed his mouth down to the fragile skin of her throat. Her head fell back, and her fingers tangled in his hair to hold him close.

His mouth was hot on the pulse that throbbed in her throat, and when the tip of his tongue brushed her skin she shivered, her fingers tightening on his shoulders as she clung to him for security in a dizzying world. Luke's mouth stilled. He exhaled a deep sigh, then nuzzled her throat and sat back.

"You're cold." He started the engine with a roar. "I've got to get you home and dried off."

Thea said nothing, but it wasn't the rain and cold that had made her shiver.

He released the brake and maneuvered carefully to turn the Jeep around on the wet, narrow road. Treacherous under the best of circumstances, it was positively hair-raising in a downpour. As Luke rounded a curve where the road clung to the cliffside, the tires lost their grip and slid across the wet, oily pavement. The wheels caught on the gravel shoulder above a sheer drop of at least fifty feet, and Luke wrenched the Jeep back into the right lane. He moved on down the hill, giving his full attention to reaching the bottom safely. Thea hung on to the roll bar, her heart in her throat.

When they left the park the road leveled out, widening into a quiet residential street. Luke stopped at a red light, sat back in his seat and looked over at Thea.

"Whew!" He flexed his fingers on the steering wheel. "I'm glad that's over."

She was busy unclenching her fingers from the roll bar.

"Thea?" He waved his hand in front of her eyes. "Can you say something?"

She opened her mouth, then coughed. "I don't know." She laughed weakly. "The fact that my heart's in my throat might be something of a problem."

"A heart could get in the way, couldn't it?" He turned and laid his arm along the back of her seat, behind her shoulders.

"I suppose it could," she whispered. Luke leaned close, but she looked straight ahead. "The light's changed."

"Hmm?"

"The light. It's green." She stared fixedly through the streaming windshield.

"Oh. Yeah." Luke moved back into his seat, shoved the gearshift into first and let the clutch out. The Jeep lurched forward with a jerk, and he swore under his breath.

Thea said nothing.

"Is this as close as I can get?" Luke asked when he pulled into her driveway and parked in front of the garage.

"Yes." Three yards of rain-swept lawn separated them from the front porch. "We'll have to run for it, but it's better than being washed down a hillside."

"Good point." He pulled the damp blanket from the back seat. "Here. Wrap this around you."

"But what about you?"

"I'll be okay. Got your keys?"

"Right here."

"Good. I'll carry the food. Ready to run for it?"

"Ready." She grasped the doorhandle. "One, two, *three!*"

She flung open the door and sprinted across the sodden grass to the porch. The wind gusted and the rain slapped at her as she fumbled with the lock, but finally she got the door open, and they dodged inside, then slammed it behind them.

The quiet was almost deafening, the rain only a distant drumming on the roof, and for a moment they were both content just to stand there and catch their breath.

"Whew!" Thea peeled off the blanket. "Welcome to sunny Southern California." She began to shiver.

"You've got to get out of those wet things and get dry." Luke extracted her from the yards of wet wool and dropped the blanket in a soggy heap on the tile floor.

"So do you. I don't—I don't have any clothes for you to put on," she said awkwardly. "I can get you a dry blanket or something, though, and put your stuff in the drier."

"Thank you." Luke smiled, but she didn't relax. "I'd appreciate that. What do you want to do with this?" He nudged the blanket with his toe.

"It can go in the drier later. Come on." She kicked off her shoes and padded off barefoot. "You can change in here." She pushed open the door of the guest bath and switched on the light. "There are towels in the cupboard, and I'll bring you a blanket, okay?"

"Okay."

Thea knew she was babbling and blushing, but she was helpless to do anything about it. She seemed nervous because she *was* nervous. She was alone in her house with a big, dripping, sexy man who was going to take off his clothes and have a meal with her. She pulled a soft blue blanket from the linen closet and returned to the bathroom.

"Will this be okay?" She pushed it into Luke's hands without meeting his eyes.

"It looks fine. Thank you."

He stepped back and closed the bathroom door. Thea must have stared at the white-painted panels for a full ten seconds before she collected herself enough to go to her room and change.

When she emerged, wearing jeans and a sweater and with her hair hastily blow-dried, the bathroom was empty. From the other end of the house she could hear the drier humming and dishes rattling.

Luke was in the kitchen, wearing the blue blanket like a toga. While the microwave heated something that smelled of basil and tomatoes, he was scooping fettuccine Alfredo from its carton into a dish.

He'd combed his hair smooth, but it was drying into unruly waves that clung to the back of his neck and fell onto his brow as he bent over the dish. A wedge of his back was bared, smooth and tanned, tapering from wide, muscular shoulders to narrow hips, where the loosely knotted blanket rode low on one side.

She made no sound, but he turned as if he'd heard her call his name.

"Hi. I hope you don't mind my taking over your kitchen, but the veal parmigiana got kind of cold."

"Veal parmigiana?"

"Yeah. Tonight's party has an Italian menu."

"You're welcome to take over my kitchen if it means we can eat soon. Did you put your clothes in the drier?"

"Just my jeans. I'll get them dry first, then I'll put the rest of the stuff in." He grinned at her and hitched his toga higher on his shoulder. "This is a lovely blanket, but I'll be a little more comfortable in my clothes."

"Have you checked on the jeans? They might be done by now if you put the drier on high."

"You think so?"

"I'll check." She pulled the jeans out and felt the seams for dampness. They were dry, so she shook them out to cool them.

"Well?"

"They're done. Where's the rest? I'll put it in now."

"On the chair by the table." He indicated the pile of damp clothing with a jerk of his head. "And thanks."

"I can't let you catch pneumonia, after all."

"You're all heart." He took the veal out of the microwave and put in the fettuccine. "I'm just glad I don't have to drive home in a blanket."

"No kidding. You could get arrested for indecent exposure." She laid the jeans over a chair. "What can I do to help with dinner?"

"It's lunch, isn't it?"

"Not anymore. It's almost dark outside."

"Time gets away from you, doesn't it?" He turned back to the food. "Those two are salads, one vegetable, one fruit. If you get plates out, the hot stuff will be ready in about five minutes."

"Okay." She thought of a way to surprise Luke, and she smiled as she took out dishes and cutlery. "You bring the hot food in when it's ready, okay?"

"Five minutes." He bent over the microwave again and didn't see her grin as she walked out of the kitchen.

She didn't stop at the dining room table, but carried the plates and food into the living room. A basket of wood stood on one side of the raised hearth, fireplace tools on the other. Thea worked quickly and quietly to lay logs in the grate, twist sheets of newspaper for tinder and turn on the gas jet that would start the wood burning.

A plaid stadium blanket was folded over the recliner in the corner. She spread it out on the floor in front of the fireplace, laid the utensils on it and was serving the salads when she heard the kitchen door open.

"Thea?"

When Luke's footsteps stopped in the archway, she looked up. He'd donned his jeans, and he was carrying a tray filled with steaming dishes. He was backlit by the dining room chandelier, and Thea couldn't see his face, only the outline of his body, gilded by the light.

"What's this?"

"A picnic." She patted the blanket. "We couldn't have a picnic in the park, so we'll have one here."

Luke looked at what she'd done, at the blanket, the neatly set places, the plates and cartons of food. He set the tray in the space Thea had left for it, then sat beside her, one knee raised and his arm resting on it.

"A rainy day picnic after all. Thank you."

"It's nothing special." Thea ducked her head, letting her hair swing forward to curtain her face. "Stefi and I have picnics in here sometimes, just for fun."

"I think it's very special."

He cupped his hand under her chin and lifted her face. Thea couldn't have moved if she'd wanted to, and she could barely breathe. When his mouth touched hers, her eyes drifted closed and she gave herself up to the kiss and the magic. She was swaying toward him when he released her and sat back.

"And now," he said briskly, reaching for the fettuccine, "let's eat!"

It took Thea a bit longer to shift gears, but the demands of her hungry body couldn't be ignored.

A half hour later, Luke sat amid a litter of empty dishes, finishing a cannoli. "Indigestion? Don't be ridiculous!" he exclaimed indignantly.

"This was ridiculous." Thea lay back on her elbows, breathing deeply. "Tell your sister everything was wonderful. But I ate entirely too much, and if I don't get indigestion it won't be from lack of trying."

"Mind over matter. I refuse to have indigestion."

"I wonder how much medicine has been sold to people who refused to have indigestion."

Luke rolled onto his side and tickled her ear with a napkin. "Cynical little wretch, aren't you?"

"Stop that!" She pushed the napkin away. "It's not cynicism."

"Oh? What would you call it?" He let the napkin drift over her hair, following a tendril that trailed down her arm and brushed the floor.

"I prefer to think of it as realism." Her tone was lofty, but she ruined the effect when she laughed and pulled the napkin out of his fingers. "That tickles!"

"I know." He caught her hand. "I love to watch you twitch."

She pushed herself up on one arm. "I do not twitch!"

"Do too." He gave her hand a tug, pulling her down onto the blanket again, into the comfortable curve of his arm. "You twitch cute, and you laugh cute." He drew her closer, her shoulders cradled in his arm, her legs brushing his.

It seemed like a dream, but the entire day had had an air of unreality. Working together in the quiet office, attempting a picnic on a rain-drenched hillside, picnicking by the fireplace as darkness fell outside—it was all a fantasy. And the most dreamlike aspect of it all was the man there with her. He was too good to be true, and he was all wrong for her.

He was handsome enough to have any woman he chose, so why did he want to spend the day with her? Gorgeous actors didn't usually seek out single mothers with little girls. He could have an actress on one arm and a model on the other, but he was holding Thea Stevens instead. He could be at a Hollywood party, hobnobbing with producers and directors and studio people, but he was lying on a blanket in front of her fireplace.

With her. And what was she doing with this man? He wasn't her type, any more than she was his. Actors weren't interested in women like her. He was young and carefree and happy-go-lucky, and they had nothing in common. This was a crazy situation. It was a sweet sort of craziness, though, and not even the knowledge that it was all wrong could pull her out of his arms.

"You're cute when you twitch," he repeated softly, settling her more securely in his arms. "And you're cute when you try to look like a schoolmarm."

"Schoolmarm? I do not!" She tried to sit up, but his arms tightened, holding her still.

"Yes, you do, and it's cute. But what's beautiful," he murmured, rolling onto his elbow, his face above hers, shadowy in the firelight, "is the way you look when I'm just about—" he brushed his lips over her forehead, touching his mouth to her cheek, savoring the velvet softness of her skin "—to kiss you."

Thea's eyes widened when he moved his body above hers, but as their lips met and clung, her eyes fluttered closed. All her being was concentrated on that kiss, warm and sweet and unexpectedly tender. She'd expected passion, quick and hot, but he explored her lips gently, slowly savoring the possibilities.

It was magic, more than she could have dreamed of, warm and exciting and a little bit terrifying. She hadn't been in a man's arms since Marty had died, and she hadn't thought she ever would be again. She had dedicated herself to her daughter and to the career that supported them, and she had pushed any thought of a man out of her mind.

It took Luke to put those thoughts back. He kissed her, and she could only think of more kisses. He touched her, and she could think of nothing but the next touch. He wrapped her in his arms, and she couldn't think at all.

She could only feel. They might have been all alone in the world as the rain drummed on the roof and the early winter night closed around the house. The rest of the world and its cares seemed a million miles away.

His mouth brushed hers, teasing and tasting lightly, too lightly. Thea relaxed, savored, and then wanted more. She locked her hands behind his head, parted her lips to him and demanded more, pulling him closer.

For a moment Luke resisted, uncertain. Thea brushed the tip of her tongue across his teeth, and his resistance collapsed.

There was still restraint as he met her demand and deepened the kiss, but now there was passion, as well. It warmed her skin, heated her blood, melted her from the inside out, and she moved and shifted beneath him, molding herself into his embrace, soft and pliant and eager.

She was beyond rational thought, overwhelmed by sensations. Luke covered her body with his, and their legs tangled. Their hands were busy, eager. She explored him, sliding her palms over his shoulders and back, learning the texture of his skin, warm and firm and smoother than she had expected. She caressed his shoulders, investigating the curves and contours of his powerful muscles, then trailed her palms lightly over his chest, her fingertips catching in the cloud of dark gold hair. When she found his flat nipples, Luke tensed, muttering something incoherent against her mouth, and she felt the long-forgotten thrill of her feminine power to excite.

As she caressed him, Luke tugged on the hem of her sweater, running his fingers over the narrow strip of skin he bared. It was warm to his touch, and he pushed his hands beneath the fuzzy wool to savor more. Her back was slender and strong, and her spine flexed as he traced its fragile line with his fingertips. When he reached her shoulder blades, he froze for a moment on discovering that she wore no bra.

He knew how her breasts would feel in his hands, small and round and heavy, warm and sweet, and as tempting as Thea herself.

Tempting. Unbelievably tempting. Too tempting to resist. As slowly as he could, Luke stroked her back, then followed the curve of her ribs and brushed his knuckles against the underside of her breast. When he took the soft, warm weight in his hand, she gasped, her back arching instinctively to offer him more. The taut nub of her nipple brushed against his palm, tangible evidence of her excitement, exciting him even more.

Luke struggled to retain the last threads of his rapidly unraveling sanity. He'd meant to hold her and kiss her and cuddle her a little. He hadn't expected to find this fire within her. She was warm and eager, without artifice or pretense, and she aroused him beyond imagining.

She squirmed closer, arching her back, pressing her body up against his. Luke stroked her breast, then bent his head, trying to find his way past the bulk of her sweater. The soft, woolly folds baffled him. After a moment's struggle, he swore under his breath and lifted Thea a few inches so he could peel the sweater over her head.

Her hair fell around her in a wildly tousled cloud, jet-black in the firelight. It drifted over her shoulders and onto her breasts, and her skin gleamed rose and cream in the flickering light. She watched his face, her eyes wide and dark with passion, while Luke looked at his hand on her breast. It was square and tanned, and the contrast with her pale, soft breast was powerfully erotic. He felt her fingers tighten on his shoulder as he caressed her, her nails digging into his skin. He welcomed the small pain; it distracted him from the other ache.

And then she eased her grip and let her hands slide down from his shoulders. Small and soft, they drifted over his collarbone and tangled in the thick hair that covered his chest.

She smoothed her palms over it, then tunneled her fingertips into it, exploring and savoring the contrast between them. He felt very masculine under her touch, in a basic, almost primitive way. She felt so small, so soft and fragile, that she brought out all his tenderness and protectiveness. She brushed her fingertips across his chest, found the flat nipples, and Luke groaned aloud. He lowered his head, met her mouth with his and pulled her into his arms, rolling onto his back so that she sprawled across him, her hair falling over his chest and shoulders.

He'd expected quiet warmth and tenderness; what he found was a passion that left him breathless and gasping, fighting for control like a callow teenager. He wanted nothing more than to tear off the rest of her clothes and bury himself in her for the rest of the night.

But that wasn't possible.

When she moved again, sliding her hands down his back, toying with his waistband, he knew he had to stop things while he still could. Slowly, with an effort that was almost painful, he gathered the threads of his self-control, fighting down the clamor of his body, struggling with the soft hands that stroked his skin, the small, slim body that moved bewitchingly against him. Her voice was even harder to resist as she made inarticulate protests when he tried to pull back.

He had to move away, in spite of her. For her.

He caught her inciting fingers, then lifted his body away, reaching for her sweater, helping her into it and tugging it into place, brushing her tumbled hair out of her eyes.

"Luke?" Her eyes were dark with passion and confusion. "What's wrong?" She reached out, and he clasped her hand securely, reassuringly.

"Nothing's wrong, sweetheart." His smile was strained, but it was the best he could do when he could smell her perfume on his own skin.

"But why...?" She came closer, and he moved away, only a fraction, but enough to bring her to a halt. She stilled, trying to hide her feelings. He could see the hurt and embarrassment that grew as her passion cooled.

He reached to stroke her cheek, but she flinched, and his face twisted in self-derision. He was making things harder for her, rather than easier.

"It's too soon, Thea," he said softly. "You don't have your feelings sorted out yet."

She dropped her head and stared at her hands. She wouldn't pretend that she didn't know what he was talking about, but she still couldn't look him in the face.

"When the time is right," he told her, making the promise to himself as much as her, "it'll happen."

"Nothing is going to happen," she told the floor. Then she lifted her chin to look at him defiantly. "Nothing is going to happen."

Luke rose to his feet. "Not tonight." He laughed raggedly. "I'd better go. I don't think I can trust myself to spend the rest of the evening with you. You're too beautiful." He tried to help her up, but she avoided his touch.

"Don't," she said in a voice that shook. "Don't make jokes. Please." Her eyes were unreadable. "I'll get your clothes."

She hurried into the kitchen, returning almost immediately with his shirt and briefs in a bundle. "They're dry." She pushed them into his hands.

Luke pulled his shirt on, leaving it open. "Thea?"

"What?" Her voice was tight, strained.

"Don't be embarrassed, please."

She stood stiffly, avoiding his eyes.

Luke sighed and stepped close to brush a quick kiss on her lips. "You're a very beautiful woman, Thea, and very desirable, and I'll probably kick myself for this in the morning, but if I don't say good-night to you now, I won't be able to. I'll see you on Monday."

"Yes, Monday." She watched the floor beneath her feet with determined intensity.

He hesitated. "Will you be all right?"

"I'm a big girl, Luke." She looked up at last, her eyes clear and her voice firm. "I'll be fine."

He studied her face for several seconds, then nodded. "Yes, I think you will." He stepped away and laughed. It was a harsh sound. "It's me I'm worried about!"

Chapter 8

Thea moved automatically to clean up, her brain awhirl with thoughts that had nothing to do with leftovers and dirty dishes. She pulled the blanket she'd lain on with Luke around her shoulders, took a floor pillow from a stack in the corner and used it to cushion the bricks so she could lean on the hearth and gaze into the fire, the glow of the flames warm on her face.

So much had happened. She could barely comprehend it all and couldn't even begin to absorb it. She couldn't pretend that she didn't want Luke Adams. And she couldn't deny that if Luke hadn't pulled away she would have made love with him that very evening. The thought was both thrilling and terrifying.

The passion that lay beneath the placid surface of her emotions was new and foreign to her, a side of herself she'd never suspected, even during her marriage. In many ways she had still been a child when she and Marty had married, a virgin bride, waiting as much in fear as in anticipation for her wedding night.

Yet after a brief acquaintance, with no mention of love by either of them, she would have made love with Luke Adams! She pressed her palms to her burning cheeks, not knowing if the heat there came from the fire or her thoughts.

She slid lower, resting her cheek against the big pillow. What was the matter with her? She couldn't possibly be in love with a man she'd known little more than a week. And she had a responsibility to her daughter. She owed it to Stefi to fall in love with the right kind of man, not with a carefree actor but with a reliable, dependable person.

Somebody dull, a little voice in her mind suggested. She pushed the thought away. Reliable didn't necessarily mean dull. Of course not, said the little voice. But hardly exciting. Luke was exciting.

She lay awake long past midnight, then slept late on Sunday morning. When she woke up she felt groggy, and she had a headache. A shower and two cups of coffee helped, but the cold light of day helped more.

Yes, she was attracted to Luke Adams, but that didn't mean she had to act on her feelings, she told herself. She simply wouldn't let the situation get out of hand again. She could work with Luke; they could even be friends. But she wouldn't put herself in another situation like last night's.

She owed him an apology, though. She had to clear the air, and she had to do it today, before the tension between them became so awkward that it affected their work together.

She felt better with that decision made. She'd call Luke and get things straightened out, and then she'd fix herself lunch from yesterday's leftovers.

He wasn't home. The phone rang four times; then his answering-machine message instructed her to leave her name and number. She complied and slowly replaced the receiver. Where could Luke be at noon on a Sunday? Having another of those oddball meetings of his? She slid off the telephone stool and went to make lunch. She would call him again later on. He'd probably be home by two o'clock.

But he wasn't. And he wasn't home at three, or four, or even five, when she left to pick Stefi up.

She didn't call again until nine, after she'd listened to her daughter's minute-by-minute recounting of the weekend's events, a detailed description of what everyone had worn and done and said, and even a listing of the toys they'd played with. Stefi was bubbling with excitement and suffering from the kind of fatigue that would wind her up to manic activity before she collapsed into exhausted sleep. Thea had no chance to think until Stefi had been tucked into bed.

Ten minutes after that, she walked quietly into her daughter's room and found her sound asleep, her face buried in her pillow, her knees tucked under her and her small backside high in the air. With the gentle deftness of long practice, Thea rearranged her into a comfortable position, straightened the covers and left her with a kiss on the cheek.

The house seemed very quiet with Stefi asleep. In the kitchen, Thea poured herself a last cup of coffee, then turned and looked across the room at the telephone. Should she?

She moved toward it but stopped in the middle of the room. She was beginning to feel like a fool, calling again and again and only reaching a machine. But would she feel any more of a fool for trying one last time? She shrugged. If he wasn't there, she'd just have to wait and talk to him when she saw him in the morning.

She punched out the number quickly, and the telephone on the other end rang once, twice....

"Hello?"

His answer startled her so badly that for a moment she was bereft of speech.

"Hello?" he repeated. "Is anybody there?"

"It's me!" she said hastily. "It's Thea."

There was a moment of silence, followed by, "Thea, hello!" His voice warmed into a smile she could sense through the phone wires. "Are you okay?"

"Of course I'm okay. Why shouldn't I be?"

"Well, I thought—" He paused and cleared his throat. "I didn't think you'd want to talk to me today."

"Didn't you check your messages?"

"Not yet. I just got in, and the machine is in the other room. You left a message?"

"Yes." She swallowed, suddenly tense. "Yes, I did. I wanted to apologize."

"Apologize? What for?"

"For last night," she answered very softly.

"Thea, I'm the one who should apologize. I didn't mean to push you."

"No. Luke, this isn't easy for me to talk about, but I don't want you to blame yourself for anything. You didn't push me, and I shouldn't have treated you the way I did. I was acting like a kid. I'm sorry."

"You have nothing to be sorry for," he said. "And we're not going to talk about it again. I enjoyed our picnic."

"So did I. I had some of the leftovers for lunch."

"You should have invited me over to help clean them up."

"I would have, but you weren't home."

"Yeah, I'm sorry I was out when you called. I had a meeting."

"You sure have meetings at weird hours."

"Yeah." Thea could almost hear him shrug. "But, like I once said, most actors do."

"It's too bad they keep you so busy."

"That's how these things are." He spoke quickly, with a sharp edge to his voice. "They call it tennis, but it's a meeting all the same."

"Well, since you just got in, I won't keep you." She spoke quickly, "I just wanted to... to clear the air. I'll see you in the morning."

"At eight?"

"That's right."

His voice dropped to a husky murmur. "I'm actually looking forward to eight in the morning, because that's when I'll see you again. Good night, Thea."

He hung up, and Thea slowly cradled the receiver, her fingers slipping reluctantly off the smooth plastic, which was warm from her touch. She was looking forward to the morning, too, with the excited anticipation of a teenager in the throes of a crush.

By eleven, they had shot the first scene and were breaking to change the set. While Thea and Bobby hung another backdrop and rearranged the furniture, Vanessa and Luke read through the script. He would be walking on crutches, and Thea stood frowning in the middle of the set, trying to decide if there was room enough for him to demonstrate the full range of movement.

"Luke?"

"Yes?"

"Could you bring the crutches over here? I want to see if this set's big enough. If you need more room to move, we can pull the camera back and reset."

"That shouldn't be necessary." He walked across the set a couple of times, supporting himself with the crutches. "It's big enough. I can get the rhythm going if I use the full width. Do I need to walk farther than this, Van?"

"Not in this scene." She perched on a chair. "I wish we could show an extended period of walking in the tape, but we didn't script it in."

Thea considered for a moment. "We can't really work it into the scene, but how about behind the opening and closing titles? We could use one of the hallways upstairs and either dolly the camera along with Luke or just have him walk toward it. We could shoot two or three minutes of that and use the same film for both titles.''

Vanessa thought about it, and her face brightened. ''Yes.'' She pushed a lock of dark hair shot with silver off her forehead. ''That would be perfect. We could even use it as an example during the film itself. Thea, you're a genius!''

''Of course she's a genius!''

Thea spun around at the sound of another voice. Allison Schuyler was standing in the studio doorway. She seemed to glow in the dim light from the hallway, all blond hair and creamy skin and luminous blue eyes, slim and elegant in a pale silk dress that bore the unmistakable touch of a designer. It looked incongruously out of place under a baggy lab coat.

''Are you just now figuring that out, Van?''

''Ally, hello!'' Thea hurried across the cable-strewn studio to hug her friend. ''What are you doing down here? Aren't you supposed to be over on Four West this rotation?''

''Mm-hmm.'' Ally returned the hug, then tucked her arm through Thea's and walked back toward the set with her. ''And I came all the way from the other end of the hospital, through endless corridors and hallways and tunnels and stairwells, just to bring you this!''

''This'' was an envelope she produced with a flourish from the pocket of her lab coat. She slapped it into Thea's hand and waited, grinning, for her to open it.

''Ally, what is this?'' Thea turned it over in her hands. It was a heavy cream-colored envelope, sealed, with her name written on the front in Ally's clean, angular hand.

Ally was bouncing on her toes with excitement. ''Open it and see!''

"I don't know..." Thea drawled the words, teasing, enjoying the sparkle in Ally's eyes, the glow that radiated from her skin and illuminated the gold in her hair.

"Go on, open it!"

"Okay, okay!"

Thea tore it open, and pulled out the folded sheet of heavy vellum inside. She was invited, it informed her, to the marriage of Allison Morgan Schuyler and Cruz Fernando Gallego on Saturday, the twenty-sixth of the next month, at twelve noon, at St. Martin's Church.

"Oh, Ally!" She flung her arms wide, the invitation still in her hand, and caught her friend in a jubilant bear hug. "That's wonderful! Just wonderful!"

"I think so," Ally said with a smile that spoke volumes about what she felt. "And Van, I have this for you." She produced another invitation with difficulty as Van hugged her. "And Bobby, one for you."

He accepted his invitation with a lopsided grin. "I'm disappointed in you, Ally."

"How's that?" Ally asked with laughter in her eyes.

"I thought you were going to wait for me. I'll probably be ready to settle down in fifteen or twenty years."

"Poor Bobby." She patted his cheek, laughing. "Now you'll just have to make do with all the nursing students and the dancers and the actresses...."

She let her voice trail away in the outburst of laughter that greeted that remark and turned to Luke. "I'm sorry to leave you out, Mr...."

"Luke Adams." He shook her hand while Ally studied him.

"I'm Allison Schuyler. You must be the actor for the student films. I'm happy to finally meet you. I understand you're going to make Thea's series great."

"Thea's going to do that. I just act."

"And he does a terrific job, too." Thea smiled at him. "You're too modest, Luke."

Ally looked at them—and at the way they were looking at each other—and made a quick decision. "I don't have an invitation for you, Luke, but I'd like you to come to the wedding."

Luke started to murmur a polite refusal, but Ally wouldn't let him.

"I insist. I want everybody to come celebrate with me. And don't say a word about it," she warned him. "There will be room for one more, or a hundred! Cruz's mother is helping my granddad plan this modest little ceremony, and it's going to be in the biggest church she could find, complete with a monsignor, no less, to officiate!"

Ally's bubbling laughter was the manifestation of the overwhelming happiness inside her. "Please come," she said to Luke. "I'd really like to have you."

Luke knew when to give in gracefully. "How can I turn you down? I'd be delighted to come to your wedding."

"Wonderful! You can escort Thea."

"Ally, there's no reason to do—"

They ignored Thea's protest. Ally nodded, satisfied, when Luke agreed to the plan. She glanced at her watch and grimaced, but the grimace didn't really come off, because she couldn't stop smiling.

"Oops, look at the time! I've got exactly three minutes to get back to the ward, so I'd better run. Literally. I'll talk to you, Thea, Van. Bye, Bobby! Bye, Luke!"

"Whew!" Luke watched her whirl out of the room, a slim tornado of silk and energy. "Is she always like that?"

"Only since she fell in love." Thea wasn't aware that her smile was wistful. "She and Cruz had kind of a hard time of it at first. I don't think she's used to the idea that love really can conquer all."

"A happy ending, huh?"

"Yes." Thea turned and walked slowly toward the set. "I guess they do happen sometimes," she added, almost to herself.

* * *

"How come Luke didn't come to dinner?"

"Because he had an appointment after work today." Thea arranged the leftover veal on a plate to microwave it.

"What's that stuff called?"

"Veal parmigiana."

"Am I gonna like it?"

"I think so. I like it a lot."

"Okay." Stefi swung herself in a circle on the kitchen stool's swivel seat. "Can I have ketchup on mine?"

"If you're sure you want it."

"I do. Marybeth says ketchup's good on everything."

"Marybeth would say that," Thea remarked dryly.

"Yeah. Mom?"

"Hmm?"

"Can I watch TV until dinner's ready?"

"Okay."

"Thanks, Mom!"

Stefi raced off to the living room. Thea spooned the rest of the leftover fettuccine into a dish and placed it in the microwave to heat. If Stefi wanted ketchup on hers, Thea figured she might as well let her try it. Maybe she'd learn that ketchup didn't taste good on everything.

"Mom!" At Stefi's shriek, Thea nearly dropped the dish of noodles on the floor. "Come here!"

"What is it?" She called back, as visions of catastrophe ran through her mind.

"Come quick, Mom!"

She sprinted for the living room and found Stefi, unhurt, pointing at the television screen. Thea turned, looked, and froze in shock.

"Yes, Catherine," Luke was saying to the willowy blond interviewer, "you could call *After Midnight* my 'big break.' I don't consider myself an overnight success, though. I've been a working actor for ten years."

After Midnight? Thea was utterly confused. What on earth was that? And why was Luke, *her* Luke, being interviewed on the entertainment news?

The interviewer placed a carefully manicured hand on Luke's arm and smiled. It was a bright smile, filled with an impossible number of even white teeth.

"I understand you had some unusual parts during those years. Could you tell us about the sort of roles you've taken?" Catherine prompted, and Luke smiled.

It was the smile Thea knew so well, the smile that had warmed her heart and melted all her well-constructed defenses. She stared at the television screen, afraid to listen, unable to walk away.

"I've been a villain on a daytime drama," Luke told her, "and I've done regional theater—light classics and musicals."

"I've heard something about another role...." Catherine leaned closer. "I've heard..." She paused for effect. "I've heard that you had a role as a member of the vegetable kingdom...?" She let her voice trail away into a question.

"I was a dancing onion—" Luke grinned agreeably and followed her lead "—in a commercial for salad dressing. I'm told that commercial sold a lot of dressing."

"I'm sure you were a superb onion. Are there any other roles you'd like to tell us about?" She waited with an expectant smile, ready for Luke to regale the viewing public with a story about his next funny part.

Thea held her breath and braced herself, waiting for him to tell the world. Announcing his role in *Giving the Bed Bath* would get him a big laugh. Luke just smiled and waited for the next question. After a moment, Catherine moved on with the interview.

"You've paid your dues, as you say, but now that *After Midnight* is being released, I doubt you'll be taking many more parts in commercials. The shooting was finished some time ago, though. What have you been doing while waiting for the news to break?"

"Keeping a low profile." Luke smiled.

That was true enough, Thea thought. You couldn't keep a much lower profile than nursing education tapes.

"In what way?" Catherine asked sweetly.

"As you know, publicity about *After Midnight* has been severely limited."

"Limited?" Catherine laughed lightly into the camera. "Ladies and gentlemen, this film has been surrounded by the kind of secrecy usually reserved for defense secrets. It was shot in a remote area of Canada—"

Luke interrupted her. "Near Blackwater, British Columbia." Catherine's smile wavered for a moment, then settled into place again.

She went on, "yes. And no one, but *no one* in the press was allowed anywhere near the shooting site. Even the story line wasn't available to us until the press release this morning. Too late, incidentally, for the news to make the morning papers. Why do you suppose there was such emphasis on secrecy about this particular film, Luke?"

He shrugged. "Your guess is as good as mine. It was the producers' decision, and I haven't asked them for their reasons."

"Whatever the reasons, all this mystery has generated a great deal of interest in the film. Simultaneous press screenings held today in Hollywood and New York were standing-room-only, and reviewers are already using words like 'masterpiece' and 'phenomenon' to describe it. Do you agree with their assessment?"

He smiled gently. "I'm not a reviewer. And I don't know how they think. I'm proud of the film and of my work in it."

"And speaking of your work, have you read what the reviewers are saying about you?"

He shook his head. Thea could see his shoulders stiffen as tension showed in him for the first time.

"Well, things like 'spellbinding,' 'charisma' and 'the next Clark Gable' are being bandied about. *After Midnight* is getting rave reviews, but the highest accolades are being reserved for its star, Luke Adams." She turned to the camera. "Keep that name in mind, ladies and gentlemen, because you are going to be hearing a lot more from this man. The film is *After Midnight*, from Constellation Productions, opening in two weeks at a theater near you."

The camera pulled back, the music swelled over a promo for the next segment and a commercial started. Thea stared blindly at a young man with a pile of dirty laundry.

"Isn't it, Mom?" It was several seconds before Stefi's words registered.

"What?" Thea shook her head and pulled her gaze from the flickering images on the screen. "I'm sorry, Stefi, I didn't hear you. What did you say?"

"Isn't it great? Luke's a real movie star!"

"Yes," Thea replied weakly. "It appears that he is."

"Wow!" Stefi bounced on the couch in excitement. "A movie star! Wonder why he didn't tell us about it. Do you think he wanted to surprise us, Mom?"

"Maybe so, sweetheart."

Or maybe he knew this would change everything and he wanted to pretend a little longer, wanted to lie to me just a little longer.

"Dinner's ready, Stefi. Can you set the table?"

"Sure I can. I'm not a baby, Mom!"

"I know you're not."

Thea smiled at her daughter and walked blindly into the kitchen, pretending that her world hadn't just shattered around her.

Chapter 9

Thea ran down the hall, looked furtively behind her and dodged into the media production office like a thief on the lam. Bobby looked up, startled, from the lens he was cleaning.

"What's with you?"

"There are reporters at the main entrance." She'd seen the crowd outside the main door and knew that the news was out with a vengeance.

"I know. They were blocking the south drive until Security ran them off, but it's not you they're interested in, you know." His eyes sparkled with eager interest.

"I know."

Bobby didn't seem to notice her flat tone. "That's another thing." He swung toward her. She stood with her head down, examining her old, familiar purse with intense interest. "You've really been holding out on me. Why didn't you tell me about our boy the movie star?"

"I didn't know."

Bobby stared at her bowed head. "He didn't tell you?" She looked up, and Bobby winced. "Sorry, Thea. I shouldn't have said that."

"Why not?" She shrugged as she unlocked the door to her office. "It's the truth. There appears to be a lot we don't know about Luke Adams."

"Yeah, I guess so." Frowning, Bobby watched her pull the door closed.

She didn't even pretend to work, just put her forehead on her folded arms and tried not to think.

"Hey!" Bobby's shout from the outer office brought her out of her reverie. "Hold on a minute!"

Through the closed door she could hear a swell of noise in the outer office, the clamor of raised voices. She knew what the uproar meant and was at the door in seconds.

She walked into the outer office to confront a forest of waving arms, cameras and microphones. Bobby was behind his desk, bristling, while Luke stood facing the press, his broad, leather-jacketed back to her. She walked up to stand beside him.

"What are you doing at a hospital, Luke?" someone shouted from the rear of the crowd.

"Yeah!" chimed in someone in front. "Are you here for treatment?"

"No, I'm not here for treatment." Luke shook his head and smiled patiently. "I'm perfectly healthy."

"Then why *are* you here? Visiting friends?"

"Not visiting." He wasn't going to give them anything on a plate, and Thea found herself amused, almost against her will.

"Come on, Luke. Fill us in! What's going on?"

"I'm here to work. Can we leave it at that?"

Of course they couldn't. They pounced on the remark like a pack of starving wolves. From the uproar of questions and demands, Thea gathered that he'd told them nothing. He raised his hands, waiting for quiet. The noise diminished a little, and someone shouted to her, "Who are you?"

"I'm Dodd Memorial's media coordinator," she replied. "And this *is* a hospital, ladies and gentlemen, and a place of business. I'll have to ask you to hold your press conference somewhere else."

They ignored her, firing another volley of questions at Luke. Thea drifted from his side to Bobby's desk. "Call Security," she murmured. "Use my phone."

He nodded and slipped away. Thea didn't look around, but she heard her office door close quietly.

"Could you give us your name, miss?" The reporter who asked was a slim young man with a straggly beard. He looked about twenty-one and seemed less aggressive than his compatriots. She felt a little sorry for him.

"My name is Thea Stevens."

"And you work here?"

Since she was wearing a lab coat with the Dodd Memorial logo embroidered on it, the question seemed gratuitous. "Yes, I do. As I said, I'm the media coordinator."

"What are you doing with Luke?" a sharp-faced man demanded from the rear of the crowd. "Working?" He laid a leering emphasis on the last word, and some of the others laughed, not sympathetically.

Luke stepped nearer to her. His face was calm, but his arm brushed Thea's and the muscles beneath his leather sleeve were tense.

"Mrs. Stevens *works* here, gentlemen. And I imagine she would be very grateful if you would all leave now and let her get on with her job."

"But what is her job?" someone else asked. "And why are you working in a hospital? Are you a nurse?" There was no evident malice in the question, and it was greeted by hoots of laughter.

"Not precisely. I'm not giving a press conference to-day, folks," he said firmly. "When I have something to announce, I'll let you know."

There was a rumble of discontent, but the arrival of three security officers forestalled further questions. The men were polite but firm and they shepherded the reporters out.

In the echoing silence that followed the exodus, Thea glanced at Luke, then turned and walked into her office. She felt cold right down to her bones. He followed her, closing the door behind him as she seated herself at her desk.

Luke sat down facing her. "Good morning, Thea," he said when their eyes met.

"What are you doing here?" she asked bluntly.

"I came to work. We're shooting today."

"I had planned to shoot." She paused. "Until Stefi called me to the television last night."

"You saw the interview?"

She nodded, and he sighed heavily.

"Then I don't have anything more to tell you."

"Except maybe why you bothered to come here. You don't need to make hospital films to earn the rent." Her sarcasm made the words sting. "You're a big movie star. You're going to be the next Clark Gable."

"I'm a working actor."

"Oh, that's right! You made that point very nicely last night."

"Yes. And right now I'm an actor working on your films."

Her rigid control cracked a little. "Come on, Luke! The actors who make hospital training films are actors waiting for a break. You're not waiting for yours, you've already had it."

"Thea—"

"Don't bother trying to explain at this point!" She gave a bitter laugh as she rose and walked stiffly to the window. "I can't believe I didn't figure it out for myself." She leaned her back against the windowsill, gripping it until her knuckles whitened. "All those meetings at weird hours. Now I understand who you were seeing. Agents, producers, who else?"

"Studio people," he told her.

"Them too." She shook her head at her own naiveté. "I should have known."

"Thea, don't do this."

"Don't do what? Figure out the truth? It seems to me it's about time I did!" She shoved herself away from the window and struck her hands together. "Good grief, how dumb could I be? Even after seeing you work, I didn't put it together! You're unusually talented, but you were available for my little hospital films, and I ignored the obvious. Well, you don't need to fool around here anymore. You've got your movie, and now you can get back to it." She stalked around her desk and dropped into her chair.

"My movie's done." He got up and perched on the edge of her desk. "I don't have to do anything more for it, except the occasional simpleminded interview."

"Then your next movie," she muttered, staring at the doodles on her desk blotter. "With all the things they're saying about you, there must be another movie for you to do."

"There is, but not for three months." She looked up, and he elaborated. "I signed to do another movie before *After Midnight* was finished shooting. I was supposed to go on location next month, but there are problems of some kind with the Illinois Film Board, and they keep delaying it. I don't have anything to do now, except finish this series."

She sat back, her arms folded across her chest. "The next Clark Gable, playing a patient in some nurses' training films? Don't be stupid, Luke."

"I'm not the one who's being stupid. I have a contract that says I'm doing three films for Memorial." He leaned over and lifted her chin with a fingertip. "So I'm doing three films."

Thea wanted to pull away, but instead she gazed up into his eyes, mesmerized, as he leaned close and kissed her mouth. His lips moved softly over hers, and his tongue traced a teasing path, tempting her until her lips parted and he tasted her sweetness. He cupped her face in his hands and kissed her long and deep, and despite her anger she returned his kiss with all her heart. She didn't push herself out of his arms, but clung to him, sliding her hands from his wrists to his shoulders, pulling herself up from her chair in an effort to get closer. When he lifted his mouth, she followed, reaching for his lips until she could reach no farther. Then the contact broke and she stared at Luke, her eyes widening in dismay and embarrassment.

He touched her cheek, letting his fingertips drift from her skin as he stood. He was smiling. "I'm doing three films."

"Done?"

"All done." Thea looked across her desk at Luke and smiled. "The shooting's finished, and so are the rough cuts."

"So what's left—"

"Is the final editing and putting in the titles."

"Will you need me for anything?"

"I may. I don't know yet." She tipped her head to one side, watching him. "This should be a good news flash for your pals, though."

There was a slight tinge of sarcasm to her words, as there always was when she referred to the several persistent re-

Say  Yes to romance

---

AND YOU'LL GET:

---

4 FREE BOOKS
A FREE CLOCK/
CALENDAR
A FREE SURPRISE GIFT

NO RISK • NO OBLIGATION
NO STRINGS • NO KIDDING

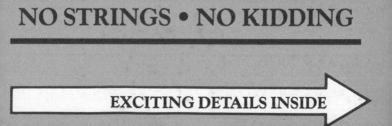

EXCITING DETAILS INSIDE

Say YES to free gifts worth over $20.00

Say YES to a rendezvous with romance, and you'll get 4 classic love stories—FREE! You'll get an attractive digital quartz clock/calendar—FREE! And you'll get a delightful surprise—FREE! These gifts carry a value of over $20.00—but you can have them without spending even a penny!

FREE HOME DELIVERY

Say YES to Silhouette and you'll enjoy the convenience of previewing 4 brand-new books delivered right to your home every month before they appear in stores. Each book is yours for only $2.49—26¢ less than retail, and there is no extra charge for postage and handling.

SPECIAL EXTRAS—FREE!

You'll get our monthly newsletter, packed with news of your favorite authors and upcoming books—FREE! You'll also get additional free gifts from time to time as a token of our appreciation for being a home subscriber.

Say YES to a Silhouette love affair. Complete, detach and mail your Free Offer Card today!

DETACH AND MAIL CARD TODAY

RUSH! FREE GIFTS DEPT.

BUSINESS REPLY CARD

First Class   Permit No. 717   Buffalo, NY

Postage will be paid by addressee

Silhouette Books®
901 Fuhrmann Blvd.
P.O. Box 1867
Buffalo, New York 14240-9952

NO POSTAGE
NECESSARY
IF MAILED
IN THE
UNITED STATES

porters who hung around the main entrance each morning. They'd pestered the hospital's public relations department until they'd been banished to the sidewalk outside. The PR director, at the end of her rope, had informed them that she would call the police and have them all arrested if they dared to show their faces in her office again.

Most of them had gone on to other stories after the first three or four days, but a die-hard group still followed Luke to the hospital each morning and questioned him each night. They'd even haunted his Santa Monica apartment for a week or so, but when that had led to nothing new they'd apparently decided to leave him alone except for the questions every day at the hospital. Luke knew them by name now.

"I'll be sure to let them know." His replies to most of Thea's barbed comments had been dry and light, with a little sting of their own. They had worked out a truce of sorts, forced by their commitment to the film series to work together, and to do it well. That didn't mean that everything was rosy, however.

"What happens after the editing?" Luke asked.

"We duplicate them, list them in the catalog, and before long you'll be educating nursing students all around the world."

"Around the world?" He raised an eyebrow.

"Mm-hmm. In the English-speaking countries, and other places like India and Africa, where English is the language of education. If they don't see you in *After Midnight*, they'll see you on crutches."

"Or being bathed, or strung up in traction."

"Or all three," she agreed.

Luke shook his head. "This is a bigger business than I realized. You're a pretty important woman, Thea Stevens."

She shook her head. "I'm only the hospital media coordinator."

"I'm beginning to think that's a hell of a lot." She shifted in her chair, uncomfortable with his praise after three weeks of sparring. "You're part of something important, and I've enjoyed being a part of it, too, even if only for a little while."

Vanessa's voice from the doorway interrupted them. "What if it could be for a little bit longer?"

"What do you mean, Van?" Luke watched her walk across to the other chair facing Thea's desk.

"Well..." Vanessa looked from one to the other, then addressed herself to Thea. "I had an idea. I was going to talk to you about this first, Thea, but since we're all here..."

She hesitated, and Thea glanced at Luke. From his blank expression, it was clear that he didn't know any more than she did. "What's your idea, Van?"

"Well, I was thinking about Luke. He's the best actor we've ever had for our tapes." She grinned wryly. "We've certainly never had a movie star before. I hate to see him go, though, and I was thinking about the psychiatric nursing videotape series we were planning to do in January."

"That's right." Thea nodded.

"The scripts are already written and approved. We don't need a lot of props or fancy sets, and the preparation wouldn't take long. Could we go ahead and do those tapes now?" She glanced at him. "And have Luke play the patient?"

Thea looked from Vanessa to Luke, shaking her head. Luke was a wonderful actor, and the psychiatric series called for a high standard of acting, but... "It's impossible, Van. You know that."

"Why?" Luke's one word made both women stare at him. "Why is it impossible?"

"I should think that's obvious." Thea's voice was sharper than she'd meant it to be, but she couldn't help it. "We don't have the budget to purchase the services of the next Clark Gable."

"I wish to God you'd stop that!" Luke slammed his palm on her desk so hard that the pencils rattled in their cup. Vanessa sat up straight, her eyes very wide. Thea jumped, then leaned back in her chair, looking apprehensively up at Luke as he rose. He leaned on the desk and glared down at her.

"I wish you'd give me a break," he went on in an ominously quiet tone. "Maybe I should have told you about the movie, maybe not, but I had my reasons for what I did. You found out in an unfortunate way, but that's old news now. Do you think you could start acting like an adult and knock off the little digs?"

Thea stared into his eyes for a long, tense moment, then dropped her gaze to the desktop. She would have liked to deny it, but he was right.

"Excuse me." Vanessa very quietly rose and let herself out of the office. When the door clicked shut behind her, Thea lifted her head.

"I apologize. I was angry and hurt when I heard about the movie, but I shouldn't have acted the way I did."

"No. You shouldn't have." He leaned across the desk and touched her cheek lightly. "But why were you hurt?"

"Because you didn't tell me yourself. Did you think I'd tell the reporters?"

He straightened. "That never occurred to me. Once I'd let you believe I was out of work, though, I didn't quite know how to bring it up."

"'Hey, Thea, I made a movie last year' might have done it."

"Yes, it might have. Look, Thea, I know I handled the whole thing badly, and I'm sorry about that. I've never been in this position before, and I'm not always sure how to deal with it."

"After watching you handle the reporters, it's hard to remember you haven't dealt with this all your life."

"Hardly!" he laughed. "No one wanted to interview a dancing onion. You've got to remember that this is all new to me, too. I'm going to make a few mistakes."

"I'll keep that in mind. Not that it will matter, since you're finished with this job."

"What about those psychiatry tapes?"

"What about them? All we can pay is scale. You can't tell me you got that for your movie."

"No, I didn't, but that doesn't mean I'm not interested."

"But why? You're the star of a major motion picture. Why should you want to do this?"

"Because it's challenging work. Because I don't start shooting on the next one until they get the location problems ironed out, and who knows when that will be. Because I get bored to death sitting around with nothing to do. Because I like to work."

"And the fact that we pay next-to-nothing doesn't matter?"

Luke shook his head wearily. "If all I was interested in was the money, I wouldn't have put in ten years of cattle calls and parking cars and eating TV dinners. Tell me about these tapes."

"They're very different from the last three. This series is about nursing patients suffering from psychiatric disorders."

"And I'd be playing the patient?"

"And Van would be playing the nurse."

"What psychiatric diseases would I have?"

"Psychiatric disorders," she corrected. "Paranoid schizophrenia, a grief reaction and bipolar illness."

"Schizophrenia? You mean a split personality?"

Thea chuckled in spite of herself. "That's the classic layman's misconception. Schizophrenia is any of a group of psychotic reactions characterized by withdrawal from reality, accompanied by a variety of emotional, behavioral and intellectual disturbances."

Luke sat in silence for a moment. "Thank you," he said at last. "I think."

"Don't worry, I still have all the research material I used to write the script. Basically, a schizophrenic patient doesn't perceive reality as we do. He may have visual hallucinations, hear voices and so on. Does that help?"

"A little. I'll take those study materials, though. I can see I'm going to need background information."

Thea leaned her chin on her hand. "You really want to do this?"

He didn't even dignify that with an answer. "About the other two tapes. I know what grief is, but what was the other one?"

"Bipolar illness. It's often called manic depression."

"Wide mood swings, right?"

"At its most simplistic. It's more complicated than that, but—"

He finished for her. "You've got all the research material. Which one will we shoot first?"

"I still can't believe you really want to do this."

He walked around to sit on the desk, close to her. Very close to her. His thigh, brushing her arm, was all hard muscle and soft denim, and the heat of his body reached hers. She edged her arm away, but he leaned across, planting a hand on the other side of her while he took her chin in the fingers of his other hand and turned her face up to him.

"Read my lips."

That was part of her problem. She couldn't take her eyes off his lips, and she was remembering how they had felt kissing hers. And she wanted him to kiss her again.

"I am going to do these tapes. I am going to do them because I want to do them."

Then he lifted her chin a fraction more and kissed her.

"Luke's gonna keep working for you?"

"Mm-hmm." Thea glanced at Stefi, who was wriggling excitedly in the passenger seat. "We have another series to do, and he's going to act in it."

"When does it start?"

"Tomorrow. He has to study the scripts and rehearse with Miss Rice so we can start shooting in a week or so."

"That's neat, Mom. I like Luke. He's fun."

"Yes, he is." Thea's reply was absentminded. Luke was many things, and he was certainly fun. He was also gorgeous and talented and almost too sexy to be real, as well as the possessor of lips that were gentle, firm, tempting.... A horn blared behind her, and she hastily stepped on the accelerator.

"And he listens to me when I talk. He doesn't say dumb things like how much I've grown and stuff, either. Can we invite him over for supper again, Mom?"

"Hmm?" Thea was intent on maneuvering through the evening rush hour.

"Can we, Mom?" Stefi repeated, loud enough to break through her concentration.

"Can we what, sweetheart?"

"Can we invite Luke over for supper again? He liked coming to our house, and he liked talking to me."

Thea had to laugh at that. "I know *you* had fun talking to Luke, but we'll wait and see about inviting him over again."

"Aww." Stefi slouched in her seat and scowled out the window.

"And don't pout. Remember what we said about that?"

"That only babies pout and if I pout you'll have to treat me like a baby," Stefi repeated in a monotone. "But, Mom, I'm not a baby! I'm almost nine!"

Thea smiled at her daughter, who was caught between her childish impulses and her desire for independence. She was growing up and away so fast it was frightening, but Thea's little girl was still there, underneath the eight-year-old's worldly facade.

"You're growing up awfully fast, aren't you?"

"Aww, Mom!" Stefi blushed and looked out the window. Except at bedtime, personal displays embarrassed her.

She didn't hesitate to make her feelings about Luke clear, though. Thea was glad Stefi liked him, but she didn't want her daughter to become too attached to a man who was only a temporary part of her life. Invite him to dinner again? She didn't think so. They were both far too vulnerable to Luke Adams's particular brand of charm.

Thea's lips twisted in self-mockery as she turned into her driveway. She knew she was vulnerable, and after that kiss this afternoon, Luke would have to be a fool not to know it, too. So why had she agreed to hire the cause of so much emotional turmoil to work with her for several more weeks?

I ought to have my head examined.

"What should you have it examdened for, Mom?"

Startled, Thea looked over at Stefi. She hadn't meant to speak aloud, and she flushed as she opened her door and climbed out of the car. "It's nothing, Steff. I was just talking to myself."

"Marybeth says talking to yourself is the first sign of in...snan..." Stefi struggled with the unfamiliar word.

"Do you mean 'insanity'?"

"Yeah! That's what she says."

"Well, you can't take Marybeth's word for everything." Thea led the way into the house, loaded down with her purse and briefcase as well as the groceries. "I don't know where she gets that stuff, anyway."

"From Terry," Stefi informed her, following with her book bag and a sack of potatoes.

"Who's Terry?"

"Marybeth's brother. He's in the eighth grade, and he knows *everything*!"

"The eighth grade, huh?" Thea grinned. "Well, I'm glad there's somebody out there who knows it all, sweetheart, because I sure don't!"

And wasn't that the truth? she thought and walked into the kitchen, chuckling.

Chapter 10

Are you ready, Van?"

"I'm ready." Vanessa glanced at her script. "Luke?"

"Give me a minute to get into it." He bent his head, turning away for a moment as he prepared himself. When he nodded, Vanessa began reading the voice-over.

"The schizophrenic patient may experience 'command hallucinations,' delusions of being controlled through voices, thought control or thought broadcasting, or by signals from televisions, radios or satellites in space." She finished the voice-over and turned to Luke.

He was a stranger to them, sitting awkwardly in the chair with a stiff and defensive posture. His eyes were blank, focusing on nothing. "They tell me what to do," he began in a voice Thea didn't even recognize.

Luke Adams had disappeared into a young man in the grip of schizophrenia, trapped in a world where reality made no sense, where unseen beings threatened and manipulated him, where voices commanded him.

His performance was chillingly powerful, terrifying yet still human. Thea forgot all about her script, and her stopwatch dangled uselessly from her hand.

When he finished the last scene, there was silence. He slumped in his chair, covering his face with his hands. Vanessa glanced at his bent head, then walked quietly off the set.

"I'll see you tomorrow, Thea," she whispered, and left.

Thea waited patiently. He sat still for several minutes more, the stage lights gleaming on his dark gold head. When he moved, it was to rake a hand roughly through his hair before he looked up, blinking as if the light hurt his eyes.

"Whew!" He sighed heavily. "I'm glad to be out of there."

Thea walked across to him. "Out of where?"

"His head." Luke shook his own head as he rose. "I have to get inside him to make him real, but it's not a good place to be." He dropped his arm across her shoulders and walked with her toward the studio door. "I never realized what a terrible life they lead. We think, 'They're crazy, but they don't understand that, so it doesn't matter to them.' But it does matter. Even if they're so ill that they're completely out of touch with reality, they're utterly lonely, and they're terrified all the time."

"Yes, they are." Thea wasn't surprised by his insight; he'd spent days reading about schizophrenia and observing patients in the hospital's psychiatric unit.

Luke held her close against his side as they left the studio, and Thea rested her arm across the back of his waist.

"We're afraid of them, we 'normal' people, because they behave in ways we consider bizarre, but we really should feel sorry for them. They're trying desperately to cope with a world they can't comprehend, and it terrifies them."

"That's right," Jessica Curtis agreed from the hallway behind them.

Thea whirled around, her eyes like saucers, and jerked free of Luke's arm. Even as she reacted, she cursed herself for jumping away from him like a guilty teenager. But why did it have to be Jessica who'd seen them with their arms around each other?

"Hello, Jessica." Luke was considerably more comfortable with the situation than Thea. In fact, she could have sworn he was even amused. "I'm afraid you just missed the rehearsal."

"I know. I saw Van leaving." Jessica smiled warmly. "She told me your performance gave her chills."

Luke brushed off the praise. "She exaggerates. I'm just trying to understand how the patient in this script thinks, what he sees and hears, and how he reacts to it."

"I can't think of a better way to approach the part."

"Did you need to see me about something?" Thea asked, and Jessica shook her head.

"I hoped to watch some of the rehearsal, but I can come back another time." She glanced from one to the other, and her smile widened. "You two have things to do."

Still smiling, she said goodbye and walked down the hall, leaving Thea staring after her. Jessica disappeared around the corner, and Thea turned to Luke.

"Did you hear that?"

"I was standing right here." He took her arm and led her into the empty outer office. "Of course I heard it."

He was definitely amused, but this was nothing to laugh about. Thea stalked across to her own office and slapped her script onto the desk. "It's not funny!"

He followed her to the desk. "Of course it is! Your boss has a sly sense of humor."

"And you think that's funny? She sees us acting like—"

"Like lovers?" he finished softly.

She whirled around to make an angry reply, but he leaned over her, planting his hands on the desk on either side of her to surround and trap her. Their bodies brushed; his face was only inches from hers, and the scathing words stuck in her throat.

Like lovers. She'd denied it again and again in her waking thoughts, but she'd awakened in the night, dreaming of it.

Luke smiled gently. "Like lovers. And your boss is more perceptive than you think."

She shook her head sharply. "But we're not!"

"Not yet."

Luke moved until his hard-muscled thighs were on either side of hers, holding her captive. As he bent to her, he slid his hands from the desk to her arms and around her back, pulling her up and into his embrace. Full and aching, her breasts touched his chest, and the contact sent a jolt of heat through her. She shouldn't do this. She shouldn't want this. She didn't want to want this, but . . .

She slid her hands up and locked them behind his neck, then let her head tip back and her eyes close. Luke brushed his mouth across her cheek and murmured low in his throat when she tightened her hands, pulling his mouth to hers.

She let her tongue touch his lower lip, and Luke abandoned himself to a kiss that left him breathless. She was sweet and open, generous and passionate, and only the last threads of his sanity kept him from making love to her there on her battered oak desk. With a strength that he'd seldom had to test, he dragged his mouth away, burying his face in her throat. Later he would smell her perfume on his own skin.

"We're not lovers yet," he whispered against her throat, "but Jessica knows more than you do, little Thea."

When he loosened his arms, she pushed herself free, stepping quickly away from him—and from temptation.

"I'm just glad there weren't any reporters in that hallway. I don't even like to think what they would have read into it."

"They're only doing their jobs." He watched her settle into her chair and open a file folder. "What are you doing?"

"My job." She glanced up, then returned to her folder with a deliberately dismissive gesture.

"It's already a quarter to six. Shouldn't you be heading home?" He reached over and closed the folder.

"Not tonight." She opened it again. "Stefi's at a Girl Scout meeting until 8:30. I'll pick her up then."

"Aren't you going to have dinner?" He closed the folder once more. When she tried to open it, he pulled it away.

"I'll have something when I get home. And will you please give me my file? This is turning into a bad slapstick routine."

"No."

When she looked up, he was smiling. "What do you mean, no?" she demanded.

"No, I'm not going to give you this file. I'm not going to let you sit here working until 8:30 without dinner, either." He caught her hand and pulled her out of the chair. "We're having dinner, and if we get there unfashionably early, we won't have to wait for a table."

"Wait?" Thea whispered across the table. She watched the maître d' bow himself off after seating them with unctuous care. "Who are you kidding? He nearly hurt himself getting you to the front of the line."

Luke looked a little uncomfortable. "I guess this is what they mean when they talk about perks."

"I guess." She shook her head wonderingly. "I know *I've* never gotten this kind of service."

"We might as well enjoy it. I don't think they're going to let us refuse."

That much was obvious. Luke had made his way through the crowd of patrons in the lobby of the popular Malibu seafood restaurant to add his name to the list of those waiting to be seated. There had been a few murmurs of recognition in the crowd, and when he'd given his name to the maître d' the small, dandyish man had grabbed two menus from his desk and hustled them to a table beside the window.

It was one of the best spots in the restaurant, and she'd caught a brief glimpse of a Reserved card before it had disappeared into the maître d's pocket. He'd seated her as if she were a duchess, offered them both cocktails and presented her with a large leather-bound menu. She opened it and stifled a snicker when she saw it had no prices.

"Luke!" she whispered.

"What?" he whispered back.

"Are there prices on your menu?"

He looked. "Yeah."

She studied hers, trying to decipher the French listings. "Which side of this thing is the cheap side?"

He grinned. "Don't worry about it. I'm a big movie star, remember? I can afford it, even the lobster stuff."

"Which lobster stuff?" She scanned the columns eagerly. "Since you can afford it, I might as well get something really outrageous."

Luke disappeared behind his menu again. "Top of the second page. First column."

Thea's French wasn't equal to a literal translation, but she recognized *homard* and *crème* and *champignons*. Anything that involved lobster and cream and mushrooms was a good bet.

"I'll have that." A waiter magically appeared when she closed her menu. Luke ordered, the waiter disappeared, and Thea sat back comfortably. Their table offered a spectacular view of the ocean and the sunset, and she stared out for a long moment.

When she turned back to the dining room, she saw a popular soap-opera hunk sitting down to dinner with a leggy, gorgeous blonde. Thea's eyes met the hunk's, and when he nodded in acknowledgement, she politely returned the nod.

"Somebody you know?" Luke was watching her.

"I've seen him on TV. He was a bad guy, but then he fell in love with the good guy's sister, only he doesn't think he's good enough for her."

"Is he?" Luke wondered, interested.

"Oh, yes. He's got a heart of gold under the tough exterior."

"He does, huh?" As Luke looked around, the man rose and walked across to their table. Luke smiled and got up, but Thea just sat and stared.

"Luke Adams?" The men shook hands. "John Dillon. I saw a screening of *After Midnight* last week, and I enjoyed your work very much."

"Thank you. Coming from a fellow actor, that means a lot." They exchanged a few more pleasantries, and when Luke introduced Thea, she somehow managed to say the right things.

"Oh, wow!" she breathed when John Dillon had left them.

"Wow, what?" Luke settled into his chair again and shook out his napkin.

"I can't believe I actually shook hands with him!"

"If you tell me you're never going to wash that hand again, I'll gag."

She stared dreamily out the window. "It's just that I was actually introduced to a TV star!"

"So what am I, chopped liver?" He looked mildly aggrieved.

"No, but you're just Luke. He's—"

"A TV star, I know." He shook his head, laughing softly. "If I need someone to bring me down to earth, I can count on you, can't I?"

Thea laughed with him. "If you want your ego fed, Luke, you've got the wrong woman. Besides, I see you every day. I've only seen him on television. It's different."

"Yeah, yeah." He was grinning as the waiter brought seafood cocktails and a bottle of Chablis. "I can tell it's different."

The meal was, if anything, better than Thea had expected. The appetizers were little works of art, the lobster sinfully rich and creamy, the salads crisp and perfect, and the dessert . . .

"There ought to be a law against this." She licked the last of her mocha mousse off her spoon. "It's too good to be legal."

"Mmm." Luke was watching her lips. He had declined dessert, opting for coffee instead. "Are you finished?"

"Yes." She flushed and laid down her spoon. "I couldn't eat another bite."

"More coffee?"

"No, thank you. It's time to go pick Stefi up, anyway."

"Okay." He walked her out with grave courtesy, barely touching her. That little moment when he'd stared at her mouth with hungry eyes might never have been, except for the possessive pressure of his hand at her waist as they passed the hunk and his lady friend.

They wouldn't allow him to pay for dinner. No, the maître d' repeated, Monsieur Adams's meal was courtesy of the house. They were delighted to have him patronize their establishment. Unable to persuade the man to reconsider, Luke gave in gracefully.

As they turned away, he bent his head and muttered in Thea's ear, "That meal cost two hundred bucks."

"Two hun—" She tripped on the perfectly smooth floor. Luke hauled her to her feet with his arm around her waist and quick-marched her toward the door.

"Two hundred *bucks*?" she whispered.

"Shh!" He tightened his arm. "You're supposed to be a sophisticated film producer. Don't blow it."

"But two—"

"Luke Adams! Over here! Luke!"

Shouts erupted as they walked out the front door. Where there had been only a couple of valets parking cars when they'd gone in, there was now a crowd of reporters, including one with a television camera in tow. Thea shrank back from the volley of shouts, and the television light flared on, momentarily blinding her. Luke pulled her up beside him, his grip on her arm almost painful.

"Stand up." He bent his head, smiling as if murmuring something sweet. "Smile at them, not at me, and don't say anything. The car will be here in a minute." She didn't obey quickly enough, and he tightened his fingers. "Stand up!"

Rather than lose her arm, she stepped up beside him. And she smiled, then kept her lips firmly together as Luke made pleasantly noncommittal replies to questions about *After Midnight*, about his next film, even about his brief soap-opera stint. When the questions addressed his plans for that evening—or, more specifically, for that night—he ended the interview.

"Where are you and the lady going?" shouted the tall, thin, sharp-faced man Thea had first seen in her outer office. He stuck a camera in Thea's face, pressed the button and blinded her with the flash.

"Home," Luke replied.

"Your place or hers?" The innuendo was obvious, and the look Luke gave him should have frozen him in his tracks.

"The lady goes to her home, I go to mine." His words were chips of ice. Thea saw his car pull up behind the reporters. "Good night." Luke strode through the pack, which parted in front of him.

"How about you, honey?" The sharp-faced reporter pushed a miniature tape recorder in her face. "Whose place are you really going to?"

Thea had stopped short rather than be bashed in the face with the mike, pulling out of Luke's grasp. The reporter smoothed a hand over his thin, carefully oiled hair and smiled at her.

"Come on, honey, you can tell me." In spite of herself, she shrank back as he advanced on her, his eyes alight with avid interest. "Where are you two really going?"

"I'm going ho—"

"Back off, Fletcher!" Luke shoved past him, not gently, and took Thea's arm again. He pulled her close to his side, but with the cameras on them, he didn't put his arm around her. "She's going home, and so am I."

He hauled Thea the last few yards to the car so fast that she stumbled, then dropped her into the seat. The windows were up, but reporters surrounded the car, waving and shouting and tapping on the glass as Luke gunned the engine and drove away.

Thea looked over her shoulder at them, then sank into her seat with a shaky sigh.

Luke glanced at her. "Fletcher's a toad. Don't let him get to you."

"Too late." She folded her arms across her breasts in an unconsciously defensive gesture. "Who is he, anyway?"

"A reporter," he said grimly. "If you can call him that. He writes for the *National Investigator*."

"That thing I see in the supermarket? The one with stories like 'My Baby's Father Is a Space Alien?'"

"That's the one."

"Will they write something about us?" Her voice was thin and tight with tension.

His mouth twisted into a grim smile as he turned left onto Topanga Canyon Road. "Maybe. Or maybe they'll just print a picture and some stupid caption. It's hard to say."

"And the other reporters? What will they do?"

"No telling. You may make the eleven o'clock news, or the gossip column in the morning paper." He grinned encouragingly at her, then turned back to the narrow, twisting canyon road. "But they won't just make up a story the way the *Investigator* will."

He swung around a sharp curve, and Thea grabbed for the armrest. "How do you stand it?"

"Stand what?"

"The press. How do you deal with reporters at the hospital, following you to restaurants, spreading your life across the headlines?"

"They also hang out on my lawn and trample the azaleas I planted myself and try to water every night."

"How do you handle that?" She wasn't laughing at his joke.

He sobered. "It comes with the territory, Thea. I'm an actor. I knew in high school that I was going to be an actor, and I knew before I did *After Midnight* that press attention was going to be part of the package. I don't have to like it. I just have to deal with it."

"But how? How do you deal with them shouting questions at you and sticking cameras in your face?" Her eyes were wide and dark, and she twisted the strap of her purse between her fingers.

"You stay calm. You answer the questions you want to answer and ignore the ones you don't like. You never apologize, never explain, and you don't let them force you into saying too much."

"Doesn't it bother you?" She stared at her purse strap, which was now in a knot.

"I don't let it bother me. It's part of my job, just like dealing with the purchasing department is part of yours. They can't get to me if I don't let them."

After a moment Thea sighed and looked out the window. "I'm glad you can do that. I know I couldn't."

"You could." He reached over and touched her cheek lightly. "You're a lot stronger than you give yourself credit for."

Thea stared blindly at the passing scenery. Luke had no idea just how wrong he was.

Chapter 11

"What a day!" Thea dropped her script on her desk and sank into her chair. She let her head fall back and her eyes close.

Vanessa sagged into the armchair across from her. "It's only 1:30."

"Don't remind me. That gives us four more hours to prove Murphy's Law."

A headache nagged at her temples, and Thea tried to will it away. After a restless night, she'd endured a day that had been a series of mistakes and problems, and the tension was taking its toll.

She and Luke had gone to pick up Stefi, who had bounced on the back seat of Luke's luxurious sedan, bubbling with excitement and firing questions at him. He'd answered them all patiently, and after saying good-night to her, he'd watched her sprint off to her room, her arms filled with Girl Scout paraphernalia.

He had drawn Thea into his arms. "Alone at last."

"For two or three minutes, at least." She'd smiled up at him, resting her hands on his shoulders.

He'd glanced down the hallway. "But you told her to get her pajamas on and wash her face and brush her teeth."

"Uh-huh. Three minutes, tops."

"Oh. Then let's make the most of them." He'd lowered his head, blotting out the porch light behind him. Then his lips on hers had blotted out everything else. She'd clung to him and given herself up to a slow, thorough kiss that had taken her breath away.

It was the sound of Stefi's footsteps behind them that had brought her back to reality. Thea had quickly smoothed her hair as she'd tried to steady her breathing.

"I'm ready for bed, Mom!"

"That's good, sweetie. You go get a story and wait for me in bed, okay?"

"Okay, Mom. G'night, Luke."

"Good night, Stefi. Sleep well."

"I will. Bye!" She had raced back to her room.

"I'll let you go read the bedtime story," Luke had offered with a smile.

"She'll pick a long one, just so she can stay up a few minutes extra."

"Smart kid." Luke had pulled her close, but this kiss had been tender rather than passionate. "Don't worry, Thea."

"About what? The story?"

He'd laughed and ruffled her hair. "About Jessica, the reporters and whatever else is bothering you."

"That's easy for you to say."

"Yes, it is, so I'm going to say it again. Don't worry." He'd kissed her, quick and hard, then loped across the lawn to his car.

Long after he'd gone, Thea had felt his lips on hers. Long after she'd gone to bed she'd lain awake, restless, remembering his arms around her, missing them. Her mind had run in circles. The weeks of coolness and pretending he was just a colleague might never have been. She felt the same things for Luke the movie star that she'd felt for Luke the journeyman actor, and not even their pursuit by the press had changed that.

She'd deliberately used the main hospital entrance this morning, swallowing the lump of fear in her throat, nodding politely to the reporters clustered there. Not to the rat-faced Norm Fletcher, though. She'd turned her back on him, told a young man from the *Times* that Luke was shooting that day and no, the studio was not open to the press, then swept up the steps and into the building. She'd been pleased with herself for the way she'd handled the situation, but it had been the last time she'd been pleased with the day.

The housekeepers had cleaned the set and rearranged the furniture for reasons Thea couldn't even guess. As a result, they'd had to review yesterday's tapes and do their best to replace the props exactly where they had been. Once they'd started shooting, an hour late, lights had burned out, Vanessa had blown her lines, and Luke had been dissatisfied with his performance. Thea had been trying to handle three problems at once when the final disaster had struck.

"Do you think Bobby can get the camera fixed before five?" Vanessa asked now.

"I don't know. On a theoretical level I know how video cameras work, but I don't have a clue about fixing them."

"So we'll wait." Vanessa dropped her head back against the upholstery. "It might do me some good, since I can't seem to remember my lines today."

"Don't be so hard on yourself, Van. Nobody's perfect."

The other woman was quiet for a few seconds. "I feel bad for Luke."

"I know. It's hard for him to get into character like that, then have to drop it for a broken camera."

"He was doing great, too. He beats himself up about his acting, but he's so good that he makes it easier for me."

"You start to think he's a real patient, don't you?"

"Yeah. All I have to do is talk like a nurse."

Thea grinned. "I'll be sure to tell him you believe he's schizophrenic."

"Thanks a lot," Vanessa said dryly, then stretched. "Want a cup of coffee?"

"I'd love one."

"Okay, I'll go over to the cafeteria and get some for all of us. You can stay here in case Bobby gets the camera fixed."

"You're sure you don't want me to come?"

"There's no need. I'll be back in a bit."

"Thanks!" Thea called after Vanessa. Then she leaned back in her chair again, concentrating on getting rid of her headache.

A tap on the door several minutes later failed to fully rouse her. "Just put the coffee in front of me. I'll find it by scent."

"If I had some, I'd be happy to put it in front of you," said Luke. "Who has coffee?"

Thea sat up, pushing her hair back, and he took the armchair. "Van went to get it. How's the camera?"

"Still in surgery."

"And the prognosis?"

Luke grinned. "Dr. Bobby's not making any predictions. He's doing a lot of muttering and swearing, though."

"Uh-oh. That's a bad sign—" The telephone's shrill ring interrupted her. "He only mutters when he's having trouble." She lifted the receiver. "Media Production, this is Thea Stevens."

Luke saw her smile vanish and her face go still and set.

"Yes," she said after a moment. Her voice held none of its usual warmth. "Yes, I am." There was a pause. "She did?"

The color drained from her face. Her thin, fair skin colored easily, but now it blanched chalk white. Luke couldn't see her eyes, but he watched her knuckles whiten and the hand that gripped the receiver begin to shake.

He tensed. He didn't know who was on the other end of that phone, but he knew something was very wrong. He left his chair and moved to the desk, waiting for her to finish.

"How long ago?" she said, her voice thin and shaky. "Do you know how? Yes. Yes, I'll come. Right—right away. Goodbye," she whispered.

"Thea?"

She didn't answer. She was replacing the receiver with great care, using both hands.

"Thea, what happened?"

Her hands moved aimlessly over the things on her desk. When she started to rise, Luke put his hands on her shoulders and held her in the chair. He could feel her trembling.

"Thea." His voice was clear and firm. "Tell me what's wrong."

She looked up at him, her eyes wide with anguish and as dark as the sky at midnight. "It's Stefi."

"What happened?" He kept his voice even and reassuring.

"She fell off a swing. At school, on the playground."

"How is she?"

"She's—" Thea's voice broke and she gulped, trying to steady herself before she blurted out, "She cut her face and they—they think she may have a broken arm!" She shoved his hands off her shoulders and lurched out of her chair, pushing past him toward the door.

"Thea, wait!"

She paused at his shout, her face distraught. "I've got to go and get Stefi!"

"I know you do." Luke caught her arm. "I *know*, but you need your purse and your coat. Will you bring her back here?"

"Yes. To the emergency room." She struggled against his grip. "I've got to go, Luke. She's hurt!"

"I know." Luke wrapped his arm around her shoulders. She was shaking hard, hanging on to her control by a thread, and in no shape to drive a car. "I know, and we're going to go get her together. Where's your purse?"

"Purse?" She stared wildly around the office, as if she'd never heard the word before.

"Your *purse*, Thea." Luke shook her shoulders briefly. "You're going to need it. Where is it?"

She responded automatically to the authority in his voice. "My desk. It's in my desk."

"In a drawer?" He'd pulled her back to the desk and was opening drawers as he spoke.

"That one."

She pointed and he found the gray leather clutch. "Are your insurance cards in here?" He didn't wait for her reply, but pulled out her wallet, flipped it open and riffled through the credit cards and snapshots of Stefi. "This the card?" He showed it to her, and she nodded. "Good." He stuffed the wallet back into her purse, zipped it closed and pushed it into her hands. "Come on. I'll drive."

Her raincoat and his jacket were on hooks on the back of the door. Luke grabbed them, throwing his over his shoulder as he pulled her through the outer office. They walked into the hall just as Bobby emerged from the studio, a piece of the camera in his hand and a disgruntled expression on his face.

"It's gonna take me the rest of the day to fix this thing," he began, then he saw Thea's face. "Thea, what's wrong?"

"Stefi's been hurt at school," Luke said as he stuffed Thea into her raincoat. "I'm going to drive Thea over there. She won't be back today."

"Don't worry, I'll handle things." Luke was already hustling Thea down the hall as Bobby called, "I hope she's all right!"

Luke waved and made for the exit. He flung the heavy glass door open, pulled Thea through and went down the steps two at a time. The cluster of reporters was there, but he didn't pause for the usual polite exchange.

"Hey, Luke! What's going on?"

Luke shouldered the reporter aside. "Later!"

Norm Fletcher stepped in front of them, tape recorder in hand, blocking their path. "Where are you going in such a hurry, Luke?"

"Let us by!" Thea's voice was shaky with tears as she tried to get past. Fletcher blocked her way. "Please, let us by!"

"Where are you going in such a hurry, little lady?" His smile was even more unpleasant than usual. "Off to find a preacher, maybe?"

Luke spoke very, very quietly. "Norman, if you don't want to see a doctor, you'll get out of the way. Now."

Fletcher looked into Luke's face and stepped quickly aside. His face red with anger, he shouted after them as they ran across the parking lot, "I'll find out where you go, Adams! I'll find out and I'll print it!"

Luke's reply was unprintable, even in Norm's tabloid. He slammed the door behind Thea and ran around to the driver's side. He was driving his big sedan instead of his Jeep, but as they hurtled off, he didn't treat the expensive car with the respect it deserved.

"Buckle up" was all he said as they shot out of the parking lot with a squeal of tires. There might have been a few traffic laws he didn't break on the way to Stefi's school, but not many. He turned into the school driveway on two wheels, and before he'd come to a full stop, Thea was out and running toward the building, her raincoat flying.

She heard Luke's footsteps behind her, but she didn't slow down, instead sprinting past a group of children on the playground and across the school courtyard to the office.

She burst through the door and stopped short, confronted by a silver-haired woman sitting at a desk, typing briskly, her head bent over her work. A nameplate on the desk announced that she was Mrs. Morris, the school secretary.

"Excuse me." Thea gripped her purse in both hands, holding it in front of her like a shield. The secretary kept typing. "Excuse me!" Thea repeated, with tears at the edge of her voice. "My little girl—she's been hurt!"

Luke reached around her and slapped his palm on the desk with a crack. Mrs. Morris jerked her head up. She had a plump, pleasant face, which was now pink with dismay.

"Oh, I'm sorry!" she gasped, pulling the Dictaphone headset off her ears. "I'm so sorry! I can't hear a thing with that contraption on. Can I help you?"

"My daughter—" Thea began, but her voice broke. She began to shake.

Luke wrapped his arm around her shoulders, pulling her close, supporting her. "Mrs. Stevens was called at work. Her daughter was injured on the playground."

"Oh, yes, that'd be little Stefi." Mrs. Morris bustled around her desk and waved to them to follow her. "She's right down here, in the nurse's office."

Thea was dimly aware of Luke's presence as they hurried in Mrs. Morris's wake, but when she saw her daughter, she forgot everything else.

Stefi was sitting on the examining table with the nurse's arm around her shoulders for comfort. She wore an inflatable splint on her arm, and the pretty nurse was holding a cold pack to her mouth. Stefi's face was dirty and streaked with tears, and she looked very small and scared.

When she saw Thea, she whispered, "Mommy," past her grotesquely swollen lower lip and burst into tears.

"Oh, sweetie." Thea was across the room in two strides and gathered her daughter into her arms, careful of her splint and her injured face. "Oh, sweetheart, I'm so sorry you got hurt."

The nurse glanced at Luke as she walked toward her desk, then did a double take. "Are you—"

"Yeah." He nodded shortly. "How badly is she hurt?"

"She's banged up, but she'll be fine." The nurse took some forms from the desk and clipped them together before handing them to Luke. "Give these to the physician who treats her. I've written down what I did. I'm sure her arm is broken, and her lip should be stitched by a plastic surgeon. I haven't been able to tell if any of her teeth are loosened, but I think they're all there. She didn't lose consciousness."

"Okay." Luke stuck the folded forms in his jacket pocket. "Is there anything else, Miss . . . ?"

"It's Mrs. Carmela Ortiz. And there's nothing else. All I did was sponge off her face and put the splint on her arm. I didn't want to do anything else to her lip, in case it made things worse for the plastic surgeon. Where will you take her?"

"To Memorial, in Pasadena. Her mother works there."

"That's good. If they want more information, they can call me. I'll be here until five."

"All right, and thank you." Luke looked over at Stefi, who was wrapped in Thea's arms. "Is she ready to go?"

"As soon as one of you signs this." She gave him a form. "On that line."

"Can I sign for Thea?" Luke asked.

"Sure."

Luke scrawled his name, and she gave him a quick grin. "My first autograph. I'll get a blanket to put around her." She pulled one from a cupboard and shook it out. "Stefi, let me put this around you so you don't get cold, okay?"

Stefi nodded forlornly and let herself be folded into the warm wool. Thea tried to lift her, but a tall eight-year-old was a heavy burden for her. She shifted Stefi and bumped the plastic-encased arm.

"Oww!" Stefi moaned.

Luke stepped up. "I'll carry you out to the car, Stefi."

Thea made a gesture of protest, and he glanced at her. "She's too heavy for you," he said quietly. "I can carry her without bumping her arm." Reluctantly Thea stepped aside. "Is that okay with you, Stefi?"

"Yes, Luke." It was a thin whisper, but Luke smiled.

"Here we go, then. You lay your big plastic arm on your lap so it won't move while I carry you. All ready?" With Carmela Ortiz's help, he lifted Stefi carefully into his arms and got her arranged securely. Thea hovered anxiously, and when he straightened with his fragile burden she darted forward to tuck in a corner of the blanket.

"Don't worry," Carmela told her as Luke carried Stefi out of the room. "She'll be all right. I have three boys who do this kind of thing a lot." She grinned. "They survive."

"Thanks." Thea smiled weakly and hurried after Luke.

He was instructing Mrs. Morris to call Memorial when she caught up with him in the office. "Who's Stefi's doctor?" He threw the question over his shoulder.

"Dr. Martin. Althea Martin."

"Is there a plastic surgeon you want them to call? The nurse said she'll need one."

"I don't know." Thea spread her hands helplessly. "Whoever Dr. Martin recommends."

"Okay." He turned to Mrs. Morris again. "Can you tell them that? We'll be at the emergency room in about twenty minutes."

"I'll let them know." She was dialing as they left.

Once they reached the car, Thea tried the door, then turned to Luke. "It's locked."

"The keys are in my right pocket." He turned to her so she could extract them. Thea didn't hesitate before slipping her hand into the pocket of his jeans.

The pocket was deep, and his keys were at the bottom. He tried to ignore the sensation of her small hand sliding down his thigh as she groped for the keys. This was neither the time nor the place for that kind of awareness. He smiled at Stefi to take his mind off less appropriate thoughts.

"How are you doing, sweetheart?"

"Okay," Stefi whispered, and tried to answer his grin. She couldn't manage it with her mouth so swollen, and Luke had to force his facial muscles to remain in a smile.

"Got 'em!" Thea announced finally. She hurriedly unlocked the door and yanked it open, then turned to reach for Stefi.

"Get in the back seat," Luke told her. "I'll put her on your lap."

"Okay." She clambered in, and he carefully maneuvered Stefi into her arms.

"You keep your arm real still, okay, Stefi?" he said.

"Okay."

He could see the determination in her to do everything she was asked to do, and he knew it was because she was a child, still young enough to believe that things happened for a reason. If she got hurt, it must be because she'd been a bad girl. She would be very good now, as if by being good she could protect herself.

Luke's jaw clenched as he tucked the blanket around her and closed the door. Walking around the car, he glanced in and saw Thea bending over her daughter, their two dark heads close together. He saw love and concern in Thea's face, and an easing of the fear in Stefi's. If her mother was there, nothing bad could happen to her.

"Madonna and child," he murmured, then swung into the driver's seat.

On the trip back to the hospital he avoided potholes and quick turns that might jar Stefi's arm, flinching every time she whimpered. He braked under the emergency entrance awning with careful smoothness, then swore under his breath at the sight of several people waiting by the door. Somehow word had reached the reporters at the main entrance.

Thea looked at them with haunted eyes. "What are they doing here?"

"Just doing their jobs." He looked back at them. "Are you okay, Stefi?"

An orderly was trotting out with a wheelchair as Stefi nodded. Luke lifted her from Thea's arms and set her carefully in the chair. From the corner of his eye he saw the reporters advancing on them, with Norm Fletcher in the lead. He placed himself between Stefi and the pack.

"Get her inside, quick," he muttered in Thea's ear. "I'll deal with them out here." She nodded, and he fished in his pocket for the papers Carmela Ortiz had given him. "Here." He pressed them into Thea's hand. "The school nurse said to give these to the doctor."

"Okay." Thea nodded and hurried Stefi and the orderly inside. Stefi looked very small, swaddled in her blanket, with her frail arm encased in the enormous inflatable splint. Thea bent over her as they went inside, blocking any camera shots. Her hand rested on Stefi's hair as if she couldn't bear to lose contact.

"Who is she?" Norm Fletcher was the first to reach him. He would have followed the wheelchair inside, but Luke was in his way. "Who's the kid?"

"The young lady," Luke emphasized the phrase, "is Mrs. Stevens' daughter."

"Is she going to be all right?" This was from a young reporter who seemed genuinely concerned, and Luke smiled as he replied.

"The school nurse assured Mrs. Stevens that her daughter would be fine."

"What happened to her?" called a young woman.

"She was hurt on the playground at school." He began backing toward the doors. "That's all I know, folks."

"What school does the kid go to?" Fletcher demanded.

Luke cursed his own lack of foresight. He should have instructed the nurse and the secretary that they were not to answer any questions from reporters. He'd forgotten, though, so now he had to get to a phone before the reporters figured out who to call. He raised his hands, putting an end to the press conference.

"That's all I can tell you. I'll see you folks later." He turned and strode inside.

Chapter 12

There was one clerk at the reception desk, writing busily. Luke strode straight to her, leaned over and planted his palm on the admission form she was writing out.

She jerked her head up, startled. "What do you think you're—" Her mouth fell open when she recognized him. "Oh! I heard you were working here, but—"

"Yes, I am." He spoke quickly to forestall any questions. "See those guys out there?" He jerked his head in their direction, and she looked past him.

"Yeah."

"They're reporters. They're going to ask about Thea Stevens' daughter. Don't tell them anything." He leaned farther across the desk. "Understand? Don't tell them *anything*."

Wide-eyed, she hastened to agree. "Okay, Mr. Adams. I won't tell them a thing."

"Good." He gave her the smile his co-star had told him would melt steel. "Where did they take her?"

She flipped sheets on her clipboard. "Here it is. Stefi Stevens, room 6."

"Thanks, darling. Thanks a lot." Luke figured that one endearment would do more to keep Stefi's secret than a hefty bribe. He was right.

He found Thea standing stiffly in the hallway outside room 6, staring at the closed door, tears sliding silently down her cheeks. Without a word, Luke pulled her into his arms.

"They wouldn't let me stay," she whispered raggedly. "They wouldn't let me stay."

Luke held her and stroked her hair, whispering soothing nonsense. Stefi was behind that closed door, and he felt a surge of protective anger on her behalf. He could only guess at the hell Thea was going through.

"They know what they're doing," he told her with more conviction than he really felt. "They're all good doctors." A nurse maneuvered a loaded cart past them, and he drew Thea out of the way. "Come on, sweetheart. We can't stand here blocking traffic. Where are we supposed to wait?"

"Out in the lobby."

"Okay." He walked her back to the double doors, pushed them open and realized he'd made a mistake. The reporters were waiting, and as they stepped through the doors, questions rang out and cameras flashed in their faces. Thea shrank back, and Luke pulled her close, pressing her face into his shoulder.

"How's the little girl doing?"

"Is she going to be all right?"

"How old is she?"

"How'd she get hurt?"

Thea shook her head at the barrage of questions. "Please," she said shakily. "Please, I can't talk to you now."

"What's going on back there?" Norm Fletcher demanded, and shoved his tape recorder in her face. "How's the kid?"

"No comment," Luke grunted. He pushed past, but Fletcher followed him, holding the recorder in front of him.

"Why are you here, Luke?" Luke kept moving, but so did Fletcher.

"Is the kid hers?" Fletcher asked, his tone heavily insinuating. "Or yours?"

Luke stopped short and swung around. As Fletcher stepped back, wary of the fury in Luke's face, Luke grabbed the palm-size recorder out of his hand and took out the tape. He stuffed the tiny cassette in his pocket.

"I said no comment, Fletcher. And I meant it." He held the recorder at arm's length, then dropped it. It hit the floor with a crunch. "If you bother me or the lady again, I won't stop with a tape recorder."

"Don't threaten me, Adams!" Fletcher yelled. "Nobody threatens me!"

With Thea held close, Luke strode to the reception clerk, who sat watching the drama with wide, startled eyes.

"Where can we wait?" he demanded. "We can't stay out here."

"The doctors' lounge," she replied promptly. "Go through that door and turn left." She stood and marched out from behind the desk. "I'll deal with *them*." She looked ready to take on the entire media establishment, and Luke winked.

"Go get 'em, tiger."

The lounge was past the treatment rooms at the end of the hallway. While they waited, Thea was alarmingly passive, barely aware of him, all her attention concentrated on the door to room 6. When it opened, she leaped up and was hurrying down the hall before Luke was on his feet.

A big, sandy-haired man dressed in hospital greens and a lab coat had walked out and was turning toward the lobby.

"Nick!" Thea called, and grabbed his arm with both hands, stopping him. "How is she?" she demanded.

He dropped a wrestler's arm around her shoulders and gave her a comforting hug. Luke watched with narrowed eyes, feeling an unexpected and powerful urge to knock that muscular arm away from her shoulders. He controlled it, with difficulty.

"She's a little banged up," the doctor was saying, "but she's going to be fine, Thea. I promise. Can we sit down for a minute while I tell you?" He looked over her head at Luke and nodded pleasantly. "I'm Nick Tyler," he said, and took his arm from Thea's shoulders to shake hands with Luke.

"Luke Adams." He accepted the handshake but couldn't quite return the grin.

"Luke's working on a film series with us," Thea explained. "And Nick's an orthopedic surgeon." In the lounge, Nick let Thea take the large, comfortable chair while he sat in a small one that creaked alarmingly under his weight.

Thea watched him, pale and tense. "Is Stefi going to need surgery?"

"I don't think so."

"But she's been in there all this time. What have you been doing?"

Nick smiled. "Thea, give us a chance! She's been here ten whole minutes. We've just talked to her and done a preliminary exam."

"And?"

"And she has a fractured arm." Nick reached out and held her hand as he spoke. "We're taking her to X-ray in a few minutes. I can feel a displacement of the radius about halfway between the elbow and wrist, and there's some problem in the ulna, too. I'll have to see the films to know what I'm dealing with there. It looks like I can set the bones and give her a lightweight cast.''

''Okay.'' Thea nodded. ''And her face?''

''Althea agreed with the school nurse, and she called John Chao. He'll be here any time now.''

''Will she have scars?''

Nick shrugged. ''I'm not the plastic surgeon, Thea. You'll have to ask John about that. I wouldn't worry too much, though. He's about the best there is.''

''Yes,'' Thea agreed slowly. ''He is.''

''Then cheer up a little.'' With a bearlike paw, he gave her shoulder a pat that rocked her in her chair. ''She's in good hands. Someone will bring you the consent forms for X-ray and so on in a few minutes.'' He stood and took a step, then paused. ''We're going to give her a sedative, Thea, so she won't remember much about this. I'll have her anesthetized, and John will probably do her face at the same time. She won't be under very long.''

''Okay.''

''Try to relax, okay?''

Thea laughed weakly, and Nick smiled. ''I don't expect miracles, Thea. Just try.''

''She'll try,'' Luke told him, and Nick nodded before returning to the exam room. Luke turned to Thea. ''Will you at least do what he said and try to relax?''

''Yes.'' She sighed. ''For all the good it'll do.''

''You can do it. Stay here and I'll get you a cup of coffee.''

''I don't want anything.''

''I'm going to get it, and you're going to drink it.'' His tone brooked no opposition. She sat back, but then they heard a child's long wail from the exam room. Thea bolted to her feet, and Luke caught her arms, holding her firmly as the wail slid up to a short scream and then another long-drawn-out cry of ''Mommeeee!''

Thea jerked against Luke's steely grip. She stood rigid and trembling until Stefi's crying died away. When it was quiet, Luke turned her around and saw tears streaking her white cheeks.

"Oh, baby." He pulled her into his arms, cupping the back of her head in his hand and pressing her face into his shoulder. "Don't cry. Please don't cry."

The dam broke. Thea pushed her face into his shoulder in an attempt to stifle the sobs she couldn't prevent. Her shoulders shook with her weeping, and Luke held her close while she cried her feelings out.

"I can't—" she gasped into his shirtfront after a moment. "I'm sorry, but I can't—" She gulped hard and drew a shaky breath. The tears began again as soon as she started to speak. "I can't stop thinking about her...hurt...and scared. She's all by herself in there, and she's so little." She hid her face again.

"I know how you feel, sweetheart. Believe me, I know how you feel, but she's a strong kid. She'll get through this."

"How?" Thea looked up at him, her face streaked and blotched with tears, wet circles of mascara beneath her eyes. She made no effort to remove herself from his arms. Luke pulled a handkerchief from his pocket and wiped her cheeks, then blotted the mascara away. "How do you know how I feel?"

"Sit down again." He sat with her on the love seat, keeping his arm around her shoulders. "I know that you feel all of her pain, and I know you're bargaining with God right now so you can take her pain and injuries on yourself."

Thea looked up, surprised.

"I know you're imagining all kinds of terrible things going on back there, and I know that her crying nearly tore you apart. They were probably just giving her that sedative, so that when this is all over, she won't remember enough to have nightmares about it.''

''Won't she?''

''I don't think so.'' Luke smiled. ''She'll want to get back to school so she can show all the other kids her stitches and get her cast signed.''

''Yeah.'' Thea sniffed. ''That's what she'll want to do.''

''Whose name will she want to get first?''

''Yours, probably.'' There was a dry note in Thea's voice. ''Just before she asks you to walk on water.''

''Huh?''

''She's crazy about you already. Now that you've rescued her, it'll be out-and-out hero worship.''

''I imagine I can live with that. Who'll be her second choice as cast-signer?''

''Probably Marybeth.''

''Oh, yeah.'' He nodded. ''Her buddy who knows everything.''

''I gather that Marybeth gets her information, such as it is, from her older brothers and sisters. It makes for some interesting conversations.''

She sounded almost amused, and Luke began to think she might be relaxing. ''I'm going to get that coffee, Thea. You wait here, and I'll be right back, okay?''

''Okay.''

He left her sitting very straight, her eyes fixed on the doors. The nearest coffee to be had was in a vending machine halfway along the hall leading to the family practice clinic. He had to search his pockets for change, then wait impatiently while the machine dropped a paper cup, poured coffee and something that was supposed to be cream and sugar into it, then repeated part of the process to come up with black coffee for him. It didn't take long, but he didn't like leaving Thea alone.

He came around the corner and heard voices from the lounge.

"Why did Luke Adams bring her here?"

"Leave me alone," Thea pleaded shakily. "Please, just leave me alone."

Luke shoved the coffee cups onto a cart and began to run.

"Is there more to this than just driving you around? Is this kid something else to Luke Adams?"

"Get out." Luke stood in the doorway, fists clenched. "Get out, or I swear I'll hammer you into the ground."

Fletcher rose languidly, a sneer on his face. "That would be a very stupid thing to do, Mr. Adams. You could end up in jail."

"It would be worth it—" Luke smiled coldly "—just to pound your face into hamburger."

Fletcher's sneer wavered, and he edged warily toward the door. "It would be the end of your career," he blustered.

"Maybe. Or I might just be a hero for getting rid of vermin like you." He advanced a menacing half step, and Fletcher dodged past him into the hall.

From a safe distance he shouted, "You'll be sorry you did this, Adams!"

"Damn!" Luke watched until he was gone, then swore and slammed his palm against the wall. "I wish I could have just five minutes with him." He turned to Thea, who was huddled on the love seat. "Are you all right?"

"Yes, I'm okay... now that he's gone."

"Did you tell him anything?"

"No." She looked up, anxious to assure him that she'd done the right thing. "I just asked him to leave me alone. But he wouldn't go away. And he kept asking things, about Stefi and you, and why you brought us here, and—"

"I know. I know." He sat beside her and pulled her into his arms. "He's a creep. I'm sorry he bothered you, but I'm glad you didn't say anything to him. You did exactly the right thing."

"I didn't want him around me."

"I don't blame you." Luke sat back. "I'm afraid I left the coffee out in the hall."

"I don't care. I'm not thirsty." She shivered. "How do you stand it, Luke?"

"Stand what?"

"Those reporters. They're like vampires. Stefi's in there, hurt, and all they can ask is why you drove us over here!"

"That was just Fletcher. I think the others were honestly concerned and not just out for a story."

"But they scared me, all around me that way. I couldn't get away from them."

"They're just people, Thea. They're doing a job, and most of them do it well. Don't let a few bad apples like Fletcher sour you on them."

She sighed. "It's not just those people. It's the idea that they can invade your privacy because you acted in a movie, and invade my privacy because I went to dinner with you or because you drove my daughter to the hospital. I hate that!"

"Remember that they can't hurt you. And keep a sense of humor about it."

"Humor? You weren't laughing when he was asking me questions, were you?"

He glanced at her, then looked away. "No. But, unfortunately, he knows I'm not going to punch him out."

"You had me convinced."

He laughed shortly. "Oh, I was mad enough, but he knows he's not worth going to jail over." He sat back and sighed. "He won't come back again, though."

"Thank goodness," Thea breathed, and looked at her watch. "How long has she been in there?"

"I'm not sure. You'll see her as soon as they're ready for you to see her." He tightened his arm around her and pulled her head down onto his shoulder. "You trust the doctors, don't you?"

She sighed. "Yes, I trust them. They're all good, and they're all good with kids, too."

"Then show me that you trust them and relax. It will all be over soon."

Thea replied with another sigh and tried to settle herself to wait.

It took over two hours. During that endless, agonizing period, Luke tried his best to distract and reassure Thea, but she continued to worry with a tenacity that even his best efforts couldn't shake.

His inability to help her frustrated him. She jumped at every movement in the hall and constantly turned her head from side to side to watch the doctors, nurses and technicians walk back and forth across the waiting room. It was exhausting to watch her.

"Thea." He spoke quietly, and she didn't look around. "You've got to quit blaming yourself."

"What?"

"You're telling yourself that if you'd done something differently, Stefi wouldn't have played on the swings, so she wouldn't have fallen off and she wouldn't be hurt."

She stared at him. "How did you know?"

"It's the natural reaction. But you didn't have anything to do with it. Stefi went on the swings and she fell off. Kids fall off swings. They also fall off bikes and roller skates. They play games and jump off the garage roof, and they get hurt. That's the way it is. It's no more your fault than it is mine."

Thea sighed heavily. "I know you're right, but it's hard to believe it."

"I know." He draped his arm along the back of her chair and patted her shoulder. "War may be hell, but parenthood will test you to the limit."

"For somebody who's not a parent, you seem to know a lot about it."

"I have a niece and a nephew. I've been to the emergency room with them once or twice, and I know what my sister's gone through."

"Yeah." Thea let her head fall back to rest on Luke's arm. She barely noticed that he shifted his position slightly to pull her closer. "It seems as if the primary aim kids have in life is to kill themselves," she said. "You can't even warn them not to do those things, because who would ever think a kid would eat a box of tissues?"

"Who ate a box of tissues?"

"Stefi did, when she was eighteen months old. I had all the medicines and cleaners and things put up where she couldn't get at them, but it never occurred to me to hide the tissues."

Luke grinned. "It didn't occur to my sister to hide the sewing chalk."

"Sewing chalk?"

"Mm-hmm. My niece ate three pieces when she was about two."

"Did they have to pump her stomach?"

"No, but she felt pretty crummy for a while."

"I'll bet she did! She must have—" Thea was actually beginning to laugh when the door to the treatment room opened and a nurse pushed Stefi out in her wheelchair. Thea shot out of Luke's arms and sprinted to her daughter.

Stefi was flanked by Althea Martin, her pediatrician, and John Chao, the plastic surgeon. Dr. Martin, a tall, lovely black woman with close-cropped hair and a brilliant smile, held Stefi's good hand as they walked, while the brand-new cast rode in a sling. Dr. Chao was listening as Althea talked to Stefi, smiling at their conversation.

Thea hugged and comforted her daughter, then took the doctors' instructions and signed forms and releases. When they were done, Luke pushed Stefi's chair over to the double doors, then peered out into the lobby.

"Are they still there?" Thea asked.

He nodded. "Where's your car parked?"

"In the south lot. Why?"

"Give me your keys."

"Why?"

He had a plan. While the reporters waited impatiently in the lobby and Luke showed his face at the door once to keep them interested, a security officer drove Thea's car to the doctors' entrance on the other side of the emergency room.

Then they installed Stefi in the back seat and drove quietly away, unobserved and unmolested. The receptionist had promised to wait another half hour before she let the reporters know they were gone. Luke had given her a kiss on the cheek, securing her complete cooperation.

It was after seven before Stefi was dressed in her pajamas, given a dose of her medicine and tucked into bed with Thea hovering over her. Luke nearly had to drag her out of her daughter's bedroom.

"She's sleeping, Thea." He took her elbows and steered her toward the door.

"I should be with her," she protested, looking back over her shoulder at the sleeping child.

"You'll be in the living room." Luke pulled her inexorably toward the doorway. "You can hear if she so much as hiccups. Come on, sit down and rest before you fall on your face." Finally, reluctantly, she went.

Luke installed her on the couch and switched off the overhead light so that the room was lighted only by a dim lamp in the corner.

"Stay there," he commanded, and went to the kitchen. When he returned with sandwiches and coffee, Thea was curled in the corner of the sofa, her eyes closed. Looking at her, he wanted only to pull her into his arms, to cradle and kiss and comfort her until the exhaustion and the pain were gone.

Instead, he set the tray on the coffee table. The small thump and rattle was enough to rouse her.

"What's that?" Thea pushed herself up and watched him arrange plates and cups.

"Supper." Luke handed her a plate. "You need to eat."

She regarded a chicken sandwich with weary distaste. "I'm not really hungry."

"You're too tired to know you're hungry. Eat."

She took a bite and chewed slowly, obedient and apathetic. The apathy worried Luke. Where was her feistiness? He watched as she ate, and smiled to himself when she started to enjoy the food.

When she'd finished, she looked up at Luke. There was something she had to say.

"Thank you. I'm sorry I didn't say this sooner, but I'm really glad you were with me today." She reached out to touch his hand. "I don't know what I would have done if I'd been alone."

"You would have been fine. You're a strong lady."

Thea sat back with her coffee mug, curling her legs under her. Her face was shadowed in the half-light. "I don't know. Sometimes it's hard, knowing you have to be strong all the time."

"But I'm here now. I can be strong for you when you need me."

Thea glanced up, then looked into her cup again. She'd seen a new side of Luke today. Today he had been the controlled one, the person in charge. Throughout the whole awful afternoon, he had coped when Thea couldn't, dealing with the doctors, the reporters, even helping her with the endless forms. But on the other hand, he was the cause of one of her worst problems.

She sat up suddenly, and Luke looked at her, surprised. "I really am grateful for your help, Luke, but . . ."

"But what? Don't leave me hanging."

"It's just... I don't know how to say this without sounding ungrateful." She took a deep breath. "I'm glad you helped me and kept me from going to pieces, but you were part of the problem."

He understood. "Because of the reporters."

"Yes. It's one thing to have pictures taken at a restaurant. It's something else when my daughter's hurt and I can't even get her into the hospital without being harassed."

"Fletcher was the only one harassing us. The rest were just doing their jobs."

"They were taking pictures of my daughter!" She glared down at him. "Pictures of her when she was hurt to print in their damned papers for the whole country to look at! I'm glad you wanted to help, Luke, but maybe you shouldn't have."

"So what was I supposed to do?" he demanded. "Leave you alone to deal with it?"

"You could have gotten somebody else to go with me. Van or Bobby or somebody. You must have known the reporters would follow you!"

"To tell you the truth, I didn't think about it. I was too busy worrying about Stefi!"

"Then maybe you should have worried about exposing her to those—those vultures!"

"Damn it, Thea, I was more worried about her health!"

"Well, having them around didn't help!"

"Maybe not. But maybe I don't care about that!"

"Then what do you care about?" She flung the words at him.

He didn't reply for a moment, but the quick heat of anger left his face as he looked at her. "Oh, God, Thea." His voice was a groan. "Don't you know?"

Chapter 13

Don't you know?'' He caught her hands and pulled her down into his arms, onto the cushions. "Don't you know what it did to me to see you hurting? Don't you know how much I wanted to make it all right, for you and for Stefi.'' He touched his lips to her forehead, and smoothed her hair back with gentle hands. "Don't you know how much I want to take care of the two of you?''

She sighed and framed his face with her hands. "Luke, you don't have to take care of us. We're not your responsibility.''

He smiled into her eyes, and caught her hand. He rubbed his cheek against it, then turned his face to press his lips to the soft center of her palm.

"Maybe not, but it felt nice to take care of you today. I think you could use a little taking care of now, too.'' He helped her shift around on the couch, and in the process of settling her comfortably, ran his hand lightly across her shoulders. He stopped at the base of her neck, probing lightly with his fingertips, and she winced.

"Good grief, you're so tight you're about to break." He shifted his position again, so that he was half sitting behind Thea, and she rested comfortably against him. "Relax," he said. "Just relax, and don't think about anything."

He pushed her blouse away from his neck, his voice a soothing murmur as his hands massaged her taut muscles. They were working the same magic they'd worked in her office, slow, easy magic.

"Let your mind drift," he murmured. "Think about flowers, about roses, and how they smell on a summer afternoon, when the sun's warmed them and brought out their scent. They're red ones, deep red, and they smell warm and sweet, the way roses are supposed to smell."

"But if I go to sleep, I won't hear Stefi."

"I'll be awake. I'll listen for her. You relax."

Luke's hands made slow circles over her neck and shoulders, now kneading, now stroking. Gradually the tension in Thea eased under his touch; her head fell forward, and her breathing slowed. She let the low, even sound of Luke's voice lead her, filling her mind with summer roses, with a meadow on a spring day, a sun-baked beach, and she drifted into sleep, dreaming of flowers and sunshine.

Luke shifted his position carefully, until her head was cradled securely against his shoulder. He stretched out his legs and rested his booted feet on the magazines stacked on the coffee table. With his free hand, he was able to reach his unfinished cup of coffee.

He took a sip, then brushed a lock of hair off Thea's forehead. She was exhausted. With luck, both she and Stefi would sleep all night. He sipped again. As he'd promised, he would be awake in case Stefi woke.

"You don't have to leave."

It was just 6:00 a.m., but Luke was dressed. Thea stood

in her dim, chilly kitchen, wrapped in an ankle-length terrycloth robe of uncertain vintage. Her hair tumbled in a raven cascade around her shoulders, and her face was pale with fatigue, against which her impossible navy-blue eyes seemed even deeper and darker. He touched her cheek lightly.

"I do, you know." He smiled. "I have to go home and take a shower. And just in case any reporters have found your house, I don't want to be seen leaving in last night's clothes."

"But all you did was sit up all night, while I was sleeping."

"And who would believe that? I could tell them I stayed up with a sick child until I was blue in the face, and they'd just believe something entirely different."

"Well, it doesn't seem fair."

"It's not." He smiled. "But then, life seldom is. Anyway, I have a meeting at eight-thirty, and if I go straight home, I can have a nap before I shower and change."

"I see." She looked up and smiled, teasing. "Do you think you're tired enough to get to sleep?"

"After being up all night?" He laughed. "I'll call later to see how Stefi is. You keep warm, okay?"

"Okay."

He moved toward the back door, then came back. Catching her chin in his fingers, he lifted her face and kissed her, gently but thoroughly. "You," he said softly, "are a very brave lady." He brushed his thumb over her lips, touched her hair, then turned abruptly away.

Thea stood at the back door, listening to the sound of his footsteps on the sidewalk, then the slam of the car door. Alone, she poured a cup of coffee and carried it to the small kitchen table. She folded her robe around her legs and settled herself comfortably to watch the sun rise. She liked this time of day, as dawn was breaking, when the world was still fresh and quiet, and she seemed to be the only one awake.

But Luke was awake, and she wasn't alone. She smiled and sipped her coffee.

"Where did Luke go?" Stefi wondered, lisping through her injured lips.

She had awakened at 7:30, surprisingly cheerful despite her broken arm and hugely swollen lip. She took her dose of pain medicine willingly, then announced that she was hungry. Thea made oatmeal, which didn't require much chewing, and Stefi attacked hers hungrily.

"He went home. He has to go to a meeting this morning," Thea replied, and took a bite of her own oatmeal, without enthusiasm. She didn't care much for it, but felt she ought to set a good parental example.

"Is he gonna come see me? I want him to sign my cast."

"I don't know if he'll be able to come over today, Stefi. And I'm not sure you can write on a plastic cast." Stefi looked at her arm, and her lip quivered. "We'll try, though," Thea added quickly. "Maybe we can find a pen that will work."

"Okay." Stefi scooped up her last spoonful of oatmeal and slid off her chair. "I'm all done, Mom. Can I watch cartoons?"

"Sure. Just remember, the doctor said to keep your arm up."

"Okay. Thanks, Mom!"

When Thea heard the sounds of cartoon rabbits and ducks from the living room, she pushed her own bowl away and picked up her coffee cup. Oatmeal was undeniably nourishing, but she preferred toast.

She sipped, smiling absently at the overgrown poinsettia outside the window. The resilience of children was amazing. Stefi's arm and face were undoubtedly hurting her, but did she wake up early, complaining of pain or showing signs of emotional trauma?

No, she slept later than usual, then got up announcing that the bandage on her lip itched, she was starving, and why hadn't Luke autographed her cast?

A new bandage had removed her first worry, oatmeal the second, and reassurance the third. With the prospect of a whole day of watching cartoons, Stefi was a happy little girl. I'm the one who'll have nightmares about this, Thea thought.

She never would have believed it yesterday, but things could have been much worse. She would positively enjoy listening to cartoons today, because Stefi was going to be fine, both physically and emotionally.

She poured out her cold coffee and peeked around the dining room archway. Stefi was reclining against the front of the couch, her cast resting on a stack of throw pillows. Not so dumb, her little girl. Grinning, Thea went to do the dishes.

Luke was coming to dinner.

He'd telephoned at mid-morning to check on Stefi, and Thea had invited him to come over after his meeting. He was due at 6:30.

By six she was as nervous as a teenager before her first date. Yesterday she'd let him help her, she'd leaned on him for strength and reassurance, and she'd slept in his arms all night. Today she was a nervous wreck.

She had cooked herself to a frazzle over a rich casserole of beef and mushrooms and wine, which would be accompanied by vegetables, rice and a salad. The food was prepared, the table was set, Stefi was taking a nap, and Thea herself was showered, made-up and dressed, but she couldn't relax.

She perched on the sofa, tuned the television to an old movie, watched blindly for several minutes, then switched it off impatiently. She straightened the magazines on the coffee table, then scowled at them. They looked too neat, like something out of a home-decorating magazine, so she disarranged them a little. She was about to do the same thing to the books on the lamp table when she caught herself.

She stalked out of the room, but was unable to resist looking at herself in the hall mirror. She didn't want to look as if she'd dressed up, so instead of a dress, she wore her newest jeans and a pink angora sweater, soft and fluffy. Her hair was loose, flowing over her shoulders. She patted a stray tendril into place and studied her face critically.

Her cheeks were pink with suppressed excitement. She touched them with her fingertips, feeling the heat, and shook her head. She was kidding herself if she thought she could wait calmly for Luke to arrive.

The doorbell rang at precisely 6:30, and Thea jumped as if she'd been shot. She hurried to the door, pausing only to glance in the mirror again. Her hair still looked fine, and her face was still pink.

She opened the door, and Luke bent to kiss her lips. "How are you?"

"I'm fine."

"I'm glad." He stepped inside and took her in his arms. When he'd had his fill of kissing her, he lifted his head and smiled down at her.

He peered into the living room. "It's awfully quiet in there. Where's Stefi?"

"I gave her the pain medicine, and it made her drowsy enough to take a nap. She's been asleep for half an hour."

"That's probably the best thing for her." He sniffed the air. "Something smells good."

"Dinner." Thea closed the door and led the way into the living room. "I hope you like—"

"Don't tell me." Luke sniffed again. "It smells like—"

"Like *boeuf bourguignon*?" she suggested. "Which is really just a fancy name for beef stew."

"It smells more like *boeuf bourguignon* than stew. This should go with it, though." He handed her a bottle of Napa Valley rosé.

"Mmm." She examined the label and raised an eyebrow. "Very nice. I'm not sure my pedestrian taste buds are equal to this."

"Then I'd better not tell you what that bottle of champagne at the restaurant was worth."

"Don't, please!" Laughing, she carried the wine into the kitchen. "My blood pressure couldn't handle it." He leaned against the doorframe, watching as she stirred the beef and took the salad from the refrigerator. "Are you hungry? This is ready."

"Do you want to wait for Stefi?"

Thea shook her head. "I'll let her sleep. She can eat when she wakes up."

They sat down to eat. Conversation was desultory, because they were both hungry.

When Thea had finished, she sat back and lifted her wineglass. "This is delicious."

"I'll tell Marilyn you said so. She told me which one to bring."

"That's not a bad deal, having a caterer in the family."

"As long as she cooks things you recognize. Some of her experiments are a little too strange for me."

"Didn't you tell me something about squid ink?"

"Luke!" Stefi hurled herself at him from the kitchen doorway. Luke managed to catch her before she hurt herself, then smiled into her battered face.

"How are you feeling, kiddo?"

"I feel fine," Stefi told him with a grin that was hindered by her swollen lip. "My arm hurt a little bit, but Mom gave me some medicine, and now it feels okay. Will you write something on my cast?"

"Sure I will, but why don't you have some dinner with us first?"

Thea left them talking while she filled a plate for Stefi, who talked Luke's ear off, ate everything in sight and went to bed at 8:30, but only under protest.

When Thea returned to the living room, Luke was building a fire. The gray, cool day had become another rainy night, and the flames took the chill off the room.

"Come here." He patted the pillows he'd arranged in front of the hearth. "I want to hold you."

The low, husky note in his voice made her knees weaken and her heart pound. She wanted to hold him, too. She'd been wanting that ever since he'd left her kitchen that morning. She walked slowly toward him. The living room had always seemed small to her, but now it seemed to take her a long time to reach him.

This was what she'd known would happen; this was why she'd been so nervous, so anxious to make everything perfect. Last night he'd held her in his arms and comforted her. When he held her in his arms tonight there would be passion. And she knew why.

This was the man she loved, and she had no will to resist. Languidly she knelt down beside him, sliding into his arms, stroking his face, savoring the textures, smooth skin, rough beard, firm flesh and bone. She stroked her fingertips across his mouth, and he tried to trap her finger, nipping gently at it, then soothing the tiny hurt with the tip of his tongue. It was scorching hot, sending a jolt of heat through her to feed the melting, spreading glow inside.

With a secret smile, Thea lowered her hand. Following Luke's example, she stroked the strong column of his throat, then brushed her fingers over the soft hair in the opening of his shirt. She hooked a finger behind the first closed button, gave a little twist, and it opened. She let her fingers follow the line of the opening shirt, found another button, freed it. She spread her palm flat on his chest, testing his firm muscles, brushing through thick golden hair, finding his flat nipple and teasing it to a stiff peak.

Luke breathed something incoherent and bent swiftly to capture her smiling mouth with his. There was no more careful control. He kissed her with all the passion he'd been holding back, plundering her mouth, tasting the sweetness.

Thea clung to his shoulders as he cradled her head in his hands and kissed her mouth, her brow, her eyelids, cheeks, and as her head fell back, down the graceful line of her throat.

He pushed the neckline of her sweater aside and traced his lips over the soft curves of her breasts above her bra. It was sheer lace and gossamer nylon, no barrier at all to the touch of his hand, or the heat of his lips. He circled one small dusky nipple with his thumb, watching by firelight as it tightened. Then he lowered his lips to taste.

Thea caught her breath and tightened her arms around his neck, but he moved again, surprising her. He slid one arm behind her shoulders, one beneath her knees, and rose with her in his arms.

"Where is your bedroom?"

He kissed her, long and deep, before she could reply. When he lifted his head, Thea touched his face gently, then pressed her lips to his cheek.

"Second door down the hall," she whispered against his skin, and kissed him again.

He shouldered the door open and carried her to the simple pine bed where she slept alone each night. Thea expected him to lie down with her, and clutched at him with a mutter of protest when he moved away.

"Can you hear Stefi if I close the door? Will she be okay?"

"She'll be okay, but I can hear her if she wakes."

"Okay. He closed it quietly, found the lock button and snapped it into place, then turned back to Thea.

She lay against the pillows, watching him in the glow that filtered through the curtains from the streetlights outside. With a small corner of her mind she realized that she should be feeling fear, nerves at the very least. Instead she was eager, as hungry as he seemed to be for the love-making that was becoming as necessary to her as her next breath.

Luke stood beside the bed as he stripped off his shirt and dropped it to the floor, moving with a deliberation designed to drive her mad. She wanted him; her hunger showed in her eyes as she watched him. But still he waited, moving slowly, when all he wanted was haste—and her.

He would wait until she was certain, until there were no doubts, no hesitations or regrets, to tarnish the magic that had been building between them from the moment they met. He'd been willing to wait for her, though it had strained both his patience and his self-control nearly to the breaking point. He would not rush her now. If she showed the slightest uncertainty, he would bury his own desire, and he would go.

There was no hesitation. When Luke's hand dropped to his belt, Thea stopped him, reaching out to open the buckle herself. Her sweater had fallen off her shoulder, and her skin gleamed with the soft sheen of pearls. Her hand shook slightly, but Luke knew that it wasn't fear that made her tremble. She freed his belt, and then he took over, stripping off his slacks and kicking them aside.

He lay down beside her, braced on one arm, with his body leaning over hers. With infinite delicacy, he traced a fingertip down her cheek, then followed the path with his lips. Thea shuddered at the first moist, scorching touch, then let her eyes close and her head fall back in surrender.

They moved as one, needing no words, not thinking, only feeling. Thea was shy at first, as she stroked his shoulders, learning the curve of muscle and the angle of bone, the texture of his skin. His back was like warm satin under her hands, his muscles hinting at a carefully controlled strength that excited her beyond imagining.

His strong hands were gentle on her skin, exquisitely careful as he eased her sweater over her head and tossed it aside. He slid one satin strap off her shoulder, then followed the line of the lace across the soft curve of one breast, down into the velvet-soft valley between them, and up again, across the other to push the remaining strap out of the way. Thea felt his touch like a brand, the mark of his possession.

She was his. She knew that now. She was his, and for tonight, at least, he was hers. She would not look beyond that.

Her bra was fastened with a single hook between her breasts. Luke opened it with a twist of his fingers. The nylon and lace floated from her breasts, and his fingertips floated over her skin. He touched her nipple, and it tightened to a stiff peak, inviting more.

He answered the invitation with his lips, and she caught her breath sharply as desire shot through her, lying low and heavy in her belly. She slid her hands up, holding his head, arching her back as her body moved instinctively, tempting, inflaming.

She wanted more. She pushed him, quickening the pace of his loving, defeating his efforts at restraint. When he touched her breasts, she wanted his mouth, and when he loved her with his mouth, she had to have more. She trembled uncontrollably, twisting beneath him, her hands restless, her mouth seeking his, blindly, desperately.

She *wanted* to push him, to take control and make him aware of nothing but her. She wanted to strip away that veneer of civilization and control, and leave only a man and a woman together.

And she did. When he touched, she touched; when he hesitated, she urged him on with soft hands and a sweet, hot mouth. She felt no shyness when he stripped off her slacks and panty hose, only feminine pride at the desire in his eyes when he looked at her. He wanted her. At this moment, there was no other woman in the world for him.

And she couldn't wait, not a moment longer. Luke would have slowed the pace, would have loved her carefully, gently, but she wouldn't allow it. She didn't want his gentleness; she wanted his passion. She tangled her fingers in his hair, urging his mouth up to hers, then twined her legs with his. With a quick movement he stripped the last scrap of clothing from her body.

She pushed at his briefs, but her hands trembled. He rolled briefly away to shed the garment and throw it aside. She wrapped him in her waiting arms as he rolled back to her, then wrapped her legs around him, pleading with her body and hands and mouth for him to make them one.

They joined together in a burst of heat. The tension built within them, and then the world whirled and narrowed to nothing but the two of them. Then there was only heat and light and sensations that burst within her into a million brilliant stars, and Thea clung to Luke and let the storm take her.

She woke slowly, reluctantly. She was deliciously warm, pleasantly achy, her limbs heavy with exhaustion. She didn't want to be dragged back to awareness. She batted at her alarm, but the bell pealed again.

"It's the doorbell, Thea." Luke caught her hand to stop her from bludgeoning the clock.

Luke.

There was no moment of confusion, of wondering where she was, or why, or even why Luke was lying in her bed, his arm pillowing her head, his legs warm and rough against hers. She remembered it all, every breathtaking moment.

The room was dark, and there were no sounds of traffic from the street outside, so it wasn't morning yet.

"The doorbell?" She groped for the clock. "What time is it?"

"Ten-thirty." He rose on his elbow and looked down at her in the dim light. "Do you get a lot of visitors at this time of night?"

"I never get visitors at this time of night."

"I'll come with you, then." He rolled to his feet and began pulling on his slacks. "You'd better answer it," he said when she hesitated, "or the bell will wake Stefi up."

"Oh, lordy, you're right!" She scrambled out of bed, clutching the sheet around her. Luke hadn't bothered with modesty, but she was shy. "Where are my jeans?"

"Here." He held out her terrycloth robe. "Just put this on."

"I don't want to answer the door in a robe." She found her jeans, then hopped on one foot as she pulled them on. "You know how that looks."

"Good point." He found her sweater and tossed it to her. "Do you have a hairbrush in here?"

"On the dresser."

She dragged it through her hair. When the doorbell pealed again, she hurried to answer it, with Luke close behind her.

"Does anybody know you're here?" she whispered.

He shook his head. "I didn't tell the service I'd be out, I just left the answering machine on. I even parked the car in your garage and shut the door."

Thea switched on the porch light before she unlocked the dead bolt. Luke stood to one side, out of sight. She opened the door on its safety chain, then stiffened in dismay.

"Good evening, Mrs. Stevens," Norm Fletcher greeted her with an oily smile.

"Mr. Fletcher." Thea's tone dripped ice, but her nerves were screaming. He couldn't find out that Luke was there with her! Somehow she kept herself from glancing back at him. She made no move to unlatch the safety chain.

"How are you this evening?"

"Fine."

"Are you going to invite me in?"

"No." She felt Luke's light, reassuring touch on her arm, out of Fletcher's sight.

"Well, then," he chuckled without humor, "how is your adorable daughter?"

"She's going to be fine." Thea felt her legs beginning to tremble and tightened her muscles against the weakness.

"That's wonderful, just wonderful. What school did you say she goes to?"

"I didn't." Thea stepped back. "It's late, Mr. Fletcher, and I don't have anything to say to you. Good night."

She closed the door on whatever his next question might have been, shot the bolt, and stood motionless until she heard his footsteps move off the porch. A car door slammed, a motor roared, and she turned and walked into the living room.

Luke followed, and when she stopped, he took her shoulders and turned her around. He bent to kiss her, but she turned her head so that his lips fell on her cheek and not her mouth.

"Thea?"

She pulled away from him, folding her arms across her breasts. "How did he find me, Luke?"

"I don't know." He shrugged. "Maybe through the hospital. Maybe the phone book. Are you listed?"

"As T. Stevens. There are a zillion 'T. Stevens' in the phone book."

"That would be enough."

"Enough for him to turn up on my porch?" She walked over to stand staring into the fire Luke had built. It was only glowing coals now, and it gave her no comfort. "Will he find out where Stefi goes to school?"

"I wish I could say no." He touched her shoulder, and she jerked away from him, hunching her shoulders forward.

"So he'll find her. And he'll try to get to her there."

"I wish I could say no."

"But you can't." She turned around, her face bleak. "Go home, Luke."

"Thea..." He walked toward her, ignoring her protest. "Don't blow this out of proportion."

"Go home. Please!"

He took her shoulders again, and he wouldn't let her pull away. "Thea, sweetheart, I'm not going anywhere until you talk to me about this."

"Talk about it?" She gazed up at him, aching and angry. "What is there to talk about? That...that *person* is on my porch, and all you can say is 'don't blow it out of proportion'?"

"You handled him perfectly. You should feel good about that."

"What I feel is invaded and violated and furious! And if that creep bothers Stefi, I'm going to feel *homicidal!*" She grabbed his wrists and tried to pull his hands away. "Let me go, Luke! None of this would have happened if it weren't for you!"

"*What*?" His hands fell from her shoulders.

"Would he—or any of them—have the slightest interest in me if I weren't with you? No." She shook her head, her hair swinging around her face. "Of course not. I told you this was crazy, Luke, and I was right. It won't work."

"It already *is* working, Thea. You can't tell me you don't care about me."

"No, I can't." She shrugged. "And I believe you care about me, but that's not enough. You are what you are. You're a star, and I can't deal with it. Reporters outside restaurants, reporters in the ER." She paused. "Reporters at my *house*. I can't deal with it, and I won't put my daughter in the position of having to deal with it."

"It's not always this bad, Thea. And reporters aren't all bad, either."

"Maybe not. Or maybe you're just making excuses."

"Why would I do that?"

"Because you want to keep seeing me. But Luke, think about what this is doing to me! They were outside that restaurant waiting for you, and they were at the ER because you drove Stefi there, and that creep was here tonight because maybe he knows you're here right now and he wants to put that in his paper. And what are they going to do if you don't leave until morning!"

She reached out then, gripping his hands with all her strength, begging him with her eyes to understand. "Please, Luke. Just go home and take the reporters with you. Leave me and Stefi alone."

"My leaving isn't going to change things."

"Of course it is! It's going to get them out of here, and that's what I want!"

"Is it?" he asked, his voice dropping to a soft, seductive note. "I thought you wanted what we shared tonight?"

He moved close and drew her into his arms. Just for a moment, she let herself be held. Yes, she wanted him, more than words could express, but this wouldn't work. It couldn't, so she pushed herself away, then bent her head, staring blindly at the floor.

"No. I don't want that, because the price is too high. I'd pay, and so would Stefi. All I want is to be left alone. Just go, Luke. Please."

There was a long, taut silence. When she looked up, Luke was watching her, anger and sadness in his face.

"If that's what you want."

She dropped her gaze to the floor again. After a few seconds the front door closed behind him with a quiet click.

She was right, she told herself. She had to send him away. He was a movie star, and reporters dogged his footsteps everywhere he went, invading his privacy in a way she dreamed of in her nightmares. It was impossible. She had done the right thing. She'd done the only thing she could do.

"Oh, Luke," she whispered. And, covering her face with her hands, she let the tears come.

Chapter 14

"Good morning!" Luke breezed into Thea's office at fifteen minutes before eight on Monday, with a big manila envelope in his hand and a broad smile on his face. The bitter argument of Saturday night might never have happened.

Thea had heard nothing from him since he'd walked out of her house. She'd spent a quiet, dreary Sunday at home, scarcely daring to go out the front door to pick up the paper for fear there might be reporters lurking in the shrubbery. She felt no better after a second sleepless night.

"What are you doing?" she demanded, wary of Luke's inexplicable cheeriness.

"I'm making a point." He tossed the envelope on her desk and dropped into the armchair. "Go on." He pointed to the envelope. "Take a look."

"But what's...?" She tipped the envelope and shook out a stack of newspaper clippings. She spread them out. "What is this stuff?"

"The press response to you and me. I bought every paper and tabloid I could find and searched each one for anything they said about me, you or us. Read it."

She shuffled through the clippings. Several were glowing reviews of *After Midnight*, with comments on Luke's performance and his next film. There was a short trade paper article on the delay in the shooting of the next film, and there was an advertisement for *After Midnight* with a picture of Luke. Two of the gossip columns mentioned their dinner at the restaurant, and another briefly mentioned Luke's bringing Stefi to the hospital. The short paragraph painted him as a white knight and mentioned Thea only as the producer of Memorial's films.

"Really racy stuff, isn't it?"

She searched through them again. "Which one is Fletcher's?"

"Here." He pushed it forward. There was a grainy photograph of Thea and Luke leaving the restaurant with his hand decorously holding her arm, and a four-line caption beneath it saying that Luke Adams had been seen leaving a popular Los Angeles restaurant with a hospital film producer. They'd also been seen at the hospital emergency room. Was a romance brewing between the star and the producer? the caption asked. More to come...

Thea laid the clipping carefully on her blotter, smoothing out the creases.

"Shocking stuff." Luke took the paper from her. "You won't be able to show your face in public after this."

"Sarcasm is unbecoming." She sighed and looked up at him. "But, heavy-handed as it is, I get the point."

"Good."

"Why do people sue them about the stories they do? This is all so insipid."

"Ninety-nine percent of the stories they do *are* insipid. They're either dumb, or boring, or dumb *and* boring. Lots of rumor and innuendo, a lot of space-alien stuff, and occasionally a story that libels someone and gets the paper in a lawsuit. That's rare, though. It's mostly sensational headlines and no substance.''

She pushed at the clippings. "And they camp out on the hospital steps day after day for this?"

"Since the publicity began on *After Midnight* they've said that I'm a great actor, that I'm only a fair actor, that I'm involved with my co-star and that I went to the University of Minnesota."

"Are you?"

"Am I what?"

"Involved with Marika McKay."

"Marika," he said with exaggerated patience, "is a very beautiful woman and a much better actress than she's given credit for. She's also crazy in love with her husband. She called him at least twice a day from the wilds of northern Canada on a radiotelephone that only worked half the time. She's expecting a baby, and she's thrilled."

"Marika McKay is pregnant?"

"Yes. And I went to the University of Wisconsin."

"And you don't care that they said those things?"

"I'd prefer them to be accurate, but if they can't do that, I'll settle for not being libeled." He stood up and took her hands, pulling her out of her chair. "Nobody believes the rest of the garbage they print, anyway."

She let him draw her around the desk and into his arms. "I know you're afraid of the invasion of your privacy, but face it, Thea, even if *After Midnight* does great at the box office, they'll forget all about me if the next film is a dud. I may be famous for fifteen minutes and go back to being a nobody for the rest of my life."

"But if they libel you?"

"Then I'll sue them for every dime they have." He smiled gently into her eyes. "I'm not that important to them right now, Thea. In fact, I may never be that important to them. And they're certainly not important to me.

You *are*. Too important for me to let you just walk out of my life.''

She shook her head. ''You should, you know. You should turn around, run the other way and find yourself someone like Marika.''

''I don't want Marika.'' His arms tightened, pulling her against his body, making her aware of every inch of him. ''I want you. And I want you to understand that I don't intend to tear your life apart. I want a normal life, too. I want Stefi to be a happy, normal kid. And I want you.''

He tangled his fingers in her hair, demolishing her prim little bun, and crushed his mouth onto hers. Thea went up in flames at the touch of his lips. She'd lain awake and ached for this for two long, lonely nights, ached just to be in Luke's arms again. She'd been angry and afraid when she had sent him away, but the anger was gone now, the fear at bay, the need and the love as strong as ever.

She locked her arms around his neck and clung to him as he kissed her deeply, filling the emptiness his going had left in her heart. When he lifted his mouth, he pressed her head into his shoulder, burying his face in her hair, running his hands over her back, from the fragile bones of her shoulders down the graceful line of her spine to the soft curves of her bottom, gently, almost reverently, as if to reassure himself that she was really there, in his arms.

''Oh, God, Thea, don't ever send me away.'' His voice was a groan. ''Don't ever do that again.''

''I don't—'' She laughed brokenly against his shirt-front. ''I don't know if I could. It was so hard to do it once, I don't think I'd have the strength again.''

Her arms tightened and, suddenly desperate, she pulled his face down to hers and kissed him again. She clung to his shirt collar, pulling herself onto her toes. Her fingertips brushed his throat, and she fumbled a moment before she opened the first button, then the second. Then the third, and she slid her hand inside to touch his skin, warm and alive and uniquely Luke. Beneath her palm, the steady thud of his heartbeat suddenly accelerated, and through the soft brush of gold-colored hair she felt his skin begin to heat against hers.

She was small and strong in his arms, the flush of passion spreading through her, her lips and hands demanding his answering desire. Luke met that demand, pulling her blouse free of her skirt and sliding his hand over her back and up to her shoulders, his palm slightly rough on her skin, strong and hard and inexpressibly exciting.

"Thea?" He drew back, looking into her eyes, which were as dark as midnight with the longing she felt. "I—" He pulled her close, rested his chin on her hair and laughed softly. "I'm glad you're not pushing me away. You don't know how glad, Thea."

She caught her breath, then let it out on a long shaky sigh before lifting her head and framing his face with her hands. "I want you, too, Luke. I still think it's crazy, but I do want you."

"Craziness becomes you." He bent his head slowly, and his breath was deliciously warm on her ear. When his lips touched her nape, she shivered, though his mouth was hot. It drifted over her skin, along the side of her neck, and moved up to nip her earlobe and brush the angle of her jaw. His fingers slipped around her throat, resting for a moment on the pounding pulse; then he tipped her chin up so he could kiss her mouth.

"Hey, Thea!" Bobby's shout was accompanied by a volley of knocking.

Luke and Thea froze, staring at the closed door with hunted eyes.

"Did you lock the door?" she mouthed soundlessly.

"No," he whispered.

She stared at the doorknob, willing it not to turn. If Bobby saw them like this . . .

"Are we gonna shoot this today, or what?"

Thea could feel Luke's chest begin to shake with silent laughter. She pulled out of his arms and reached behind herself, hastily stuffing her blouse back inside her waistband.

"I'll be with you in five minutes, Bobby." Her voice was huskier than usual, but maybe he wouldn't notice.

She flapped her hand at Luke's shirt. "Button that!" she ordered quietly. Grinning at her agitation, he complied.

"Okay!" Bobby called after a tense pause. "I'll go set up."

Thea waited until she heard the outer door close behind him, then sighed in relief. She looked at Luke's laughing eyes and could feel laughter welling up in her, too.

"This is ridiculous!" she whispered. "I feel like a high school kid."

Luke finished buttoning his shirt and smoothed a hand over his hair. "Did you do this kind of thing in high school?"

"Of course not!" She gave him a mock glare and turned away to rummage in a drawer. "But I knew Mary Elizabeth Capetto. She kissed a student teacher in the janitor's closet. His name was Mr. Trevise, and he was really cute." She laid a brush and a large tortoiseshell barrette on her desk and began pulling pins out of her hair.

"What are you doing?"

"I'll never get this pinned up again, so I'll just clip it back." She brushed with quick, hard strokes, then gathered her hair at her nape with the barrette. "Do I look all right?" She fussed, patting her hair and smoothing her skirt, until Luke caught her hands.

"You look beautiful. You always do. But I like your hair better the other way." He pulled her face up and kissed her quickly. "And I like your lips just like this."

* * *

"Ready, and . . . time." Thea clicked her stopwatch. "Action."

Vanessa read the title of the tape. "Grief and grieving. Nursing intervention in the grieving process." She ran smoothly through the introductory voice-over, then stepped onto the "office" set.

"Hello, Mr. Smith." At his cue, Luke raised his head. Thea stifled a gasp. His was the face of a man ravaged by grief, a wound so raw and new that it hurt Thea to look at him.

Vanessa's voice was warm and accepting, inviting "Mr. Smith" to explore his emotions. He'd had a dream, he told her, about his dead wife. Thea watched, awed, as the script was brought to life and he began to describe his dream.

"I was driving down a dark road," Luke said, tension creeping into his voice, "with Karen beside me in the car. She always rode with her hand on my knee." His lips curved into a small smile, as if at the memory. "I can still feel her hand when I drive. On my leg, right here." He touched his right thigh, just above the knee in a little caressing movement.

Unexpected tears stung Thea's throat. She'd put that line in herself, remembering how she'd always ridden with her hand on Marty's knee.

"It helps to remember the good things," Vanessa said.

Luke hunched his shoulders, and Thea sensed that his memories had grown more painful. "The road got darker and darker." He tensed, and his words came more quickly. "And then it was there, all of a sudden, right in front of us." He gripped his hands together, and his knuckles were white.

"What was there?"

"It was a truck, a gasoline truck." He fussed with the watch he had worn for the taping, twisting it on his wrist.

"The gasoline truck that hit Karen?" Vanessa asked.

"It was in the middle of the road," he went on, as if Van hadn't spoken. "Red and white. I tried to steer around it. I pulled on the steering wheel and hit the brakes, but they didn't work, nothing worked. The car wouldn't turn or stop and—" He broke off, shivering.

"What happened then?" Vanessa asked very gently.

"Then I wasn't in the car anymore. I was standing beside the road, watching. I saw it all, like slow motion in a movie. All I could hear was Karen, screaming." His voice dropped to a whisper. "She was screaming that I killed her."

Thea had to look away, fighting feelings that had nothing to do with the script. It was too real. At that moment Luke *was* a loving husband who had just lost his wife.

It was too real. It brought back the memories she had tried to seal away, memories of the terrible, dark months after Marty's death. She had been tormented by guilt for having survived, feeling that she had somehow caused Marty's death and should have done something to prevent it. Guilt that she had lived and he had not. Guilt about the secrets that she hadn't guessed, the things she hadn't known.

"Thea?" Bobby touched her arm. "Hey, Van, Luke! Cut, okay?" He pushed the camera away and took Thea's arm. "Thea, are you all right?"

"I'm fine." She was shaking and tears filled her eyes. "It's nothing," she said, but clearly it wasn't.

Vanessa put her arm around Thea's shoulders and pulled her toward a chair. "We all need a few minutes to relax. I'll go get some coffee for everybody. Bobby, you can help me carry it." They moved away, leaving Thea with Luke.

He went down on one knee by her chair, his hand on her shoulder. "What's the matter, Thea?"

"Nothing." She sniffed and scrubbed her hands over her face. "I'm okay."

"Did I upset you with those damned clippings?"

"No, it's not that." She drew a shuddering breath. "It's just the script."

"What about it? It's damned good."

"A little too good," she said ruefully. "We meant to write a moving script, but I'm beginning to think we did our job too well. Or maybe—" she looked at him "—it's your acting that's too good."

"Did it bring things back?"

Thea's head jerked up. "How—"

"How did I know? Logic. You suffered a similar loss." His fingers moved on her shoulders in a comforting caress. "This might be a little too immediate."

"You made it so real. I remembered riding beside Marty in the car."

"With your hand on his knee."

"Yes." Thea nodded slowly. "We didn't put a lot of stage direction in that script. Better to let the actors do the acting. That bit of business, touching your leg—"

He repeated the gesture. "Like this?"

"As if you could still feel her hand there." She breathed deeply. "For a minute, it was just too real."

"I can leave it out."

"No. It's good. The problem's with me."

"But if it upsets you—"

"It's been a long time. I've done my grieving."

"You were crying."

She smiled at him; it was a bit watery, but it was still a smile. "Consider it a compliment to your acting."

"How can I feel complimented if my acting upsets you?" He touched her cheek lightly, tenderly.

"I'm fine, Luke. And between my script and your acting, we'll make the best grief-and-grieving tape anybody's ever done."

"You're a brave lady."

His hand slid from her shoulder to her nape and guided her lips to his. She wasn't brave at all, Thea knew, but his

closeness gave her courage. She let her breath out in a little sigh of surrender as her eyes closed, and she concentrated all her senses on that kiss. God, it was insane, but
she loved him, loved his ability to understand why she
hurt, to comfort her. She didn't even want to think about
the consequences of loving him. Who he was, what he was,
none of it mattered in the face of that kind of love. She
clung to his shoulders and let him give her strength.

"Four coffees, comin' up!"

Bobby's cheerful shout broke them apart as effectively
as a bucket of ice water. By the time he'd entered with a
cardboard tray loaded with cups, Luke was standing a full
three feet from Thea, who was sitting in the folding chair
again.

"Thanks, Bobby." She accepted the cup he passed her.
"Just what the doctor ordered. How about we take five for
this coffee, finish the run-through and get on with shooting this thing?"

"I want you to go with me."

Thea stared at him. "To a party at the studio? Is this for
After Midnight?"

"Yeah. It's supposed to be the wrap party we didn't
have in Canada."

"Luke, I can't go to something like that."

"Come on." He sank into the armchair. "I thought
we'd settled all that. There may be a couple of reporters
there, but all they're going to say is that I attended the
party in the company of a lovely producer."

"Yeah, but there will be actors there, and directors...."

"And studio people, and even a producer or two." He
nodded. "Yep. They'll all be there. You scared?"

She bristled. "I'm not scared! I just don't want to go to
a studio party, that's all."

"Oh, sure." He shook his head at her. "Where's your confidence, Thea? You can handle this job and you can handle the reporters, so I know you can handle one dumb party. You know what your problem is?"

"No, but I'm sure you're going to tell me." She propped her chin on her hand and sighed. "Fire away."

He leaned back, folded his arms and gave her a bland smile. "You're afraid of things that you can easily handle."

She sighed and shook her head. "Why do you think I'm such a superwoman? I don't feel that way at all."

"Because I see what you do, and I see you do it well. Are you coming to the party?"

"Do you really want me to?"

"I really want you to."

"But why?"

He shook his head at her. "Maybe I want to be with you every minute that I can. Maybe I want to show off my woman." He smiled and reached for her hand. She curled her fingers trustingly in his. "And maybe I just don't want to go to the damned thing by myself."

After that, there was no way she could refuse. "Okay. I'll come with you. But I'm going to be nervous," she added hastily.

"Fine. We'll be nervous together."

Chapter 15

"Luke, wait." Thea stopped short in the middle of the narrow studio lot street. They were walking past the high blank wall of a vast soundstage. Luke went two steps farther before he realized she'd stopped.

"What is it?"

"I can't go in there."

He faced her, hands on hips. "You're twenty feet away and now you decide you can't go in?"

"Yeah." She stared at the door. It looked ludicrously small in the side of the enormous building. "I can't do this."

He sighed melodramatically. "Well, if you can't, I can't." He looked down at her in the slanting light of a street lamp. "I'm scared to go in there by myself."

"You are not!"

"Am too." He folded his arms, trying to pout. "I cannot go in there and face that pack of ravening wolves without your moral support." Maybe it was the archly petulant tone, or maybe it was the protest, but it worked.

Her spasm of panic dissolved, and Thea burst into helpless laughter.

"All right!" she gasped through her giggles. "All right, you win, I'll come!" She tucked her hand through his arm, and her giggles faded. "Thank you, Luke."

"For what?" he asked, turning her into his arms.

"For making this easier for me. It may be silly, but I'm nervous."

"It's not silly. I'm a little bit nervous, too." He kissed her quickly. "Don't worry. I'll be with you all the time." He wrapped an arm around her shoulders and walked her inside.

The echoing expanse of the stage was broken up into sets and storage areas. Thea recognized three sets left standing from a weekly television comedy; the familiar rooms seemed oddly lonely without the actors and looked cramped and shallow with no camera angles to give them depth. They crossed an empty concrete-floored expanse made treacherous by thick cables snaking past their feet. At the far side, on living and dining room sets built to duplicate those from *After Midnight*, the party was in full swing.

A buffet was set up in the dining room of the set, and both "rooms" were warmed by lights suspended from the shadowy rigging high above. A crowd of laughing, talking guests made themselves at home on the sofas and chairs, while all around them the huge stage was eerily empty and dark. Thea paused outside the circle of light.

Luke stopped beside her. "What is it this time?"

"Do I look all right?"

He smiled and looked her up and down. She was wearing narrow black trousers, an ivory blouse and a green satin jacket she had spent three evenings sewing.

"You look as beautiful as anyone here. They're no different from you and me. They make movies, we make movies. Now, let's get in there before they eat up all the food.''

Thea smiled in spite of her nervousness as she followed him into the fray. Luke kept her by his side, her hand in his as he moved through the crowd. He nodded to some and greeted others with a word, but some, like Marika McKay, he paused to talk with. She'd been known as a sex symbol for several years, but *After Midnight* let her show the powerful dramatic actress behind the alluring facade.

"And I owe it all to Luke." She smiled at Thea. "He gave me the chance to play something besides a sexpot."

She bent her head to her husband's shoulder for a moment. Max Kramer, highly respected television producer, was a burly man several inches shorter than his wife. He grinned at her and draped his arm around her waist, where there was a slight but significant bulge. With her husband beside her, Marika looked very much a happy woman.

"But you play such a good sexpot, sweetheart." Max gave her a squeeze.

"Yeah, but I'd like one or two people out there to know I have a brain." She turned her five-thousand-watt smile on Luke. "And you made that possible."

"I just did my part. You ought to be thanking Adam. His direction kept the emphasis on what was happening in your head."

"It was your intensity that made it believable, though. The audience can see why she feels the way she does, and they can see that it's more than sex." She laughed and winked at him. "They can see the part sex plays, too, though."

Thea glanced at Luke and was surprised to see a flush creeping up his neck. He shifted his feet uneasily, and Marika laughed. It was a low, musical sound.

"What's it like directing this guy, Thea?" she asked. "Does he behave himself?"

"Well . . ." Thea slanted Luke a teasing glance from beneath her lashes. "I could tell you about temper tantrums and script changes . . ."

"Hey!" He put his arm around her shoulders and shook her gently.

". . . but since none of that happened, I won't," she said, relenting. "He's a pro. Knows the lines, does his research, no temperament."

"Just like he was up in Canada," Marika said. "A pleasure to work with. Thanks again, Luke."

"De nada."

Max was talking to a choreographer, and when he drew Marika into the conversation, Thea and Luke moved off, drifting from one conversation to another.

She was surprised to find she was enjoying herself with these people, who were creative, witty and fun. A makeup man reduced her to helpless laughter with his account of the problems of making a group of very civilized people look as if they'd spent months in the wilderness. A character actor showed her how he assumed the appearance of evil without any makeup at all. A petite blonde with a voluptuous figure turned out to have a master's degree in chemistry. She tried to explain film emulsions to Thea, but it was a lost cause.

"Luke!" A short, stout man with steel-gray hair and a neatly trimmed beard waved and called to him. Luke took Thea's hand and led her through the crowd.

"This is someone you'll enjoy."

"Who is he?"

"Leonard March, one of the producers. He brought *After Midnight* in under budget, on time, *and* kept the actors happy."

"A talented man."

"Talented and still efficient." When they reached Mr. March, Luke kept Thea beside him, with an arm around her waist.

"Glad to see you, Leonard."

"I'm glad to see you, too, Luke." The producer turned to Thea. "And the lady. Is this . . . ?"

"Thea, I'm happy to introduce you to Leonard March, producer *extraordinaire*. Leonard, this is Thea Stevens, who is also a film producer."

"Glad to meet a colleague, Ms. Stevens." He shook her hand firmly and smiled through his beard. "I wondered where Luke was keeping himself until I read about it in the trade papers."

"Thank you, Mr. March. It's an honor to meet you."

He shook his head. "Call me Leonard. I was interested to read about what you're doing at Memorial. I'd like to watch you work some time."

Thea looked from one man to the other in confusion. "I'd be thrilled, really thrilled." She grinned at Leonard. "Of course, I'd also be scared to death."

"Nonsense!" He put his arm around her shoulders and drew her toward the prop couch. "Come sit down and tell me about the things you do. Luke—" he looked up at his star "—why don't you go circulate or something? Thea and I have a lot to talk about."

"I had a wonderful time!"

"Well, I don't like to be the one to say it—"

"But . . ." Laughing, she linked her hands over his arm and rested her head on his shoulder as they walked. "Go on, you deserve the chance to say it."

"I told you so," Luke singsonged. "And I'm glad you enjoyed yourself. Come this way." He led her to the right, past the darkened commissary and onto the studio's "brownstone street." Moonlight silvered the stoops and tall windows of the false fronts, creating a street that any New Yorker would have recognized.

Thea smiled as they walked. "I wasn't uncomfortable in the least. They're all so much fun to talk to. And Leonard was actually interested in hospital training films."

"You shouldn't be surprised." He laughed. "Everybody loves to hear the inside scoop about those medical hotshots you work with. You'll let Leonard come to the hospital, won't you?"

"Are you kidding? How could I refuse? I don't know if I'd have the nerve to work with him watching me, though."

Luke gazed up at the heavens in exasperation. "Will you cut that stuff out? You do a hell of a job, very different from Leonard's. And he really is interested."

Thea watched the bumpy pavement beneath her feet. "That's hard to believe."

"Confidence," he announced. "Your only problem is confidence."

"How's that?"

"You don't have any."

"You just keep playing the same old tune, don't you?"

"I'll keep playing it until you get the message." He stopped in the shadows, where a Victorian street led off to the left, and took her shoulders. "You're a very special lady, Thea Stevens. Why is that so hard for you to believe?"

She shrugged her shoulders under his hands. "It just is."

He pulled her closer, sliding his hands down to her waist. "It shouldn't be." He found her lips and kissed her. Thea closed her eyes just before his mouth touched hers, waiting for the now-familiar jolt. When it shot from her mouth to her center, she forgot the silent studio street, the party, the people, everything but Luke.

Several seconds later, he lifted his head. His breathing was as ragged as hers, and his eyes gleamed in the moonlight. He slid the ball of his thumb across her throbbing lips.

"Let's go home."

"What was the matter with that girl?" Luke asked a little while later as they stood in her kitchen.

Thea dumped the last scoop of coffee into the basket and glanced over her shoulder. "She's a college freshman and she met a movie star. What do you think is the matter with her?"

"I'm not sure I like knowing that meeting me reduces intelligent young women to that condition."

"Don't worry." She slid the basket into place and switched the machine on. "Under normal circumstances, she's well able to walk and talk at the same time."

"That's a relief." Luke pushed himself away from the dining room doorway, brushing his hand over the light switch as he did so. The overhead fixture went out, leaving only the small stove light to illuminate the room. "Come here."

He folded her into his arms, and she leaned back, looking up into his face.

"Why wouldn't you let me pay the baby-sitter?" he asked after a moment.

"I hired her, so I paid her."

"I didn't know they charged so much. Whatever happened to fifty cents an hour?"

"The same thing that happened to nickel candy bars."

"I should have paid her. I feel responsible for Stefi's baby-sitter. I feel responsible for you *and* for her, and you know what? I like it."

"But you don't have to—"

"Shh." He pressed his fingers to her lips. "I like it. I want to be responsible for you." He took her face in his hands. "Thea, I want to marry you."

For a moment time stopped, and so did her heart. She could only stare at him in shock.

"Come on, Thea, say something. Will you marry me?"

"I—" She tried to speak, but nothing came out. She coughed. "I don't . . . don't know what to say."

"How about yes?" She shivered, and he eased her more closely into his arms, bending his head to see her face. "Is it really such a shock?"

"Yes," she replied helplessly. "I never thought..." She shook her head, irritated with herself. "Luke, I never thought I'd get married again, and you—" She couldn't go on.

"And me what?"

"You...you're a movie actor. A star. I never thought... You want to marry me?"

"Yes, I do. That shouldn't be such a surprise. Thea—" he lifted her chin with gentle fingers "—what did you think was happening between us?"

She turned her head away. "I thought—"

"That I just wanted to have a fling with you while I was working at Memorial?" He read the answer in her face and grimaced. "I wish you had more respect for me, Thea. I've never lived that way, and I don't ever want to. I want to marry you."

She pulled out of his arms and moved away. "I'm sorry. It's just so hard to absorb this." She folded her arms across her chest. "I can't quite believe it."

"Believe it, Thea." He took her into his arms again, stroking her back. "I love you, and I want you to be my wife."

She touched his face lightly. "Me, a movie star's wife?"

"Not a movie star's wife, *my* wife." He smiled into her eyes. "Is the prospect so terrible?"

"No." She tried to return his smile. "No, it's not. Oh, Luke." She sighed and smoothed her hands over his face, unable to resist touching him. "It's not the *prospect* I'm afraid of. It's—I guess it's me. I don't know if I can do this."

"People get married all the time, Thea. I want to get married to you." He studied her for a moment, and she dropped her eyes. "How do you feel about marriage—to me?"

She was silent for several long seconds. When she looked up, she slowly began to smile. "I think I feel wonderful about it."

It took an instant for Luke to understand. Then his eyes widened, his face lit with happiness, and he lifted her off her feet to twirl her in a circle that almost wreaked havoc in the small kitchen. He set her on her feet and kissed her heartily.

"I want to shout," he whispered. "But I'd wake Stefi up."

"She'd be glad to hear the news. She's crazy about you."

"We can celebrate with her in the morning." He smiled and pulled her closer to stand between his feet, pressed into the strong, protective curve of his body. "Right now, I want to celebrate with you." He bent, looped an arm behind her knees and scooped her up to carry her across the kitchen. "Shut that off." She reached out and switched off the coffee maker.

"If we leave that there, it'll get disgusting."

"We'll deal with it in the morning. Right now, we have better things to do than clean coffeepots."

When he reached her bedroom, he set her gently on her feet beside the bed. Immobilized by a spasm of shyness, she stood where she was while he lowered the blinds and pulled the sheer curtains over them, then locked the door. When he returned to her, she was still standing by the bed.

"Thea? Are you all right?"

She shrugged, her head lowered.

"Hey—" he took her gently into his arms "—don't. Please don't be shy, not with me." He brushed his mouth over her cheek and touched his lips to her throat. "Never with me.'' He found her mouth with his own and swept everything else away.

Thea couldn't think; she could only feel the wanting and the quick rush of need. Her doubts and shyness were swept away when he pulled the silk blouse free of her slacks and ran his hands over her skin, and her hesitation evaporated as she worked at his shirt buttons, fumbling in her haste.

The need grew quickly, beating in their blood, heating their skin, driving them together. They pulled at each other's clothing, throwing it aside so they could meet each other, skin on skin, hands eager, lips feverish, desire driving them faster and higher and farther. Thea felt Luke in a series of small discrete sensations: his leg against hers, hard muscled and sprinkled with hair; his hand on her breast, warm and slightly rough, teasing her nipple to aching stiffness; his lips on her throat, hot and moist against the pulse that hammered there.

When he wrapped her in his arms and lifted her feet clear of the floor, she floated dizzily through space, then came to rest on the bed, sprawled across his chest, her legs tangling with his, her hands twisted in his hair, holding his mouth to hers. She moved above his body, teasing and tormenting, reveling in his excitement, reveling in the knowledge that for him there was no other woman in the world.

She shook her head so that her hair fell forward around her face and brushed over his throat and shoulders. Luke caught a handful and touched it to his lips, then slid his hand around to cup the back of her head and bring her lips to his. Thea clung to him, trying to absorb him, urging him with instinctive movements he was unable to resist.

Luke fought the temptation as long as he could. He wanted to love her slowly, to make it beautiful for her, but she wouldn't let him. She slid over his body, knowing exactly where to touch and kiss to drive him beyond his limits. Words of love were beautiful, but this commitment went deeper. It was her soul pledging itself to him. His control suddenly snapped, and he tightened his arms to roll her beneath his body. She moved beneath him, seeking fulfillment. He looked into her eyes, which were dark with passion.

"I love you, Thea." He brushed his lips over hers. "I love you."

Then his head blotted out the light, his mouth covered hers and, as their bodies became one, the world faded away. There was nothing for her then but the warm darkness, filled with touching and tasting and sweet madness. She clung to him as the tension built inside her and then burst in wave after wave of pleasure. Her last conscious thought was of love.

She must have slept. When she awoke, she was lying in Luke's arms, blankets covering her warmly. Luke knew when she woke, because his arm tightened around her and he settled her more securely against his side.

"How are you?" He rubbed his chin against her hair.

"Mmm." She nestled against him drowsily. "I'm wonderful."

"That's good. When do you want to get married?"

"I dunno." She yawned. "When do you want to?"

He considered it for a moment. "How about tomorrow?"

She chuckled under her breath. "No time to get a license and all that kind of stuff."

"Oh. The bureaucracy gets in our way."

"Mm-hmm."

"Then how about next Saturday?"

"Can't."

"Why not?"

"That's Cruz and Ally's wedding."

"Oh, yeah." He sighed deeply, his chest lifting and falling beneath her cheek. "Well, are we gonna get married or not?"

"We'll work it out," she mumbled sleepily against his chest.

"We will," he vowed softly as she slid into sleep again. "We certainly will."

"You know what?" Stefi paused, a spoonful of cereal in midair, dripping milk.

"What?" Luke took a bite of toast and waited for her insight.

"This is just like a real family, isn't it?"

In the heartbeat of silence that followed, Thea, standing at the sink, glanced over her shoulder and met Luke's eyes.

"Yes, it is," he said, his voice husky.

"Is it gonna be like this when you and Mom get married?"

"I imagine so."

"Good. I like this." She ate her spoonful of cereal and stirred what was left in her bowl. "Mom, can I have more milk on my flakes?"

"Sure, sweetie." Thea turned away to hide her laugh. She'd seen the look on Luke's face. He wasn't used to the way a child's mind shifted gears. From family life to milk for her cornflakes, from the sublime to the ridiculous. No matter, he'd learn soon enough.

"I've got to get going." He slid his arms around Thea from behind as she closed the refrigerator. He was already dressed in the slacks, shirt and casual jacket he'd worn to the party. Thea wore her robe over the nightgown she'd put on that morning.

She turned in his arms and leaned back, letting him support her as she smiled up at him. "The star's got to be on time."

"The star's got to read through this script, and he doesn't want the rest of the cast to think he's a prima donna. I'll see you this evening, okay, Stefi?"

"Okay, Luke. Bye!"

"Walk me to the door?" he murmured in Thea's ear. She nodded and stroked Stefi's hair as she followed Luke out of the kitchen. At the front door, he pulled her into his arms. "What will you do today?"

"What I do every Saturday." She grinned at him. "Clean house, do laundry, shop for groceries, make dinner."

"Don't do that."

"Don't clean? We'll be up to our armpits in dust if I don't—"

"Don't make dinner. I'll be done by six and we can all go out. Does Stefi like Chinese?"

"Oh, yes. Szechwan, especially."

"I know just the place. If I'm going to be late, I'll call you, okay?"

"Luke, don't worry about it. If you're late, you're late. We'll understand."

"I don't want to be inconsiderate."

She laughed aloud. "Believe me, you aren't inconsiderate. We're going to be a family, Luke. Families take care of each other, but you don't need to use kid gloves."

"Except if I want to." He slid his hands from her shoulders to her waist and kissed her lingeringly. He touched her mouth with his fingertip before he stepped out the door. "I love you, you know that?"

"Mm-hmm." She smiled a small, secret smile. "I'm even starting to believe it's true."

Luke paused on the porch, then took her hand and pulled her out with him. "Believe it." This time his kiss wasn't sweet or tender, but hot and hungry. "Believe it." He dropped his arms and strode to his car.

Thea stood on the porch until he'd driven away. The morning paper was still on the front walk, and she smiled as she padded out in her bare feet to get it. It had landed near her neighbor's yard. Mrs. Cudahy had dozens of roses and azaleas. Some of the bushes were enormous, taller than Thea, thick and bushy from the elderly lady's religiously observed program of fertilizing and watering.

Leaves rustled, though there was no breeze, and Thea glanced over to see branches and blossoms moving deep within the rose bed. She picked up the heavy newspaper and suppressed a smile as she walked back to the house.

She'd always suspected that Mrs. Cudahy used that rose bed as a sort of urban duck blind from which to observe the neighborhood comings and goings. If she looked hard enough, Thea was sure she'd catch a glimpse of a flowered housedress in there somewhere, but she didn't try. She'd let Mrs. Cudahy enjoy her little hobby in peace.

She couldn't resist waving at the rose bed, though, just before she stepped back into the house.

Chapter 16

"Thea?"

Thea stopped in the hallway and turned to see Jessica hurrying toward her.

"Thea, I was hoping to catch you before you started work."

"Is there a problem?" Together they walked toward the elevator that would carry Jessica upstairs to her office.

"No, not at all." Jessica smiled at Thea's quick concern. "I stayed late on Friday night and screened the psychiatric-nursing tapes."

Thea glanced sideways, but Jessica's calm half smile gave nothing away.

She tensed, bracing herself for the bad news. "What did you think of them?" Her voice was only slightly unsteady.

Jessica's smile widened a little. "Before I answer, tell me what *you* think."

"Well..." Thea looked at the tile floor as she walked. "I think we did good work. And Luke's performances are excellent. He made the series what it is."

Jessica nodded consideringly. "That's about what I thought you'd say. I knew you'd be too modest to tell the truth."

Thea looked at her warily. "What do you mean?"

"I mean they're near-perfect."

Thea flushed and looked at her hands. "Jessica, I don't know what to say...."

"You don't have to say anything. They're some of the best educational films I've seen, and you produced them in a remarkably short time, and well within budget. Did you know that Luke has declined to accept payment for his work?"

"What?" Thea looked up, startled.

"That's right. He called this morning to tell me that he's returning his paychecks. He said he'll consider them his contribution to nursing education and he'd like them to go to the School of Nursing scholarship fund."

"Oh." Luke had said nothing to her about that.

Jessica smiled indulgently at her confusion. "That's about how I felt when he told me. Thea, your casting was inspired. Luke made a tremendous contribution to these films, and the sales value his name will give the series is a real bonus. I'm delighted that you were perceptive enough to recognize talent like his before you knew of his movie work."

"Th-thank you." They stopped at the elevator. "Jessica, I don't really know what to say."

"Maybe this will help." Jessica took an envelope out of her briefcase and handed it to Thea. The elevator doors slid open, and she stepped inside. "Call me after you've read it."

In her office, Thea sat down and opened the plain envelope with her name typed on the front. Inside she found several folded sheets, her six-month evaluation. She took a deep breath and began reading.

When she'd finished, she laid the pages on the desk and dialed the phone with great care. The conversation with Jessica was short and astonishing.

She had received the maximum score of ten in all the job-performance categories, and Jessica's comments were more than glowing. She was accepting Thea as a permanent employee of the hospital, giving her the highest overall job rating and recommending a merit increase as well as the standard six-month raise. She specifically commended Thea on casting Luke for the tapes and for her ability to take suggestions and work with others.

Thea shook her head. To think she'd been worried that Jessica had seen Luke offering ideas about the scripts. She'd feared that would make her seem incompetent, but instead she'd seemed even more professional.

She'd worried herself to a frazzle over nothing! She sat for a moment, staring into space, then burst out laughing.

Luke walked around her desk and kissed the top of her head. "Can I share the joke, or is it private?" Thea caught his hand before he could move away.

"Do you know who you're looking at?"

He looked her up and down. "I thought I did, but I guess I was wrong. Who *am* I looking at?"

"At the no-longer-a-probationary-employee media coordinator." She tapped the sheets in front of her. "Jessica gave me my evaluation this morning."

"And?" he said when she paused. "What does it say?"

"See for yourself."

She handed him the evaluation, and he quickly scanned the pages. He looked up at her face.

"Thea, this is terrific! Congratulations!" He pulled her out of the chair and into his arms for a big hug. "I knew all along you could do it!"

"Well, I wasn't too sure." She smiled happily up at him. "I still don't believe it."

"Believe it." Luke pulled her closer and brushed a thumb across her lips. "Believe in yourself and your ability." He bent his head, and his mouth replaced his thumb.

"Did you guys see this?" Bobby was too excited to knock tactfully. He was in the office by the time he noticed he was interrupting something, and he was too preoccupied to care. "Oh, hey, sorry about that." He waved a tabloid at Thea. "Did you see this?" He stabbed the page with his fingertip. "Right here, see?"

They looked. A large photograph of Thea and Luke dancing at the studio party filled the top of the page. Beneath it was a splashy banner headline: New Love After Midnight For Luke? There were three columns of accompanying text and several smaller pictures.

"What is this?" Thea nearly tore the paper in half in her eagerness to find the front page. "The *Investigator*?" She turned frantically to the article. "What do they say?"

"That you're my new love, evidently." Luke was reading over her shoulder. "And that we went to that party."

"I didn't see anybody from the *Investigator* there."

"I doubt if they wanted you to. They probably sent someone we don't know."

"My house!" Thea's voice dropped to a shaky whisper. "When did they take a picture of my house?"

"I, uh, I'll just go polish a lens or something." Bobby backed out of the office. Neither of them even saw him go.

"And why did they take a shot of your house?" Luke's voice was low and hard, and he pulled the paper out of Thea's hands. The caption was innocent enough, just a couple of lines about her quiet neighborhood. The story was continued on the next page, though, and he didn't like what he found there.

The photograph was grainy, shot from a distance with a telephoto lens, but there was no mistaking the subject. It was Luke, kissing Thea goodbye on her front porch, eyes closed, mouths touching. The caption referred leeringly to a suburban "love nest."

Luke just shook his head, but beside him Thea gasped an oath under her breath. He looked down at her in surprise; she almost never swore. Her face was white, and her hands were shaking.

She was horrified by the picture, but what she read in the columns of print below it was her worst nightmare come true. There was a second headline, halfway down the page: Mobster's Widow? Or Innocent Victim? Another grainy shot of Thea's face accompanied it.

"What in *hell*?"

Luke took the paper from her nerveless hands, and she moved away, walking to the window. When he'd finished the story, he dropped the paper on her desk.

"Thea? What are they talking about?"

"You read it." Her voice was flat and dead. "You know what it's about."

"Your late husband was in the mob?"

She turned around, her face white and set. "No, he wasn't."

"Then what is that—" he flicked the paper with his fingertips "—all about?"

She swallowed. "If I tell you, it has to remain absolutely confidential. You can't tell *anyone*, not your mother, not your father, not *anyone*, about this."

"All right."

She knew she could trust him with her secret. Thea wet her dry lips with the tip of her tongue. "Marty wasn't in the mob. He was working for the Justice Department when I met him, but I didn't know that. I knew him as a regional salesman for a cigarette company. I never even wondered why a man who didn't smoke would sell cigarettes. He was a good man, and I loved him. It was only after his death that I found the badge, the papers, the gun that he'd kept hidden."

"What was he doing?"

She leaned against the window, her face on the cool glass. "Infiltrating an organized crime operation that was selling cigarettes without paying the excise tax. I won't go into how it worked, that's too long a story. Suffice it to say that being a cigarette salesman was a perfect cover. They told me he was close to breaking the case when he died."

"Was he—"

"Killed by the mob?" She glanced over her shoulder. "The Justice people didn't think so. It appeared to be a case of drunk driving, pure and simple. That's why all those stories the *Investigator* quotes were printed in the local papers."

"But you were being called a mob widow. Why didn't they tell the truth?"

"It was to protect me and Stefi."

"*Protect* you? You must have gone through hell."

"It was better than being killed."

"*What?*" He stared at her, shocked.

Thea's smile was small and bitter. "If the mob *had* had Marty killed, Stefi and I would have had to change our names and move away, because I would be a target, as well. When they were sure the accident wasn't a hit, they presented me with two options: print the truth, change my name and go into hiding, or stay where I was, ride out the publicity and let the mob think I knew nothing. I had a home and friends, so I chose to stay."

"And you let them go on printing stories about your husband the mobster?"

She nodded. "Eventually other stories replaced him on the front page, things died down and I was allowed to get on with my life in peace. Until now." She looked across the room and met his eyes. "Until you."

"Has enough time passed that you can go to the press and tell them the truth?"

"Organized crime has a long memory, Luke. I can never tell the true story. All I want is to put a stop to it, right now."

"How can you do that?"

She turned away, looking blindly out the window. She felt cold, numb, empty. "By taking myself out of the limelight, Luke. By not seeing you anymore."

"Thea, no!" He caught her shoulder and spun her around, holding her upper arms. "You can't mean that!"

"What else can I do?" Her voice was flat, her face lifeless. Her unnatural calm frightened Luke more than tears and hysterics could have. "If I hadn't been with you, they would never have unearthed that stuff. If we break it off right now, they won't have a reason to print any more of it. I'm sorry, Luke, but—"

"No!" His hands tightened unconsciously and his grip became painful. Thea almost welcomed the pain; it penetrated the icy numbness inside her. "No, I won't accept that!"

"It's not your choice, Luke." Tears began to sting her eyes. "It's what I have to do."

"There's another way, Thea. There has to be!"

"Like what?" she demanded.

"You can wait it out. It will blow over soon, and they'll find somebody else to write about."

"No, Luke." Her eyes were closed, and she shook her head blindly. "You don't know what it was like. I can't go through that again!"

"You wouldn't be alone this time."

Her eyes opened, and he nodded. "I'll be here with you. You don't have to face it alone. It blew over before, and it will blow over again."

She looked into his eyes for a long moment. "Think about what you're saying, Luke. The taint of a mob connection could hurt you, too."

"There isn't any mob connection!"

"But no one knows that!" she shouted. Then she paused, trying to collect herself. "You can never tell anyone that it isn't true. Nobody can ever know it isn't true."

"Don't try to protect me, sweetheart. I can take care of myself, and I can help you get through this. We can do it together."

Thea looked up at him, aching to believe that was true. "I wish I could believe you." Her gaze slid away.

"You *can*. Even if no one else knows the truth, you and I do. We can get through this together." He eased her into his arms. "I love you, Thea. I want to help you through this and everything else."

"Oh, Luke, I love you, too!" She slid her arms around his neck and held on. "I just know how ugly this can get, and—"

He silenced her with a kiss. Thea melted against his body, taking the comfort and strength he offered her.

"Hey!" Bobby knocked thunderously on the door. "You guys gonna come out of there and do some work, or should I just go home now?"

Safe in the circle of Luke's arms, Thea looked at the door. A smile tugged at her lips. "He's right. It's time to get to work."

"Yeah." Luke laid his cheek against her hair for a moment. "We'll talk about this later."

She was afraid to let herself believe it. Thea drove away from the hospital, wrestling with her emotions. She wanted to think that love could conquer all, but she was afraid to think it might be possible. If only she and Luke could have talked again. He'd had to leave as soon as they'd finished recording dialogue, though; he'd been called to the studio for a meeting.

The last thing he'd said before he left had been "Trust me." Well, she was trying to trust him, though the memory of the weeks after Marty's death made it difficult. She'd been so utterly alone then, but she had Luke now, and perhaps that would make the difference. She wanted desperately to believe it would.

Thea didn't leave the room until she was certain Stefi was sleeping. The little girl's cheeks were still streaked with tears, and her nose was red from crying, but she was relaxed at last. Thea couldn't say the same; a cold rage filled her. If Norm Fletcher knocked on her door that night, she would kill him with her bare hands.

Moving quietly, she covered Stefi with her comforter, then padded out of the room, leaving the door ajar in case Stefi had nightmares. Luke would be there soon, and she needed a few minutes to prepare herself.

He arrived a little while later. "How is she?" He kept his voice low to avoid waking Stefi. He reached out to hug Thea as he came in the door, but she stepped away.

"As well as could be expected."

"Well, what happened? You didn't tell me much on the phone."

"Some of the kids at school had seen that paper." Thea's voice was flat and cold.

Luke glanced toward the hallway and Stefi's room. "Oh, God, Thea, I wish I could have spared her that."

"So do I. I got the story in bits and pieces from Stefi and from the supervisor at day care. From what I gather, they told her that her father was a gangster, that he shot people with a machine gun and he deserved to die."

Luke swore under his breath, and Thea gave him a cynical half smile. Her voice was bitter.

"That wasn't all of it, either. Norm Fletcher was waiting for her after school. He tried to question her." Emotion began to creep into her voice. "He actually tried to get an eight-year-old to talk to him, Luke! He took pictures of her!" She stepped closer to him, her fists clenched at her sides. "I won't have her picture published in that stinking piece of garbage with some caption about her being a gangster's daughter! I won't have it!"

"They won't publish it."

"Who's going to stop them?"

"I am." He was striding to the telephone in the kitchen as he spoke. Thea heard him punch out the number quickly. She heard the low rumble of his voice, and then the sound as the receiver was replaced. She didn't look up as he walked back into the room.

"They won't publish any pictures of Stefi."

Thea gazed fixedly at her hands. "I don't want them to print anything about her, not her name, or her school, or anything."

"They won't."

"How did you do it?"

"I promised them that if they published a picture of a minor without consent, I would put them out of business."

"Could you?"

"One way or another, yes." He sat beside her on the couch, and Thea edged slightly away. Luke looked at her stiff posture and set face, then sighed and sat back. "They won't harass her at school or anywhere else."

Thea looked up at last. "No, Luke, they won't." She stood, her back to him, her hands clasped tightly in front of her. "They won't have any reason to, because she won't be interesting to them anymore."

"Thea—" He was on his feet beside her and would have touched her if she hadn't stepped quickly away again, out of his reach. She hunched her shoulders as if she felt a cold wind on her back.

"She won't be interesting to them because she won't have any connection with you." She turned and faced him. "*I* won't have any connection with you, Luke. I'm not going to marry you."

"Thea, you can't mean that." He fought the sudden cold terror that settled in the pit of his stomach.

"I mean exactly that. I'm not going to marry you."

"Don't be stupid, Thea. You can't make a decision like this on the spur of the moment."

"I can make any decision I want, Luke. On the spur of any moment I want."

He caught her arms and pulled her close, in spite of the fact that she stiffened and tried to pull away. Fear made him rougher than he'd intended. "You're going to marry me, Thea."

"No." She shook her head, trying to pull away. "Not anymore."

"You *are*! We talked about this, about making it work. We can do it."

"I can't." She looked up into his eyes. "I tried to make myself believe that, but I can't. I can't have my daughter put through this anymore. I've been through this kind of hell once, Luke, and I just can't do it again."

"Thea, I'm more sorry about this than you know, but the kids will forget all about it by tomorrow."

"Maybe. And maybe not. But even if they do, as long as I'm involved with you there will be other articles and other days."

"And you're willing to call off our marriage because of this?"

"*This* is something I can't live with, and I won't force my daughter to live with scandal." She reached up to touch his face lightly. Her eyes were too bright, and her voice was shaky. "I want to marry you, Luke, but the price is too high."

He studied her face for a moment, his eyes bleak. "And that's your final word?"

"What else is there to say?" she whispered.

"Maybe nothing." His eyes were dark and stormy with emotion. "Maybe this."

He dragged her against him and kissed her, his lips hard, bruising, as he plundered her mouth. Thea's response was unwilling but undeniable. She clutched his arms and kissed him back, taking just as he took, with the same angry, desperate need.

When he released her she was shaking, and she staggered a little without the support of his arms. He dragged his hand over his face, then gave her a grim smile.

"I thought I knew you, Thea, but I was wrong. I never would have pegged you for a coward."

Chapter 17

Thea studied her image in the mirror and scowled. She looked exactly right for an afternoon wedding. Her dress was of rose-colored silk, with a slim tulip skirt and a pretty peplum jacket covering her bare shoulders and emphasizing her tiny waist. Since this would be a Catholic service, she wore a hat, a sliver of rose satin with a froth of veil that just touched her eyebrows.

Yes, she looked just right for Allison Schuyler's marriage to Cruz Gallego, but she couldn't manage a smile. Luke had walked out of her house five days before. In those five days she hadn't seen him, hadn't even talked to him on the telephone. It appeared, despite his protests and arguments, that he'd accepted her decision not to marry him.

Thea was unhappy without him, but Stefi was inconsolable and stubbornly unwilling to listen to Thea's awkward explanations. As a treat, she was at Marybeth's today and would spend the night. Thea hoped Stefi was having a good time, because *she* didn't expect to.

She trudged to the front door, opened it and stopped short. He was waiting for her, leaning against his car, which was parked at the curb. She pulled the door closed behind her and stood on the porch while he walked across the lawn.

"What are you doing here?"

"I'm taking you to the wedding."

"No."

"Yes."

"I don't want to be photographed with you, Luke."

"Ah, yes, the wicked press might be there." He took her arm and virtually hoisted her off the porch. "I talked to Ally I'm not on the guest list, the press couldn't care less about her wedding, and the wedding photographers won't take any pictures of me." His voice was as calm as if they'd discussed this just the day before.

Thea met his gaze for a moment as she weighed the pros and cons of a struggle on the front lawn. Then she tucked her keys into her purse and walked with calm dignity across the grass.

Mrs. Cudahy's rosebushes rustled as she stopped beside Luke's car. Thea didn't know whether it was Mrs. Cudahy or Norm Fletcher lurking beneath the flowers, but she gave the unseen watcher a brilliant smile as Luke opened the door, and then she slid gracefully into the car.

They drove in silence, Luke glancing over occasionally to watch Thea sitting stiffly in the passenger seat and staring out at the road ahead. He parted his lips more than once, but didn't speak. There was nothing he could say.

Luke parked behind the church, killed the engine and caught Thea's hand before she could leave the car. "No matter what's gone on between us, Thea, this is Ally's day. We owe it to her to be happy for her."

Thea met his eyes for a moment, then nodded. He was right. The problems between her and Luke shouldn't be allowed to tarnish Ally's wedding day.

The vast, vaulted church was decorated with roses and lilies and lighted by seemingly hundreds of candles. Bach and Handel on the organ mingled with the quiet hum of conversation and the rustle of silk. The air smelled of candle wax, perfume and flowers.

Seated near the front on the bride's side of the church, Thea felt the tension seeping out of her. In this place, on this occasion, she couldn't dwell on her own unhappiness.

When the church was nearly filled, there was a quiet murmur behind them. One of Cruz's brothers was escorting his mother down the aisle. She was a beautiful woman, small and slender, wearing an elegant mint-green dress with a matching bit of fluff as a hat.

Behind her walked a tall, angular man of about fifty, with a sharp-featured, aristocratic face and thinning sandy hair. He wore formal clothes and took a seat in the second pew on the bride's side.

Beside her, Luke moved slightly, and Thea glanced up. "Do you know the man who just came in?" he murmured.

Thea looked at the tall, lean man again. There was something vaguely familiar about his face, but she knew she'd never met him. She shook her head. "He's on the bride's side, so he must be a relative of Ally's."

There was a breathless pause while the organ played softly. Anticipation shivered in the air. The music slowed, paused and then moved into a Bach prelude.

The ceremony flowed around Thea, beautiful, dreamlike. Cruz and his brothers assembled at the altar, his sisters preceded Stacy Alexander, the maid of honor, up the aisle, and then the music swelled into the triumphant wedding processional from *Lohengrin* as Allison walked toward her groom.

She was radiant in billows of white satin, and Cruz watched her with his heart in his eyes. Thea's throat tightened, aching for things that might have been, and she saw the rest of the ceremony through misty eyes, not hearing the traditional words and music and prayers but feeling them. The rings gleamed in the candlelight as they were exchanged, and then Cruz carefully lifted Ally's veil and took her into his arms for the kiss that would seal their marriage.

Thea blinked, her eyes stinging. She would not cry on this happy occasion. When Ally walked back down the aisle on her husband's arm, Thea was smiling. Ally saw Thea standing with Luke and gave a little smile of approval before she swept past them. Stacy, walking with Cruz's brother Carlos, flashed Thea and Luke a grin, and then everything was a blur of color and noise and smiling faces.

Ally had announced that she intended to *celebrate* her wedding. She meant to see that everyone else did, too, so the reception was at a hotel and consisted of dinner, followed by dancing.

The wedding supper was an uncomfortable meal for Thea and Luke. They had little to say, and it was a relief when the cake-cutting was announced. No one expected them to make conversation while that was going on.

Ally opened the dancing with her grandfather. When they had waltzed once around the floor, Cruz led his mother out. One more circuit, and then the bride and groom paused to change partners. Applause erupted when they kissed in the center of the floor.

Luke watched them and made a silent vow. One day he would be out there, dancing the first waltz with Thea.

He had been scrupulously careful not to touch her, but now he took her hand, his grip tightening when she tried to pull away.

"Dance with me."

It wasn't a request. He pulled her into the crowd of guests that had begun filling the dance floor. Thea moved stiffly, unwilling to dance, but equally unwilling to make a scene. Luke ignored her resistance and hauled her into his arms, pressing her close against his body as he began to move.

Thea pushed at his shoulder. "I don't want to dance."

"I don't care." His arm tightened into a steel band around her waist, molding her body to his from breast to thigh. "It's a wedding. We're dancing." He swung her around, throwing her slightly off balance so that she had to cling to him for support, then he rested his face on her hair and gave himself up to the music.

It was almost too sweet to bear. Thea closed her eyes as she relaxed in Luke's embrace. She'd spent long, agonizing nights aching for his arms around her; now that they were, it was all she could do to keep from crying. Luke drew her closer as they danced to the slow, seductive music, their bodies pressed together, her cheek against his shoulder, his face on her hair.

If only... Angrily she blinked the tears away. "If only" was for children. When the music faded, she pulled herself out of his arms, walking quickly off the dance floor.

"That's him!" She heard a teenager squeal from across the dance floor. "It's really him!"

Thea quickened her pace. He couldn't come after her now. He'd be busy with his fans.

"Oh, Mr. Adams," the girl gasped, "could I have your autograph, please? I saw you dancing and I thought, is that him? And then you turned around and I could see your face and I knew it really was you and—"

She almost felt sorry for Luke, surrounded by palpitating teenagers. Almost. As it was, his misfortune provided her with the opportunity to escape.

She dropped her purse on the first table she reached and sank into a chair. Ally was drifting around the floor in a cloud of white satin and lace, dancing with the tall man who had sat at the front of the church. She smiled and said something to him when the dance ended, then walked off the floor toward Thea.

"Hello, there." Her smile could have lighted the room. "Can I sit with you for a few minutes?"

Thea pulled out a chair. "It's an honor to sit with the bride."

"At last, a chair!" Ally gathered her voluminous skirts and carefully seated herself, then made a few small movements with her legs. "Oh, that's better!" She grinned at Thea. "Nobody can see, but underneath this skirt I've got my shoes off."

Thea grinned back. "I'll never tell."

"I knew I could count on you." Ally signaled a passing waiter and took two glasses of champagne from the tray he carried. She handed one to Thea. "Cheers."

Thea sipped, then set her glass on the table. "Ally, who were you dancing with just now?"

Ally glanced at the dance floor, her smile thoughtful. "My father."

"Your father?" Thea looked and saw him in the midst of the dancers, a woman in his arms. She looked at Ally. "I thought your grandfather raised you?"

"He did. You thought my father was dead, didn't you?"

"It sounds awful, but—"

"I understand. In a way he was dead for me." Ally sighed. "It's a long story, but the easiest thing to say is that we were estranged. I wouldn't even have sent him a wedding invitation, but my grandfather insisted." She smiled at Thea. "And he came."

"It looks as though things are working out."

"Well, I don't know if we'll all live happily ever after, but it's a start."

"I'm glad," Thea told her quietly. She could see how much all this meant to Ally. "We saw him in the church. I didn't know who he was, but I can see that you resemble him."

"I've been told I look like my grandmother, but there's probably a likeness to him, too." Thea looked for Mr. Schuyler again and recognized the woman he held in his arms. She stared.

"Ally?"

"Hmm?"

"Is your father dancing with Marsha Mott?"

Ally gave her a satisfied smile. "He sure is."

"But isn't she the one—"

"Who gave me such a terrible time on my clinic rotation? Yes, that's her."

"Why is she at your wedding?"

"That's another long story. She disliked me because of something that happened a long time ago. She knew my father."

Dancing and smiling, Marsha Mott looked nothing like the hard, angry woman Thea remembered from the clinic. "Was she in love with him?"

Ally smiled. "It's obvious, isn't it?"

"Did you set this up, Ally?"

"Yes." She wasn't the least bit abashed. "I'm so happy I want everybody else to be happy, too." She turned her satisfied smile on Thea, who hastily shook her head.

"No you don't, Ally! There are some things you can't fix."

Ally shook her head and looked for Luke. He was still surrounded by star-struck guests.

"It's too bad," she said softly, "that because he was born with a talent, he's had to become public property. He could no more abandon his talent and his art than he could cut off his arm, but it's taken away his right to his own life."

Thea glanced at him. He was being as courteous as always, laughing and chatting with his fans. "He's dealing with it."

"He's dealing with it just fine," Ally said gently. "But you're not, are you?"

Cruz fox-trotted past them, a lavender-haired matron in his arms. He signaled with his eyes, and Ally sat up again.

"I think my hubby wants me to put my shoes back on and rescue him." She grinned wickedly at Thea. "Are wives allowed to cut in on their husbands?"

"Would you care if they weren't?"

"Not a bit. See you later."

As Ally rustled away, Thea's smile faded into thoughtfulness. She turned so that Luke was in her range of vision. As she watched, he accepted a slip of paper from a gangly youngster with braces sparkling on her teeth. He spoke to her, smiling, then scribbled rapidly.

He seemed to have an endless supply of patience, even with a hard-faced woman who was waving a napkin in his face while he tried to finish talking to the girl. He smiled, took the napkin with good grace and signed that in turn.

"Am I glad to see you!" Bobby sank into the chair Ally had vacated and glanced around furtively. He had dressed up for the wedding, wearing wool trousers, a leather sport coat and, to her wonderment, a tie.

Thea followed the direction of his eyes but saw nothing unusual. "You act like a crook on the lam."

"I'm hiding out." He picked up her glass and drained what was left of the flat champagne. "You remember Corinne?"

"The little blond nursing student?"

"Tall redhead. The blonde is Billie."

"Oh, yes, of course." Her voice was dry.

Bobby gave her a hunted look. "Not funny, Thea. I never should've brought Corinne to a wedding! She's been talking white lace and promises all night. I had to get Cruz to dance with her just to get away for a minute."

"It's not time to push the panic button yet, Bobby. Everybody gets that way at weddings."

He gave the dancers a harassed glance. "She thinks we'd have cute kids!"

Thea stifled a spurt of laughter and looked him over. "Well, you would. They might even have red hair." She patted his shoulder. "Don't worry. If she asks you to marry her, I'll tell her you're too young to settle down."

"There's a mean streak in you, Thea," he said reproachfully. "Do me a favor, though. If Corinne comes over here, tell her you need to talk to me about work, okay?"

"Anything for a friend in need." She grinned.

Bobby muttered something and gazed glumly at the dancers. "Who's that?" He pointed.

"Who's who?"

"Who's Van dancing with?"

After a moment Thea spotted her, looking regal in deep green silk and dancing with a tall, rugged-looking man with unruly dark hair. When they turned, she saw his face.

"He's the detective, the one who worked on those drug thefts in the clinic last summer. Cal. No, Clay. Clay Williams. I didn't know Van knew him."

"She doesn't, does she?"

Van was dancing with none of the grace Thea knew she possessed. Her body was stiff, and her hand, rather than resting on her partner's shoulder, was braced against it. Suddenly she stopped short in the middle of the dance floor. Thea and Bobby couldn't hear her words, but her vehemence was clear. She shoved herself out of Clay Williams' arms and stalked off the floor.

Bobby whistled softly. "Wonder what that was all about?"

"Want to go ask her?"

He shook his head. "*I* don't have a death wish. Speaking of which—" he got to his feet "—here comes Corinne. I'm gonna hide out in the men's room for a while."

"Good luck!" Thea smiled as she watched him flee with Corinne in hot pursuit.

"Thea?" Luke reached around her and snapped his fingers under her nose.

She jumped. "Don't sneak up on me like that!"

"Come on." Luke pulled her to her feet. "Ally's about to throw her bouquet, and you're going to miss it."

"No, Luke!" She tried to pull away. "I don't want—"

"Ladies and gentlemen!" The bandleader held a glass to the microphone, tapping it with a spoon. "Ladies and gentlemen, the groom is about to throw the garter!"

Luke forged a path through the crowd. "Hurry up, or you're going to miss the fun."

"I don't want to do this," Thea protested as he hauled her across the dance floor to join the group by the bandstand.

"Listen, I escaped that mob just for this. You're gonna do it." He eased through the crowd and held Thea in front of him, his hands on her shoulders, her body touching his lightly.

They arrived as Cruz was removing Ally's blue garter to a raucous accompaniment of cheers, laughter and wolf whistles. There was a burst of applause as he slid it over her calf and ankle and held it aloft. The bandleader called for the unattached men to come forward.

"Go on." Thea gave Luke a shove. He hesitated, and she shoved harder. "This was your idea. Get up there!"

He joined the men, who ranged in age from Ally's grandfather to a little boy of five in a natty blue suit with short pants. Cruz turned his back to the crowd and tossed the garter over his shoulder. His brother Alfonso, seventeen, was shoved forward by another brother and caught it, then blushed scarlet at the teasing he got from the others.

Stacy brought Ally's bouquet to the bandstand, and a drumroll commanded their attention. "The bride," the bandleader announced dramatically, "will now throw her bouquet!"

Luke plucked her purse from her hands and pushed Thea forward. "Get up there."

"Luke, this is silly."

"It's a wedding. Silliness is expected." Ignoring her protests, Luke pushed her into the front row just as Ally turned her back to the crowd. She counted to three and tossed the bouquet in a high arc over her head.

Ribbons streamed and a few petals scattered as it floated directly into Thea's unwilling hands. Trapped, she smiled stiffly, held it up to cheers and applause and waited for the attention to shift to someone else.

As Ally left the bandstand with Cruz, she caught Thea's arm and leaned close. "I threw it to you," she whispered. "And you'll be the next bride."

Before Thea could protest, Ally was gone, swept toward the door by her new husband. As she vanished, she looked back at Thea and winked.

The crowd closed around Thea, carrying her to the doorway, where there was a blizzard of rice and shouted congratulations, and then Ally and Cruz drove away in a car decorated with flowers and paper streamers.

The guests were drifting back in for more dancing, but Thea hesitated by the door.

"Don't you want to dance anymore?" Luke asked her.

Her smile was tired and strained. "No. I came for Ally, not for a dance. I'd like to go home."

"Then we'll go."

She relaxed in the seat as Luke drove away, fingering the bouquet of white roses and orchids, her eyes closed, her mind a tired blank. They had driven for several minutes before she looked around her. "This isn't the way to my house, Luke."

Chapter 18

She sat up straight and looked around. They were miles from her home, moving fast in the wrong direction. "Luke, this—"

"I know it's not the way to your house." He signaled, then turned onto a freeway entrance ramp. "We're going to talk."

"I don't want to—"

He turned and fixed her with a cold stare. "We're damned well going to talk!" His low tone was more intimidating than a shout. Thea opened her mouth to protest, thought better of it and subsided into her seat.

He drove for miles in a cold, angry silence, heading out of the city and north up the coast. He finally stopped beside a narrow stretch of beach that lay below rocky bluffs rising steeply from the shoreline. There was little traffic on this stretch of the highway, where it wound along the coast, squeezed between the beach and the hills. The moon was full and high, laying a silvery trail across the water and reflecting off the foamy surf.

Luke swung the car onto the sandy verge and braked roughly. He got out, slammed his door with enough force to rock the car and marched around to yank Thea's open.

"Come on. We're gonna walk."

Feeling stubborn, and just a little scared, she sat where she was. "I can't walk on a beach in these shoes."

"So take 'em off."

He caught her hand and pulled her out of the seat. When she didn't move quickly enough, he bent to lift her feet one at a time, pulling off her high-heeled pumps and tossing them back into the car. "Come on."

He strode out across the beach so fast that Thea stumbled in the deep sand, trotting to keep up. He walked rapidly for perhaps a hundred yards, then slowed his pace and let go of her hand. They walked a few more yards, their feet shifting and sliding in the sand.

Luke stopped and looked out at the restless ocean. "Why won't you marry me?"

"I told you." Thea dug her toes into the sand.

"Yeah, but that was a crock! You're a coward, Thea."

She looked quickly at his averted face, then dropped her head. "Maybe."

"Maybe!" He laughed harshly. "Is that all you have to say about it?"

"If I'm being a coward, I have my reasons."

"I know your reasons, how you want to lead a quiet life and you don't want to deal with the press and the old scandal, and how you want what's best for Stefi."

"That's right." She ignored his sarcasm, her voice quiet and level.

"Do you really think it's best to let her see her mother run from her problems?"

"Luke, I didn't have a choice—"

"You *always* have a choice!" he shouted, grabbing her shoulders and jerking her around to face him. "You always have a choice, Thea! You can choose to stand and face this, or you can run—from the reporters and from the past and from me."

"I have to protect Stefi—"

"Bull!" His hands tightened on her shoulders, and he shook her slightly. "The damage is already done, Thea! You're not protecting her anymore, you're protecting yourself from a little embarrassment!"

"Am I?" She struck his hands off her shoulders. "This is hardly a *little embarrassment*!"

"The things they said have all been said before. Nobody has accused you of any wrongdoing. It was clear that you knew nothing about what was going on. Marty is dead, Thea. No one can hurt him now. He made his choices, and he lived with them. Maybe he should have told you the truth then, but you know it now. You know he wasn't a criminal, even if nobody else does."

"That's not a whole lot of satisfaction when the kids at school are telling Stefi her daddy was a mobster!"

"No, it's not." Luke's voice was quiet, in contrast to hers. "But Stefi is old enough to know the truth about her father. And she's old enough to understand the need to keep a secret."

Thea turned away and began to walk slowly again. "She's just a little girl. She shouldn't have to deal with this."

"She's not that little." Luke measured his steps to hers. "She can be trusted with this. She'd rather know her father was working to undermine the mob than think he was a part of it."

"I'm sure she would. But think of the temptation to tell everybody."

"She's a strong kid. She can handle it."

Thea stopped. She lifted her head and stared out at the ocean, her hair streaming in the wind. "Can *I*?" she wondered, her voice barely audible. "Can I handle it?"

Luke reached out to catch her hand. "You don't have to handle it alone, Thea. I'll be with you, and we'll face the problems together."

She looked up. His face was all planes and angles in the moonlight. "But why would you want to marry someone who will always be known as a mobster's widow?"

Her voice and expression revealed real puzzlement. Luke was silent for a moment; then he chuckled under his breath and drew her to him, sliding his arms around her waist.

"Don't you know that I don't care? I don't care what they call you, as long as they call you Luke Adams' wife." He brushed her windblown hair away from her face. "I know who you are. I know the truth, Thea, and nothing the papers print can change that."

"They'll say things about you. They'll imply that you're a criminal."

"I don't even have any unpaid parking tickets! They aren't going to call me a criminal."

"I don't know." The wind gusted, and Thea shivered. "I just don't know."

He turned to lead her up the beach. "Come over here and sit down. You're going to freeze."

In the shelter of a group of boulders, he pulled her down to sit beside him on the sand, which was still warm from the sun. Thea crossed her ankles and sat with her knees pulled up and her arms around them, while Luke stretched his legs out and leaned back, bracing his hands behind him in the sand. She could feel his warm bulk beside her, though several inches separated them. They sat in silence for a few minutes, watching the ocean and the moon.

"What is it that you don't know?"

Thea thought for a moment before she answered. "I don't know if I can do it, even after they get tired of writing about the mob connection. I don't know if I can live with a different life-style, the press attention..." She paused. "I don't know if I can be a movie star's wife."

There was an instant of stunned silence; then Luke burst into a roar of laughter. Thea stiffened, staring at him.

"The last time I checked," he gasped through the laughter, "Charlton Heston and Paul Newman were both happily married. I'm not asking you to marry a movie star, Thea, I'm asking you to marry *me*! Just me, Luke, the guy you hired."

"Yes, but—"

He interrupted her. "No buts. I love you. That's a fact. I'm in movies. That's also a fact. I'm not naive enough to think it won't make a difference to my life, and I'm not stupid or arrogant enough to think it will be easy to handle. I know damned well it's going to be hard, but I'm prepared to deal with it." He looked at her, his eyes grave.

"I'm not some teenage hunk-of-the-week, thrown into the public eye before I even know who I am. I've worked hard to get to this point, playing dancing onions and husbands with dirty collars. I've seen the downside of acting, and I can keep the glittery side in perspective."

"Oh, Luke, who can know how they'll deal with that?" She sighed. "I'm sure all actors think they can handle fame until they find out that it's harder than they expected. You don't need my notoriety added to that."

"That's a flash in the pan, Thea. It's old news already." He chuckled softly. "And if you think fame and money will twist me in some way, remember that fame is fleeting and the money may never come. I'll still be me."

"You seemed like a kid at first," she muttered, tracing patterns in the sand with a fingertip. "We're both twenty-nine, but you seemed so young, happy-go-lucky, with nothing on your mind but fun. You didn't really seem like a grown-up."

"It was obvious that you didn't approve of me, but I didn't realize how little you knew me." There was an edge to his words.

Thea looked down, uncertain. "I saw another side of you the day Stefi was hurt. I was a wreck. I don't know what I would have done if you hadn't taken charge of things. I'll always be grateful you were there."

"But?" He touched her cheek, urging her to look at him. "Come on, I can tell there's a but in there somewhere."

"But you're a movie star now!" she said helplessly. "You're not just another actor. And I'm a single mother who's just started the best job she's ever had. My big achievement is that I'm finally going to have a few dollars left over after the groceries and the mortgage. It's like we're on opposite sides of an ocean."

"We don't have to be." He turned toward her, his legs brushing hers as he touched her shoulder. Thea felt each individual touch and tried to ignore her response. "We don't have to let that happen."

"Don't be naive!" She laughed cynically. "You know how I live. I wouldn't know how to deal with all the attention. And I don't want Stefi involved in that movie-star life-style."

"*What* movie-star life-style?" He rolled onto his knees and pulled her up to face him. "I like pizza with extra cheese and picnics in the park and dumb jokes. I didn't alter my way of living just for you!"

He relaxed a little, sliding his hands up and down her arms in a gentle caress. As her skin warmed, something deep inside her warmed as well. "I am who I am. Where I work, or what I earn, isn't going to change that." His hands slid around her waist, and he pulled her against his body. "Only one thing's going to change—your name. And it will. You're going to marry me."

Thea's eyes snapped open wide. "I'm going—"

Her quick protest was smothered beneath his mouth. His kiss was hot and insistent, demanding a response. They knelt in the sand, mouths locked together, bodies straining to be closer. Thea clutched Luke's shoulders and slid her hands around his neck, tangling her fingers in his hair, clinging to him with all her strength.

Her hesitancies, all her doubts and fears, meant nothing. She'd tried, but she couldn't pretend her love didn't exist, couldn't pretend it would ever die. All her reasons were good ones, but they didn't matter as long as there was love like this.

He took his time with the kiss, savoring her lips, slaking the ache inside him. There was hunger and passion, but there was also tenderness and love. Slowly, his breathing ragged, he lifted his mouth and looked into her eyes.

"That gulf between us isn't so wide," he whispered. "Hasn't it occurred to you that we can compromise? We can take our two lives and make them into one, just like Cruz and Ally are doing, just like every husband and wife have to do."

Thea gazed into his eyes, aching to believe him. "How?" she breathed.

"With love." Luke smiled, his fingertips moving over her throat in a soft caress. "That's all it takes. Just love and a little common sense. I love you, and I love Stefi. I'll protect her just like I will you, and I won't ask you to live a life that makes you uncomfortable."

"No fur rugs and marble bathtubs?"

"No fur rugs and marble bathtubs. No wild parties, no butlers and maids. If you want, we can live in your house so Stefi doesn't have to change schools. I don't care where we live, I just want to live with you."

He stroked her cheek, then drew his thumb across her lips. They parted slightly at his touch in an instinctive invitation. He resisted it with an effort. "Thea?"

"Hmm?"

"Do you love me?"

This time she didn't hesitate. "Yes." Her voice was a whisper, but it strengthened. "Yes, I love you."

Laughing softly in triumph, he pulled her into his arms and found her mouth again. Thea clung to him, and he lowered her to the sand. They kissed in a flare of passion, demand meeting demand.

Thea's hands moved restlessly, eagerly, touching Luke's hair, his face, his shoulders, seeking to claim all of him. Rolling her closer, so their legs tangled together, he tugged her silk jacket open and stroked her shoulders and then the soft curves of her breasts above her bodice. His fingers were warm and slightly rough on her skin, and Thea arched her body into his, seeking more, seeking to meld them into one.

It was Luke who slowed the pace. His breathing heavy and rough, he dragged his mouth from Thea's, pressing hot kisses along her jawline and onto her throat before he pulled her face into the curve of his shoulder and laid his cheek on her tumbled hair.

"Luke?"

Thea reached up to pull him back to her, but he caught her hand and kissed the palm, then pressed it to his chest. She could feel the heavy thud of his heartbeat as he held her. Her blood cooled, her own racing heartbeat slowed, and she nestled against his chest, rubbing her cheek against him like a contented kitten.

"Mmm." The sound rumbled in his chest like a big cat's purr. He rested his chin on her hair, then kissed the top of her head. "Did I hear you right?" he asked softly.

"When?"

"When you said you loved me."

She levered herself back so she could look into his face. "I've been trying to talk myself out of it, you know. It sounds crazy, but I love you, Luke Adams, even though you're a movie star."

He laughed. "Most people wouldn't consider that a drawback."

"You know what I mean." She pressed her lips to his throat and felt his pulse jerk. "Can we really live like normal people?"

"We can," he replied gravely. "With love and trust and a lot of determination, we can be just as happy filthy rich as we could be if we were poor."

It took a moment for that to penetrate.

"You stinker!" She burst out laughing and mimed a cuff at his ear. "You gave me that whole speech just for the sake of a punch line!"

"No." He pulled her into his embrace again. "*This* is the punch line." He kissed her, hot and hard, parting her lips and plundering her mouth, branding her with his taste and his scent. When he lifted his head, Thea was dazed and shaken.

"And this is another punch line." His voice was rough with desire. "Will you marry me, Thea Stevens?" He gazed into her eyes and touched her face lightly. "Will you marry me and keep me from getting a swelled head and a star complex? Will you keep me grounded and centered in the real world? Will you be my wife and my partner and my lover, my friend and my family?"

"Oh, yes." Thea traced her fingertip along the angles of his face, loving him. She spoke slowly and deliberately. "Yes, I'll marry you. And I'll keep you from getting a swelled head, if you'll help keep me from being insecure and defensive. And if you'll love Stefi and love me. And be my husband and my partner and my lover, my friend and my family."

"I will." The words were a vow. He kissed her gently to seal the promise. "Forever. And you know what?"

"What?"

"I think we'll make a pretty terrific team."

Thea smiled. "I think you're right. And you know what?"

"What?"

"I think we ought to get off this beach and go somewhere more comfortable."

"What time is it?"

Thea moved her wrist from behind his head and looked at her watch. "A few minutes after midnight."

"You could be right." He ruffled her hair, and sand sifted out of it. "I'm afraid we're going to take quite a bit of the beach home with us, though. Would you like to go somewhere comfortable and get yourself desanded?"

"Mmm." Thea shifted her shoulders and felt grittiness inside her dress. "That sounds nice." She looked at him through the thick screen of her lashes. "Where do you have in mind?"

"A little place I know of. In Santa Monica."

"Ahhh. Would that by any chance be—your place?"

"Could be."

"Do you mind if I get sand all over your bathroom?"

Luke grinned. "Not as long as you don't mind if I get my sand mixed up with yours." He rose, pulling her up with him. "Let's go mess up my bathroom, Mrs. Adams."

"Mrs. Adams." With his arm around her shoulders, they strolled back up the beach. "I like the sound of that." Thea wrapped her arms around his waist and let him pull her along.

He stopped suddenly, and Thea swung around him, coming to rest against his chest. "Do you have to get home to Stefi?" he asked.

She shook her head. "She's at a slumber party. I'm picking her up at ten tomorrow morning."

"Good." Luke smiled. "We'll pick her up together and give her the news. Do you think she'll be happy?"

Thea laughed softly. "She'll be ecstatic! She's been glowering at me ever since we had that awful fight." She tightened her arms around him, linking her hands behind his waist. "She'll be happy, but she won't be as happy as I am."

"Or as happy as I am."

Luke bent his head and kissed his woman, soon to be his wife.

*   *   *   *   *

Silhouette Intimate Moments

COMING NEXT MONTH

#241 THAT MCKENNA WOMAN
—Parris Afton Bonds

Marianna McKenna was used to the bright lights of Hollywood until a tragic misunderstanding made her a convicted felon, sentenced to work at the Mescalero Cattle Company. But there she met Tom Malcolm and found that even the darkest cloud has a silver lining.

#242 MORE THAN A MIRACLE—Kathleen Eagle

Elizabeth had lost her son, and only Sloan McQuade could help her get him back. Sloan was sure it would take more than a miracle to do the job. But then, it had taken just that for him to find the only woman he could ever love....

#243 SUMMER OF THE WOLF
—Patricia Gardner Evans

From the moment Christian saw Erin he was no longer the hard-bitten loner he had once been. He had fallen—and fallen hard. But his job was to protect Erin, and her safety had to come first—even if it meant hiding the strength of his love.

#244 BEYOND FOREVER—Barbara Faith

When Catherine Adair came to Egypt, it was her chance to fulfill all her goals as an archaeologist. But when she met David Pallister, everything changed. He was determined to see past her cool, professional exterior to the passion beneath—and for the first time in her life, she was willing to think of herself as a woman in love.

AVAILABLE THIS MONTH:

#237 AFTER MIDNIGHT
Lucy Hamilton

#238 THE ECHO OF THUNDER
Linda Turner

#239 WILLING ACCOMPLICE
Doreen Roberts

#240 ROGUE'S VALLEY
Kathleen Creighton

Silhouette Intimate Moments

Rx: One Dose of

DODD MEMORIAL HOSPITAL

In sickness and in health the employees of Dodd Memorial Hospital stick together, sharing triumphs and defeats, and sometimes their hearts as well. Revisit these special people this month in the newest book in Lucy Hamilton's Dodd Memorial Hospital Trilogy, *After Midnight*—IM #237, the time when romance begins.

Thea Stevens knew there was no room for a man in her life—she had a young daughter to care for and a demanding new job as the hospital's media coordinator. But then Luke Adams walked through the door, and everything changed. She had never met a man like him before—handsome enough to be the movie star he was, yet thoughtful, considerate and absolutely determined to get the one thing he wanted—Thea.

Finish the trilogy in July with *Heartbeats*—IM #245.

Silhouette Special Edition

NORA ROBERTS'S 50TH SILHOUETTE NOVEL

In May, SILHOUETTE SPECIAL EDITION celebrates Nora Roberts's "golden anniversary"— her 50th Silhouette novel!

The Last Honest Woman launches a three-book "family portrait" of entrancing triplet sisters. You'll fall in love with all THE O'HURLEYS!

The Last Honest Woman—May
Hardworking mother Abigail O'Hurley Rockwell finally meets a man she can trust...but she's forced to deceive him to protect her sons.

Dance to the Piper—July
Broadway hoofer Maddy O'Hurley easily lands a plum role, but it takes some fancy footwork to win the man of her dreams.

Skin Deep—September
Hollywood goddess Chantel O'Hurley remains deliberately icy...until she melts in the arms of the man she'd love to hate.

Look for THE O'HURLEYS! And join the excitement of Silhouette Special Edition!

SSE451-1